When Corey explains that he
with 'no destination in mind
possible', you know resistance
to take a seat on that ride. Cor
disturbing, equally soulful and thought p
blends the real world of his past with the ethereal backdrop
of his troubled mind. The result is a young man who may
have died, is certainly broken and definitely cannot come to
terms with the tragedy until he understands what the
tragedy is.

Buckle up for the ride, reader, because when you jump
into Corey's mind with him, be it the train ride from hell or
the ethereal world filled with rabbits and cats, endless
tinned food, a disturbing friend and a purple jumper, you
join him in one of those perennial nightmares when you
just can't get to where you need to be.

Your emotions will be wrecked and you won't be able
to put this down—which is good, because *All the Waves,
Calling* has one of the cleverest, most satisfying endings of
a novel I have read in a long time.
—*Jackie Buxton, author (Tea & Chemo, Glass Houses) and
editor*

All the Waves, Calling is a beautiful and atmospheric novel
which will grab you from the outset and refuse to let you
go. Intriguing and unique, it tells the story of Corey who, in
looking for an escape from a painful past, boards the 'Train
to Nowhere'. When the train derails on an unknown beach
in the highlands, we follow Corey as he befriends Skye, the
only other survivor, and the two of them embark on a
strange and unsettling journey to find answers. This novel
reads like a fever dream, never allowing the reader to feel
grounded, instead we feel Corey's confusion in the
aftermath of the derailment and his journey for answers in
a world where his past and present collide. Jamie D. Stacey
knows how to keep the tension high; he understands what
it means to become lost in grief and how to navigate a

difficult subject with a gentle and sensitive touch. I thoroughly enjoyed reading this novel and I know this story will stay with me for a long time to come.

—*Sam Payne, fiction and CNF editor at Janus Literary*

This moving journey into one man's struggle to come to terms not only with grief, but also the inability to deal with his loss, is an incredible achievement. At times confusing, at others harrowing in its raw intensity, overall it is a tribute to the resilience of the human spirit. Highly recommended.

—*Lorraine Mace, author of the D.I. Sterling series*

Corey has travelled far. A terrible accident has left him in a Highlands town made, it seems, of mist and shadows. It is deserted; but it seems that, prior to their exodus, the inhabitants knew a cataclysm was brewing. How else to explain the tinned food with which one house is stacked to the rafters? Inexplicable, though, are the ubiquitous portraits of cats: still-life counterparts to the feral cats that have apparently made the town their own.

Corey strives to make a somewhere from this nowhere—aided by the enigmatic Skye who is, variously, fellow-forager and guide. But is she something more? Is she the means through which he can face his history, his rudderless mother, estranged father—his wife, Claire, with whom he knew at first joy, then the unspeakable misery of an unborn child?

But has Corey travelled at all? Is the whole nightmarish experience a way of forcing him to confront the demons he has dodged for so long? 'The reason I'm here,' he finally realizes, 'it's all to face my bad dreams.' At last he does…and so his known world returns to him —but much expanded now, radiant with all the colours of hope.

—*Michael W. Thomas, author of The Stations of the Day, Under Smoky Light and Sing Ho! Stout Cortez: Novellas and Stories.*

All the Waves, Calling

Jamie D. Stacey

All the Waves, Calling

First published in 2023 by Black Pear Press
www.blackpear.net

ISBN 978-1-913418-80-9

Cover design Mike R. Newman

Black Pear Press

'Talking is a lifeline... "Are you alright?" '

—*Time to Change Wales*,
https:www.timetochangewales.org.uk/en/campaigns/talking-lifeline/

'This is no town of cats, he finally realises. It is the place where he is meant to be lost. It is another world, which has been prepared especially for him. And never again, for all eternity, will the train stop at this station to take him back to the world he came from.'

—Haruki Murakami, *1Q84*

all the waves, calling

If only life's answers were as black and white as the dark Scottish Highlands outside and the bright lights of the train inside, and the train ran on time like bills through the letter box, and the letter box was as empty of bills as my wallet, and my wallet was as heavy as the sigh of the wind trapped in the window, and the window could just close like the last few chapters of my life, then it wouldn't be such a bad train journey after all.

If only. That's what I tell myself.

The train drags on, trails the howling wind, hacking my ears as I slam the window shut. It doesn't shut. There's a draft. Typical.

Jerks, halts, then the train spurts some more. A final *chug chug chug* sees it lunging forwards. It roars, it squeaks. Can't decide if it's a lion or a mouse. I fall unconscious again. Can't decide if I'm here or there. Just nowhere, tucked away in some forgotten corner of these British Isles. Just me, a shitty old Nokia, half a KitKat, loose coppers, two half fags, and company I don't need. If only my head could keep still against this damn, shaking window…

If only I'd grown up somewhere that wasn't an estate or Swansea, if only I'd had a better job or one at all, or if Dad had actually been one and Mum wasn't half of who I've heard she used to be, if my friends hadn't left for the four corners of the world or the four corners of Wetherspoons, or if only I'd have taken an earlier train or one that hadn't been Arriva Train Wales to Newport.

If only all babies were born and cried and sang; if only you'd never met me, Claire.

But then what do they say? If this, if that… Any train and I'd still have ended up here, eventually. At least I chose this train, this day. At least there are KitKat and fags.

I'm on our beach. The sea—this vast unknown—stretches and yawns and is calmer than most nearby places. And this spot, this feeling. This is not an easy place to find. It's a secret. No map or geography or Google will know. I know. I can hear the song of the sea, the dancing waves all bright and blue. I wander, the soles of my feet sinking into the salt and pepper sand. Soon I look back, see the impressions left behind by my feet; there are other footprints walking alongside, smaller than my own. I look around, but there's no one else to be seen—

A loud thud. Another pull and the train screams as my head smashes against the window and I stutter awake. I bite my lip, hold it all in.

'Jeez, that had to hurt!' The bubbly fat beside me blurts out. Can't remember his real name, not that it matters.

'Shut it, Bubbles,' says the guy opposite. Larry, or at least I think that's what he said. The less annoying of the two, tries to keep his distance. 'We don't all pack enough belly to hold us down when some train goes amok.'

'It…It's not just *any* train, Larry.' Bubbles says, licking his lips as if savouring his words. Maybe hunger. I don't offer him anything. 'Not just *any* train…'

They're lost on me. I know physically they're right next to me, sharing this table around Seat 42 Carriage B, but I still feel them slip away. They knock back a few words. I sink into my corner, wait for the night to swallow me whole. Just forget it all. Instead my head lolls from one side to the next, my eyes wandering the carriage for the umpteenth time. Damn carriage. It's closing in, suffocating. I have to accept it. Hand as a pillow, I rub my head against the window and struggle for some forty winks to salvage some energy, some motivation maybe.

Minutes to midnight. My phone buzzes, again. Again,

I leave it. It's been a whole day, a few hundred miles. Someone is phoning; someone is too late.

The train lumbers on, caught in some spasm as it drags itself along the tracks. These damn, endless tracks. I feel my body pulled with the underbelly of the carriage, scraping across steel scales clamped to the earth, dragging me from one place—

'Ow!'

Another jolt. Fat Bubbles moans while Larry observes the carriage. Just the odd late-night passengers though. Most seats empty, only ghosts for company. Another jerk. Not that I notice much, I only look when the train shakes me awake and throws me in their direction. Another jump. Otherwise I keep to myself.

I glance at my phone. This damn phone that whinges and cries like a helpless child. I skip the missed calls, check the time. Still some way to go, to nowhere.

'I miss home, Larry, miss home I do,' Bubbles says. 'How much longer—is it much longer?' No one replies. 'Midnight,' he continues, looking up from the cheap plastic watch strapped so tight to his wrist that the skin folds over it. 'It's almost midnight, Larry.'

'Yeah,' Larry says. 'It's been nearly 15 frickin' hours now, but the train bloody stopped for half of it…'

His voice trails off. A few other words are batted back and forth, nothing I hold onto. My head sways, slips between sleeping and waking. My body still reacts to the push and pull of the train, still drawn to the noises crowing nearby. Still—

'Are we nearly there, Larry, are we nearly there yet?'

Again, like a big kid, Bubbles looks up to Larry who shakes his head. A yawn escapes between his lips. Bubbles follows suit.

'At least another hour, I reckon.'

'At least another hour…'

'And that's providing the train don't stop again,' Larry adds. 'Damn kids ripping up copper cables outside Newport. Every time Newport, and every damn time it's our train…'

I hold back my own yawn. Newport. A city that feels years away already, let alone every other place behind me. I'm half-conscious but my body still slumps in the chair, the rough and itchy and grimy fabric a reminder of reality. Bubbles stoops over the table, eyes wide like a baby's, lost in the nothing of the window.

'I don't see nothing, Larry, nothing.'

His stupid words have me glancing outside once more, but the night swallows everything, like Glasgow onwards never existed. I could be anywhere now. Not that it matters anyway, not that I know this place, this nowhere.

'Shit…'

Even Larry is tired. He wants to be home, as he says. Home…

A buzz. It's not someone phoning though, instead it's the phone crying—it's going to give out before the day ends. I drag it out, mere minutes of life left. This dinosaur Nokia has finally had it. I click straight to my messages, but I'm just re-reading old ones.

I flick through contacts, most now no more than the strangers on this train. Another name, another number, this time my thumb hovering over the call button. I rub the sides of the plastic headset in my hand, back and forth. I press down on the number and dial.

Ring, ring.

I hold the phone on my lap.

Ring, ring.

Watching, waiting.

Ring—

I hang up. Pocket it along with the few rattling coins

left. Damn—and now Bubbles is looking my way.

'Alright?' Larry says, turning to me. 'Where'd you come from all of a sudden, huh? Thought we'd lost you not long after we crossed the border like.' Bubbles lets out another groan and copies him parrot fashion, or like a cat clawing at my ears.

I hold my breath. I feel my chest sink, press against my lungs until it becomes hard to even open my mouth.

'I'm fine.'

Fine. A word that's neither here nor there. They're not really interested anyway, not really looking at me. I'm fading away.

'You look tired too.' I force the words out, try to make a connection, I don't know. 'Miss home, huh?'

Larry's eyes skirt the dull grey of the window frame, then my outline beside it.

'Yeah, as a matter of fact I do, actually.' His gritty tone betrays the struggle in his voice. I can just about hear him. 'You know, it's been a long time I've been away now like. Port Talbot stinks, I know, but it's like they say, yeah? Home is home—'

'—No matter how poor it is!' Bubbles rallies.

'Too right,' Larry says. 'You know, few people head this far north, take the *train to nowhere*.' What did he just say? His voice changes, nothing but a whisper when he says those last few words. 'It's a shitty little train and all, and you've either gotta be pushed into this corner of the world or looking to disappear, if you ask me.' He pauses, as if waiting for some response. I say nothing. 'Well, being so far away, yeah, I miss home. The works, the lads, and the little kid running circles screaming bloody murder, the missus chasing after him making sure the house is proper tidy and don't stink of shit. A proper Valley's girl born and bred she is…' He holds his breath, as if the weight of everything before holds the words

5

back. 'And I'm stuck up here again.' He pauses, without explaining why he's even here, not that I care. 'You got any of your own?'

He means well. They all do. That's what I have to tell myself, that it's fine.

It's as if the last couple of years won't let go, no matter how far north I disappear to. Even the accent, like he's dragging gob from the back of his throat with every other word, it all follows me even here. To *nowhere*. I brush my hand against the pocket holding my phone, then decide against it. Do nothing.

I laugh, or rather a long, exasperated huff that shuffles alongside the silence.

'Almost there,' I say, by way of breathing.

Larry nods. 'Home sweet home.'

'Home sweet home,' says his big teddy bear shadow.

Sweet nothing. There's a hint of sadness in the way the words kind of fall from his mouth. Or maybe that's me.

'You know,' he continues, 'besides a good cwtch, the thing I'm gonna miss the most is her cooking.' Larry lets himself smile. 'Hate the canteen crap and triangle sandwiches. Bloody triangles. Does my head in.'

'Bloody triangles.' Bubbles thrashes his head about, threatening to dislodge it from his neck.

The light flickers, my eyes close shut. I can feel myself slipping away from them, from the train, from…

'Come on like.' Bubbles nudges me. I grit my teeth. 'Come on.'

'Look,' Larry says, trying to defend the fat blubber. 'The way this train is banging on, nothing'll let you rest. Just saying, may as well spend the night with us. Nothing but bad dreams falling asleep here.'

Bad dreams, I wonder. My phone buzzes again—a last call, an impending battery death. I do nothing, I've

6

already decided. Besides, Larry is looking my way so I nod and play along.

'Good,' he says. 'Come on, Bubbles, get them cards out of your pocket.'

The big fella obliges, his giant paws fumbling inside his trousers, pillaging a deck of cards dirty on the edges and sticky like sweaty palms. Most of them are still there, though. As the cards are dealt, I can't help but fix each one in turn; red card, black card; red card, black card; six, four, two; five, three…All low numbers. I got all low numbers.

'Hey, what's your name again?'

Corey, I don't say. It's Bubbles, blowing his big mouth. Not that I know his name either. I mutter something, anything, the first name that comes to mind. Like I own my name anymore.

I catch his lips moving, repeating, merely an echo lost in the background. I just want to sleep. But Larry's right about one thing; the push and pull, the heaving and howling, this damn train won't let up…And Bubbles pushing up against me…And my phone buzzing, calling…

The train lurches to the left.

'Come on, it's your turn like.' A voice rises like a wave. Other words follow, other sounds scamper around like frightened rabbits.

'Leave him alone,' another rising wave. 'Don't bother. He don't talk much, this one.'

Total darkness outside, dim lights inside. Calmness chokes the carriage, like we're the only ones here. And now I'm hesitating; I'm back at the station, 8 o'clock this morning, handing over the last £201.50 in my scrawny bank account to scavenge a one-way ticket to the back of beyond. No destination in mind other than the furthest possible place. Two trains, a delay, a missed train, then two more trains, a bus, another train, and already 23 more minutes late. To nowhere...

A hand tugs at my side.

'Hey!'

'Woah, easy now.' It's Larry's voice, but it's Bubbles nudging my side, his wet breath blowing into my eardrum.

Despite it, I don't respond—don't give them the satisfaction—and Larry returns to his cards, Bubbles following suit. Ha, suit. I can afford a smile this late into the night. The cards slap against the table. I'm left alone.

The train heaves and pulls through each contraction. My head hits the window. I choke on a curse. I look outside, lose myself in the darkness that has swallowed the landscape; even the moon, gnawed to a bone.

Someone mutters something. I turn, catching a card now balancing in the air, and past that ace of spades I notice a young woman opposite. She's wearing the strangest purple underneath a black and rather boring coat, turned away towards her window, laughing. Moments later she looks my way. She seems to focus on me and I lose all concentration. Eventually, I turn away, back to the table, the cards dealt out once more.

She wore purple, I remember.

'What's the game?'

Larry says nothing while Bubbles has his face pressed against his cards. But hey, it's their game. It's enough to distract them, make them forget; Bubbles no longer hungry, Larry no longer missing home. I want to forget too.

The train swerves to the left, but my head swings to the right. A pull in one direction. Towards her. Hidden in her corner, still looking at me, that woman in the loud purplish jumper buried under everything else.

'Darn it! How you so good, Larry?'

But Larry doesn't reply, at least not right away. His eyes are focused on the cards as he shuffles, real neat and tidy before dealing them once more.

'So, you in?'

My eyes flicker. In the corner of my eye I feel her watching me.

Bubbles leans over. 'You in the game, you in?'

I nod. Bubbles smiles, Larry lets him deal. A four. A three. A two. It's the final countdown.

'It's still far...' Bubbles blubbers, in no direction in particular, his mouth spraying the cards some. 'Are you from far?'

I check my cards, pinching the braised edges, pressing my skin against the rough material. I want to know I'm awake.

'Not many blokes get this far, is all he's saying,' Larry intervenes. 'Out here, middle of nowhere. Need to have a damn good reason...'

He's trying again; different words, same conversation. I abandon my cards.

'Hey, wait...'

'I fold. Not my luck tonight, sorry.' I pull my hoodie over.

Bubbles looks disappointed. Larry too, but he's trying to hide it. When I'm halfway down the corridor I hear Bubbles cry out, the sharp smack of Larry's hand fresh on him, then his voice which follows after me.

'Ain't no messing with the dead.'

I walk away, the feel of the ace of spades still fresh on my fingertips. I don't want to win. What can I win? The answer to life isn't in the ace of spades. I'm not going to close my eyes, open them to wake up on some sunny beach from years ago...

The train lurches to the right.

*

In the smudged face of the mirror, just above the leaky toilet, hangs my portrait. I stay still, lock myself in place until there's nothing left but my shadow. No one would have recognised me at that school reunion last week. Even I can't, that much I understand now. *Tell me what's wrong, I don't know who you are anymore—I'm fine, Claire.* I'm fine. Except when I'm not fine. I'm falling forwards into the mirror, and I have to tear myself away before it's too late. It's too late. The cold kiss of the mirror singes my forehead, and I let it, waiting a few seconds before pulling back.

I had no friends waiting for me there, I convinced myself. I don't need to know about their wives, their children, their happy lives...

It's then I notice the graffiti. Of course there is. A mess, a sprawl, one long scribble. I just make out a rabbit—all white—scratched into the wall above the toilet, of all places. A stupid rabbit, of all things. It's then I make it out, a word, all big and loopy like a kid's.

Peekaboo.

I hesitate. The word echoes in my head, like I heard a voice. But there's nothing. Just some rabbit and some scribbles.

I head out the door only to stagger to the left, seizing the frame with both hands. Another stroke rips through the train and the inside howls.

I need to breathe. I lean against the exit, yank the window down before fetching out yesterday's chewed cig along with the lighter from my back pocket. I flick on the old Red Ronson, letting the burning fluid inside fill my nostrils before rubbing the old cig between my fingers, then bring it to the tip of the flame. A snap as I release the lighter and tap the cig against my lips. It's still moist, still has warmth to it, and I let the heat fill my lungs and breathe.

The lights hanging overhead flicker on and off, like some annoying game of peekaboo. I rid myself of the remains of the cig and pocket the lighter. Fragments of light spit, the world caught in blinks and beats. I wander a short distance when another spasm throws me forwards. I crash onto the floor, smacking my head. The world bleeds black—

Peekaboo!

My eyes water from the throbbing beneath the skin where my face scraped against the floor. It's just a fall, I'm fine. The lights had gone out, not me.

The train—and life—drag on.

I pull myself back up, clinging to the wall for support. I limp back through the darkness. Hitting against the dud of an automatic door alerts me of where I am, and passing through I expect to grasp the back of a chair anytime soon, but nothing. Instead the space grows around me, expands and gives way to an infinite nothing. Damn, must have turned the wrong way; now complete darkness strangles the corridor, or room, or wherever this is. Darkness and silence as thick as tar. The stink of piss from the toilets has gone at least. The vibrations clamouring the length and width of the train have gone too. I could be dreaming, floating, were it not for some sharp prick jabbing my skin—

A sound, a whisper? A lullaby. Notes that feel…familiar. Something is approaching, something in the air. Even my heart beats faster, the blood in my veins swells, and a tangy taste lingers on my tongue. Something passes in front of me. I see—

The lights buzz then blister; at least enough light to

11

make out where I am, where I'm heading. The door to the next carriage is just ahead. I take a few steps forward—

I stop, the lullaby cuts and there, almost a shadow in the dying of the light—

Her.

My foot grinds against the floor and she twists around, the exit at her back. She grasps one of the handles, jerks it to release the frame. A final tug and— despite the moving train—the door snaps open, a gush of wind hitting me, the rush of darkness vast as the open sea.

It would be all she has to do, just another step.

Her fist curls inwards. Her heart crosses the threshold. My own stops and the night crashes into her like waves and I feel myself plunging with her—

'Don't.'

Still. Her hand still clings to the handle, the rest of her fading fast in the dark waters. She stands still, her body caught between inside and outside.

Between nowhere, and somewhere.

'Don't,' I repeat, the word heavy, falling with the dull thud of an anchor from my lips.

Her body hangs over the edge, hangs onto my words, just. She doesn't move. But she can't look me in the eyes either.

'I'll do it,' she says at last. 'And you can't talk me out of it.'

She edges closer, closer to falling straight through. I'm falling with her, I—

'Jump. Just jump. It's not like I can stop you, right?'

My words seem to cut right through her, my voice sharp, strong; like it's not my own. She's looking straight at me, a strange stroke of confusion caught in her face. Now I'm the one who struggles to look her in the eye.

Nothing. Her lips part—as if on the verge of speaking—but she says nothing.

'But if you jump, I'll jump too.' At least that's how it feels, seeing her there, hanging onto nothing, it's like I'm there too. 'It's you.' I feel myself caught among the waves, struggling to surface. 'At the back of the carriage. It's you.'

The woman with a hint of purple.

She holds back, like she's unsure. Then a faint nod—a millimetre of movement—as if anything more...

'It's me.'

I don't understand. For a moment her voice is like a child's, light, like it's forgotten the weight of past and present. Her strange voice, the situation stranger still. And this stranger in me; what am I saying, what am I doing? I think about the cig, about...But she's watching me now, caught between the darkness out there and darkness in here.

'It's you.' I echo.

Her foot shuffles, slipping back inside the carriage; the other drawn to the edge, her head turned outwards towards the howling wind as if for comfort.

Then a flicker of a smile, like first light.

'I'm no longer alone.'

I don't understand. Maybe it's the long day, or it's late, or maybe it's this middle of nowhere that surrounds me. And this stranger. She struggles back further inside, her back facing both the darkness outside and the cold inside. She glances here and there, between nowhere and—she shuts the door. A twist, a tug, then the darkness locked outside, and inside now an erratic light as everything comes to.

Peekaboo, says the dark outside. I'm long tired of these games, but I breathe again.

The train lurches to the left...

*

I trip through the corridor, passing through the automatic door that needs a good kick to open. No one notices, these ghosts on a train. Beside me she keeps close, and as we head down the carriage I feel my phone buzz. I've lost count how many times someone has tried, and against my earlier judgement I'm now slipping my hand inside my pocket—

'Hey!'

It's Bubbles, his big frame now a large, ridiculous shadow lodged in the corridor. Flickers of light rescue his portrait, swaying like a boat lost at sea.

'Okay, you okay?' he gives a sort of hurried, anxious yelp. 'We was worried, we was.'

'I didn't notice.' I glance in the direction of Larry who, his face lit up in the spasms of artificial light, hardly acknowledges me; he barely so much as glances at the woman now beside me, if at all.

'What's going on?' he says.

'I don't know.' My mind is elsewhere. My heart beats fast, something that—maybe absurd—feels fresh and exciting all at once. 'Did we stop again?'

Bubbles snaps his head. 'No, no!'

Larry comes up beside him, keeping his calm, and Bubbles holds back a cry.

The train jerks to the right again, throwing us across the carriage. Even Bubbles can't hold himself upright, crashing into the chair beside him. I feel my phone moaning inside my pocket once more.

'What the bloody heck is that?' Larry blurts out.

'W-what if…?' Bubbles is spinning around. 'Are we gonna die, gonna die?'

A powerful smack catches him on the back of the head, and I notice Larry retracting his red palm in the violent glint of the full moon.

'That's enough. Pull yourself together!'

Of all of us, Bubbles is the only one really afraid of death.

'Ouch…Shit, Larry!' But Larry does no more than hold his stare, and Bubbles buckles. 'Okay, okay. Let's play cards, Larry, play cards.'

Larry nods.

They both take the nearest seats with a table. I remain standing, the young woman behind me, silent. Larry, meanwhile, has already taken out the pack of cards and gives them a quick shuffle before dealing them out. One card balances in his hands.

'You in?'

I hesitate. Bubbles is already hovering over the table. Both then turn to me.

Peekaboo.

That word. That echo in my mind. I'm about to speak up when I notice the woman shuffle behind me. I catch her eyes drifting, notice her arms folded and hugging her frame. Unsure, anxious maybe.

'No, not this time,' I say. Then, turning to Larry, 'Maybe later.' His image is already fading.

'Sure…'

I catch him dealing the last card, and in the spit of light I make out the ace of spades slip into his hand. He's already smiling. Except this is no ordinary ace.

It's the white rabbit.

This damn phone, the buzz pushing against my leg. Then something brushes against me, but it's only her. She doesn't speak, doesn't dare maybe. She's drifting down the corridor, but I hold back. The train rocks. I trip.

She holds out her hand, and piercing the windows on either side the white eye of the moon fills her own.

Corey.

I'm sure she spoke, and I'm sure that's what she said. I say nothing in turn, question nothing, just follow her as she now paces down the corridor, heading back to the connecting bridge, back to the door where...

I notice the other passengers for the first time but the flickering light reveals only hooded expressions, dark outlines, and everyone's staring at me. Everyone. At me. These ghosts turned shadows. No one so much as blinks as we brush past, as the train around us shrieks. No one moves. No one speaks.

And I wonder if there's anyone here at all.

I stumble a few times. A few stowaway bags and other rubbish fall from overhead compartments, the train rattles and shakes like it's banging on God's door. All the while, though, I focus on her, never let her out of my sight; watch her as she reaches the broken door, watch as it resists her pull, watch as a few jerky movements later the mechanism breaks and—

A spasm, a scream; like the earth is contracting, casting the whole train aside.

I'm thrown forward with the train as it screams out of control. An eruption blares behind as a hundred shadows shriek. Lights spot and bleed as a darkness devours the train and all the faceless faces on board. The train beneath me, around me; the whole world jerks left then right then—

In the bruised purple light, I see her twisted image and there, outside, a row of dunes—of waves—close in on either side. Out of nowhere a hand grabs mine but she's slipping away, like water falling through my fingertips.

I close my eyes. I want to return to our beach, Claire, to wander among the sea of blue and bell, to follow those footsteps—

I'm torn awake. Then I see. Her eyes. The last thing I see, then the train screaming and, like a trigger, all past and pain hit me. And then, a feeling stranger to me still. I'm afraid of dying.

*

I watch as the big blue heart beats, the pulse carried through waves that crash and die on our shore. Swash, backwash, I watch them coming in, listen to the beat of the sea—watch, as my footprints are erased and forgotten.

There's litter on the beach. Empty cans of Coke and opened packets of Lambert and Butler, the silver foil spilling out like vomit still clinging to someone's mouth. That's what all of this amounts to. Vomit, an unwanted excess that ruins the otherwise smooth speckled sand on the shore. The waves come in, claim it, only to spit it back out again, unable to rid itself of all these memories.

Where are their footprints? They were here a few moments ago. Before the next wave comes in—the next beat of the heart—mine linger in the trailing sand. But they are gone; despite me hearing them, the sounds they made, despite their black and white images so clear I can see them now when I close my eyes. There are memories everywhere, scattered across the shore. A purple felt bunny—torn at the edges, no doubt from that black feline—a book of rhymes and lullabies, a promise written in the sand...But no footprints. No other trace of who they were. Like they never existed.

Like any of us existed, Claire.

And like that, there's nothing left but a trail of litter all about me.

welcome to the town of cats
(13 days to go…)

Alive…

A torrent of noise smashes against my right ear. The other pressed hard against…My side feels crushed. My head—is that blood…? Try to move. This thing digging into me…Can't make out the faintest shadow. Damn this darkness…Shaking, my body's shaking…Yet…

I'm alive.

A spasm in my leg alerts me and I realise I'm pressed down on the ground. Like I've been thrown here. Hard, real hard. I struggle to shift my weight on this surface which slides under my movement, scratches the exposed skin of my face. I stretch out my hand and touch the soft, crumbling earth surrounding me. I take a fistful and stare. In the emerging light I look down at the tiny grains falling through my fingers.

Sand. The beach.

Then a light up ahead flashes into view, bone white. Several long, catalytic bursts of artificial light blink in the fading darkness. Up above a white gash breaks across the black skin of the sky, and below wave after wave of dunes dance in the glow. And there—a mess of metal and glass and tracks—half the carriages clinging to the sleepers with another buried into the sand. Pressed down I sink with it. Beads of cold sweat run the length of my spine, then I feel my skin flush red and raw like a newborn and I feel exposed. I stay still, watch as the last hint of light inside the train gives out.

Watch, as the past passes away.

Eventually I drag myself up. I run my hands over my body, my face, my eyes. Everything is fine, except I can't stop shaking. My hands are fidgeting, craving; a bottle, a fag. I need something to numb it all, dim reality. I thrust my hands into my pockets. I still have the lighter. Fat load of good that'll do me now with just a few stubs left. I pull out half a fag anyway, but the train and its entrails sprawled out nearby kill any desire. I take my phone out; it doesn't even turn on, dead as the dark that lingers in the space between the train and me like some great chasm, some grand unknown. I slap it against the palm of my hand, as if that would work. And this damn ache, my back feels wrecked, and this damn cold biting my skin, and—

I shout. I don't know why, I just shout. Nothing. No reply, and my voice drowns in the ocean of darkness. Then silence. Then…

A shout, then—like a chorus—cries erupt in random directions, all places, thrown about by the evening wind. At least that's what I think I hear. Maybe it's my echo. I'm shouting. Crying. Can't help it. This sudden surge in my stomach and it just comes out. Like the urge to throw up. My head slips back. The moon, chewed up and spat out by the throng of clouds, leaves little in view but an outline of what remains in front. The darkness creeps in, and I squint, desperate to find something, someone.

I look at the wreckage and the dunes, look for a sign. Is anyone here, anyone at all? They weren't all ghosts on that train. Larry? Bubbles?

Her?

I feel my body dragged down, falling through the sand. The darkness licks at my skin, like a wolf teasing its prey. Several more shouts—my shouts—wander up and down the dunes; keep me awake, keep me alive, the echo like someone else is here with me. Ahead, a few more flashes of light reach out into the night, like a beacon, an SOS.

I'm still here though. Still buried in the sand, still

staring into the carriages and finally the black screen of death on my phone. The moon above breaks through the clouds once more, an afterthought living in the screen.

I lie, unmoving, still.

Alive, and alone.

*

They say the angels bring us into this world. They bring us here, the sun or the moon bright against their backs, and they carry us here on their wings like a dream. When they let go of us, leave us in this world, they place their fingers on our lips, whispering us to be quiet, to hold back all the secrets of the heavens.

She's waiting for me to speak my first word, my mum. She holds me by the window, almost leans into it, the cold glass pressing against my lips.

'Shhh,' the moon, now chubby and soft in the sky, likes to remind me.

Eventually babies grow, become toddlers, become children...become adults. We forget about the angels, forget about the secrets, and the moon doesn't need to speak to us anymore.

But we all suspect, don't we; all suspect we know something, are tied to something, connected to a bigger universe.

She's waiting for my first word, my mum. She holds me by the window, almost leans into it...

I'm thinking about what my first word was all those years ago. I don't know. All I can think of is nothing, a blank space. I look up and see the moon tonight, now a silver scythe hanging overhead, clouds gripping it at the hilt.

Claire tells me it's a frightening image, that the moon doesn't have to be seen like that. On our second date, she tells me that her first word was 'moon'.

*

I march—don't know why—just march across the dunes, away from the wreckage, but not too far that it disappears entirely. I need to get away from here, get away from all this death and destruction. The distant call of the sea acts as my guide. The crash of waves somewhere brings a strange comfort, like there's someone close by. And this totem of reality, a reminder that I'm still awake, still alive.

Questions leap out. Where am I? How did the train crash? Where is everyone?

Have to keep moving, keep myself distracted. But I don't stray too far before the faint outline of the sprawling carriage lingers into view. I can't pull myself away, but I can't approach it either. Instead, I look to another direction, any direction, and drag the soles of my feet across the crumbling sand; try to forget their voices, forget the tracks and the train, forget...

Her.

Strange, this image of that young woman on the train keeps returning in my mind. The last thing I remember was her on the train, the purple sweater under her coat, her laughter...Her one foot hanging off the edge.

I stop. Beneath me the sand sinks, a small fissure dividing me and some other side. I hold my stare. Then my body escapes me and I fall onto the swarm of shingle peppered black and white, absorbing the starlight. I throw my head upwards. The mass of clouds has now all but gone, and all that is left is the bright halo disk in the sky, a myriad of stars stood guard around it.

I smash a fist into the sand. Then another. It has the desired effect. I run my hands through the sea of sand and grab a fistful, then watch as the individual grains slip through my fingers, fall with no sound. I wait until the last few grains escape, then clench my hand and strike the sand hard again. It steals the impact, swallows my anger, my fear, and my hand below, threatens to swallow me whole. I gasp, pull each finger out one by one, escaping the mouth of the dunes. Then I look up, but it's still just me and 101 questions for company...

'Anyone there?' Even sitting in that shrinking box back home there was the familiar glow of the computer screen, the words and images left behind by other people, digital footprints I could hold onto, that I could kid myself meant something. I turn to the black, empty canvas surrounding me, reach out as if I could paint something, or someone. 'Anyone at all?'

How long? Minutes, even hours since I came to? Maybe. I can't tell when the train derailed, my mind scattered, and life buried itself in the tracks and sand. It all feels so...

I hear the sand blowing nearby and twist around, losing my footing in another fissure carved into the dune. A shadow emerges. I hold my breath.

Silence. A faint blur, an outline, and finally the shadow takes shape. It leaps—then drifts—across the sand, not stopping until she's close. Close enough to see the life in her breath, the heart in her eyes. That hint of purple.

Her.

Her stare, my stare. For a while we're just that, with the hush of the wind and the chanting of waves in the distance. She stares right at me, maybe even through me. All the while the moon, fat and full, slips down the side of her face.

She smiles, a faint, but recognisable smile. At least that's what I think I see, anyway. After all this, I can't be sure.

'Hey,' she says, her voice real, and yet I feel the need to catch it and hold onto it if I could.

I frown, unbelieving, unable to. Just a short while ago I was back on the train. The so-called *train to nowhere*. And now I'm here, with her and ten thousand shadows for company. I want to think I'm dreaming, but the damn sand in my shoes scratching my feet reminds me of reality.

For a long minute she remains still, silent, watching me as if my reaction to everything around means nothing. Meanwhile, I try to hold her stare, hold her in place.

'Who are you?'

The words pass between my lips, but I can't be sure if there's any sound, at least going by her reaction. I don't understand, maybe I can't. I'm struggling to make sense of anything right now. The crash, the fall, my head. But she's still looking, as if waiting for me to respond. She looks different. That smile, however faint, the way she holds herself; is this even the same young woman I met on the train, the woman who...? It is her, definitely. That bizarre purple, that contrast between her smile one moment and nothing the next—

She runs up and throws her arms around me. Only to break away moments later.

'Oh,' she breathes at last, a soft sigh lost in the breeze, this transfer of pent up energy inside her as her chest rises and falls like a wave then settles. 'Just someone like you, lost in the dunes, looking for some place to go.'

She's strange, like she's playing with me or denying the gravity of it all. Yet she seems serious. As she speaks her image focuses, and I've no reason to doubt.

'It is you. From the train. The one who...'

She doesn't reply, but her eyes brighten and I lose myself in thinking. She's watching, waiting. I don't even know what to say.

'Why did you...?' I can't catch my words. 'How did you...?' I can't hold onto them. I give up, lost in the folds of this unknown northern landscape, this ridiculous place, and even more ridiculous series of events. And her. I throw my arms in the air. 'Just where the hell are we?' But she ignores the shout, and something tells me I won't get much else out of her.

'Oh, anywhere, somewhere...' Maybe she notices the hint of annoyance in my face, because she continues, 'Somewhere in the dunes, somewhere far away from nowhere...' Calm, she's seemingly untouched by the chaos left behind us. 'It's cold,' she adds matter-of-factly. Then, turning one foot in the other direction, and her voice leaping forward unexpectedly, 'Come on. We should get going.'

I can't speak, let alone move. But she looks ready to run.

'Hold on...' I try to be assertive, but my words are lost under my teeth grinding and I say nothing else.

Her body turns to face me fully once more and she takes another step closer. She could be seven again, looking up at me with eyes wide and wondering how close the moon is tonight. Then her head leans to one side, her lips parting.

'It's okay,' she says, her voice different, soft as sand. 'I'm scared too.' Strange, but her admitting that just makes me feel better. 'I'm Skye, by the way. Since you were wondering.'

She pauses, then surprises me again when she draws close and wraps her arms around me, holding on. I don't move. I feel the warmth of her jumper, of her hands. And in this most surreal of places I wonder, with her head pressed against my chest, just how loud my heart is beating.

Against all the odds, I'm alive. We're alive.

*

They're worried I'm mute, which is to say someone has to pull the words out of me when they expect me to talk. The speech therapist

24

is saying this to my mum again, across the desk as I sit there wondering if a voice can be trapped in a jar. A bottle. A can. I'm holding a can now, its lips still sealed, and if I press my ear up against its cold exterior, I can hear the voice fizzing inside, waiting to be set free.

I remember our front door, which is to say I am putting together the sounds it made and the voice it had; the turning of the key struggling through an old lock, the chain and bolt grinding like clenched teeth, the letterbox that others open and shut as they are pleased. How many people pass in and out of this door, this mouth of our home, of our lives, the gatekeeper of everything outside and everything inside?

I collect jars. Old jars and new jars, glass jars and plastic jars, jars with tall slender bodies whose words inside must have suffered from vertigo, to jars oddly shaped where words inside could bounce and leap and mix about. But mostly everything stays still. Safe. Inside my jars.

Safe. Secure. I hide everything in my sealed jars.

I'm seven years old, which is a number greater than the words I utter in the morning. I'm seventeen years young, young enough that everything everyone says to me still leaves its mark. I'm twenty-seven, the wrong side of my twenties, and I'm here again. I'm…

'Boys tend to suffer more from these kinds of problems,' the therapist continues, and she catches me looking at her and sort of smiles.

I'm mute, they say. But I can speak, I know I can, but everything—all thought all feeling—stays in my jars. Few people can look inside.

But you, Claire…

*

'I don't understand.' My thoughts break free. I repeat them over and over, as if the mere sound could comfort me, even offer answers. 'I don't understand. Just what the hell happened?'

25

Silence. In perhaps the half an hour or so since our paths crossed again, I've found that Skye prefers to ignore everything and just skip along the dunes in her cold comfort of nature; the occasional gust of wind, the clap of the sea in the distance, and the sand shifting beneath our feet are all useful distractions. I get it though, the shock. She's just unable to answer my questions. So many damn questions, questions that twist and stretch in my head, questions that swell under my skin—questions, I realise, I hardly registered once the train derailed. It was the shock, the bang on the head. But now...

'You're quite the talker,' she says for the second time, slowing down for me to catch up to her agitated pace.

I'm not sure how to reply.

'I just...don't understand,' I repeat, dune after dune. 'Where are we, what next? Do we just walk up and down the dunes until we casually bump into someone? And then what? High five we survived! Hey look, I get that you're shaken and all, but any idea where we are and what to do next? Maybe got a phone that works? And heck, just where is everyone anyway or, better yet, how did the train even crash in the first place? In the middle of nowhere? How—'

I stop. She's looking right at me, this look that she gives, and I just stop.

'We're both alive. That's what matters,' she says bluntly. Then she twists away. 'Let's hurry!' That urgency. Of movement. But no words. Turns out I am the talker after all.

Yet that doesn't stop her thoughts lingering in my mind. That despite it all, we are *alive*. The word hangs in the air, catches in my throat. I could choke on it, the irony.

'The train...' the words derail from the growing tracks between us. 'How on earth could that possibly happen, how could—'

'How this? How that?' she says. 'Not how, but why. We don't know. Not yet.'

'Why...We don't know, not yet,' I repeat. I'm trying to catch up. She has me now. Either way, she's right about one thing. Whatever the question, we don't have the answer. 'What now then?'

Standing atop the crescent of a dune, the moon overhead smiling this crooked smile—a smile nonetheless—looks on.

'It's lonely here.' Almost a whisper, barely escaping her lips. She keeps to herself, to her moon, her eyes fixed on its crooked smile. 'You're here,' she adds. Then, turning to face me, 'and I'm here too.'

I'm here, yes, but the whole world has abandoned me—abandoned us.

It's then I hear the call of waves and I notice, for the first time, the sea up ahead. Squinting, I trace the crest of the waves in the twilight glow. I hear the swash and backwash, the water sliding across the coast, drawn by nature's pull, a soft splash that whispers...

Corey.

'It's beautiful.' I snap awake. Here in the now, Skye's voice leaps then falls with the waves. It's annoying, though, that she ignores everything else.

'Beautiful,' the word echoes across my lips. I play her game. Then another wave smashes nearby and I throw my arms in the air. 'Stranded here, sole survivors of a train crash, scattered who knows how, miles or so from the nearest station.' I stutter a laugh. 'What are the odds, eh? Guess we're lucky, one in a million. Beautiful.'

But the darkness hides a side of her face, like she's back there on the train and I feel the guilt hit me like the tide.

'No, wait. I'm sorry. You're right, it is beautiful. The sound of the sea, the night sky, it's all so…poetic.'

'Poetic?'

'Yeah…I don't know. A mysterious place, unusual circumstances, the sea and the moon. All floating and dreamlike. Shakespeare like.'

Again, with the darkness, it's difficult to tell. I feel like she's going to mock me but there's a hint of a smile.

'That's nice,' she says, her voice soft as sand once more.

The wind picks up, blowing some shingle our way and biting cold my skin. I clutch my hoodie tighter.

'We should go.' She's already turning away. What's her rush? 'I'm cold too.'

But go where? Continue in the direction of the unknown, drown in the slap and clap and promise of the sea? Or return to the wreckage, however far back? I guess it could be worse. Then my dead dinosaur Nokia reassures me. It couldn't be worse.

'Maybe we shouldn't stray too far from the wreckage. Someone will come sooner or later, rescue teams or something.'

'That could be days.'

The end of December, the middle of nowhere, she's right. No trains, no maintenance work, no repairs on the tracks.

'But *someone* would notice the train didn't arrive, right?'

She doesn't seem convinced.

'The beach,' she says finally, as if reading my thoughts and weighing in. 'We might find something if we follow the coast.' A suggestion, maybe, but her voice is pressing.

There's something impossible in her choice, ridiculous even. That she's drawn to the sea, to abandon all hope there, turn our backs on the wreckage and forget

28

it ever happened. Is that it? Is she afraid of what's behind? She's in a hurry to escape it, leave everything behind. Is she still thinking about what happened, what nearly happened?

Here in the Highlands, hopefully, the far north, somewhere, but even then I don't know what the hell is here or isn't. I make out this small flicker of red burning the sky above. The wreckage or a mirage, I don't know.

'You're holding yourself back.' It's not an echo in my mind, but her voice pushing against me. 'You're afraid of what you might find.'

'What?'

'I said let's go,' she says, ignoring the rest. But her words—or my echo—have their effect.

'Yeah...'

'Something wrong?'

I'm still drawn to the burning sky, the crooked smile etched in the crowd of stars, and the questions—just how did this happen, and why?—whose voices are whispering in my ears.

'It's just that...'

Is there anyone else? Could Larry or Bubbles have made it? They were right next to me when it happened. Bubbles' breath tickling my neck, Larry shouting after us, the playing cards...But would it be safe to go back, would anyone come for us? Questions, more questions, I question myself right now. Question her, too. After everything I expect her limbs to give, her spine to crouch and curve and for her to ride a rainbow unicorn to the moon. A strange image but stranger still this question mark over her head, over mine, over here and there. Damn, maybe I did hit my head harder than I thought, or maybe I just need a drink, or a working phone, or a pack of Lambert and Butler. But what can I do? There's nothing here, and who's telling what she might do; I've got to follow her, go in some direction.

'You think too much.' It's her, along with another question mark.

'It's nothing.'

She stops.

'If we go back, we'll die.' Her words strike me. 'We can't go back.'

What did she just say? But then she slides her head to the side, like she's a curious child once more, and I realise it's just me and her and this damn train on a beach. Or what's left of it. And I haven't the faintest idea which of us survived the crash more intact.

'Let's go.'

I go—to protest—when something brushes against my leg and I jump. Something small skitters off among the dunes and the dark. I turn to her but she's already pacing away. Without another thought I set off after her.

As we march I find myself returning to the sea, losing my mind as my feet carry me forward, one step after another, after—

'Hey, look!'

Just ahead a strange, crimson glow hovering over the coastline, a smear across the thick charcoal landscape stained a shocking red that burns like the light of a fag.

'What is it?'

'I don't know...A town maybe?'

Impossible. A town here, in the middle of nowhere?

'It can't be. We're stranded in the middle of God knows where, somewhere in the Scottish Highlands between two stations, and we've taken the only train that passes this way for days.' I stop. 'It can't be. We would have stopped here if it was a town.'

And yet...

'A small town then,' she counters. 'We should look.'

I have to say something. Anything.

'And what about the train? The others?' She's ignoring the big white elephant on the beach. 'We should wait it out.'

The words, the questions, everything just stumbles out of my mouth. I throw everything at her, trying to make her understand, try to—

'You said it yourself,' she says. 'The only train for days. The middle of nowhere. No one will come, not until we've frozen to death, not until the sea has swallowed us whole. Not until it's too late.' She steps closer, her voice quiet, direct. 'This was your choice.'

I thrust both hands in my pockets to stave off the cold and distract myself. But her voice lingers in the air. I don't say anything. As much as I find her hard to believe, as much as I want to question it...

She didn't jump. The train crashed. I found her. And that's why I'm here, when I could have stayed at the wreckage, because I *chose* to follow her.

'Ten more minutes. Then I'm heading back.'

'Right.' Her only reaction.

'Right,' I say. Did I want her to react differently?

We resume our pace, and as the seconds slip into minutes and the minutes into what feels like one long hour, I'm ready to turn back when I realise there is no turning back now. The crimson sky ahead glows then fades, and I start to doubt my own eyes, doubt myself. I can't be sure if we're heading in the right direction. Whatever the right direction is anyway. At this point I'd be grateful just for direction. For all I know we've turned back on ourselves, walked in circles and ended up back to nowhere. There's even a hint of light dancing about, maybe the lights flickering in the carriages or someone's phone calling out. At least that's what I tell myself. I can still hear the sea close by. Up ahead the same glow flickers like a fag end crackling, like it's calling me. Then vanishes, enshrouded by darkness.

I focus on the same wisp of light now all too black against the darkness, then a shuffle beside me, and I catch her rushing into that very same void up ahead.

I shout. She's already gone. Nothing but silence, nothing—

'Here! Look!'

I struggle up the steep slope after her. I'm brought to my knees. When did I become so unfit? I haul myself upright and then, all at once, a bright light scrambles into view. That same wounded crimson now swells then scatters over the horizon, breaking up the darkness with streaks of light warming the night.

I catch my breath. The night, thick and heavy, rushes in and I gasp, my breath now blurring the impossible. There, nestled in a valley, the stone and concrete characters of a town emerge, the moonlight bouncing off an island of clouds spread above like wings.

'What...'

But she's not listening. I see it though, see the dark shapes that fill the white void of her eyes.

I think of home, of Swansea, like I want to be back there. Back under the folds of my blanket, back behind a screen, counting the few unemployed pennies I have which is more than the few friends I don't have. Swansea, that ugly, lovely town; that pretty, shitty city. So what's this place, no less than what home has become. At least Skye is here.

Inside my right pocket I feel the creased edges of some card rub against my fingers. My one-way ticket to nowhere.

This is it then. For better or for worse. There's no turning back now; after all, this was my choice. That much I understand.

There's no turning back now.

*

Claire isn't giving up. And even I'm starting to have faith. Maybe it's the fear, the cold, that I don't know which way to turn back anymore. The Gower peninsula stretches its long limbs and snores lullabies far into the night. Maybe I just want to believe her.

She's racing up ahead, her backpack bobbing up and down. She stops when I call, turning a fraction so that I hover in her periphery.

Hurry. *The word grabs me.* Let's go.

I move, slow, with uneven steps, like I'm a baby learning to walk.

It's been a while we're marching now. She stops and, observing the fragile light flutter on the horizon, she lets out a deep sigh. I'm sorry, *I say*, maybe we should turn back—

She shakes her head, a violent surge.

Glimpsing up ahead, I notice the remains of the landscape blink and blister against the feeble night light. I take a step forward, drawn by the next crash of the waves. We both stand there, freezing on the water's edge.

Where are we?

Speaking with her hands, she grabs my arm and thrusts a heavy something into my hands, the rough edges nicking my skin. I hesitate, but she's already started. Useless, I watch as she conjures a flicker of light. A small ember licks then snaps at the air, shadows now bouncing around us.

There she is, plank of wood resting on the sand in front of her, now alight with embers that crackle in my ears.

'Well, come closer then,' *she smiles.* 'Warm up your hands before they fall off.'

'Right.'

I shuffle forwards and offer up my hands, black in the darkness—or by the cold I don't know—but the flames soon tickle them back to life. The warmth feels like a long-forgotten hug which

I let embrace me. We sit in silence for a while, admiring the snap and crackle. Reminds me of the fag stubs in my pocket. I take out one of the halves, light it up, and pull a few drags before gesturing to her. She doesn't reply, doesn't even notice, her mind absorbed in the flames. Somehow, I don't feel like I need it anymore and I tuck it away, instead watch the whispering heat for a few more minutes as it's tamed by the wind and dark. Like the remnants of something. I forgot my phone, and I wonder what the time is, if only to have some better sense of things, how long we've spent wandering, how fast—or slow—the universal clock moves without us.

I turn to find Claire, her smile, and a cupcake with a single candle.

'Happy birthday, Corey.'

*

Skye thrusts one of the remaining planks of burning wood into my hands—a beacon that keeps the shadows off me—this evidence of her skill, her survival. She made quick work of the fire, our next route, and my lack of just about anything. We progress along the coastline and, in her wake, with this odd light still up ahead, I start to feel the waves washing away the rest of the world; the wind calms, the sand beneath my feet hardens, and I feel a sense of warmth trickle over me as everything grows brighter. I throw a glance behind, the whole world still steeped in its night veil.

It's not far now. Black, beastly figures—houses or blocks, I don't know—stretch and sprawl across the line ahead, punctured only by the long trail of rushing water nearby. A single dark, scrawny tower climbs upwards, lost in the pull of the night. And yet nowhere is there a sign of rail tracks; nowhere are there traces of a train, a station, or indeed anyone at all.

This train to nowhere.

'It's incredible.'

I catch up to her. She throws her head upwards, as if drawn to some peculiar beauty. I can't help but look too, though I'm not sure I see what she does. Little questions pull on my ears again and start whispering. Where does this light come from? What is this place? Is anyone here? But answers escape me, mock me. Only more questions, the fidgeting night, and her.

Then her hand grabs mine.

'This way.'

I hesitate, but she breaks free and soon her footsteps fade and that pulls me to her. The darkness is everywhere, save for that promise in the distance and the torch in our hands. I glance one last time back into that vast oblivion behind us, until shutting out that world completely.

'Here,' she points at a wooden post, half-buried in the ground, hunched over like some old lollipop lady who's lost her smile. I can't make out anything. No words, no indication. Neither does Skye. She simply brushes past it and is already gone.

It's like falling through history, walking the past. The sand gives way to a sprawl of cobbled stones, the worn edges caught in the moonlight. A few buildings packed together—outlines, rather—emerge in the spit of light just up ahead. Bricks, doors, and a winding path slip in and out of view. The path rises, then falls, like the beating heart of some hills, slow and slight. It's then I think that this could be any sleepy little town, anywhere. It could be a town in the Valleys, a village in the Rhondda. Or our *Silent Hill*, our *Final Fantasy*.

'It's still night, no one will be outside,' she says.

'Or maybe there just isn't anyone at all,' I offer.

'I thought you liked being alone.' I look her way, but she takes a few more steps, once again embracing the darkness; drawn into it, encouraged by it, curious, I think.

I don't dare move. 'There's always *someone*,' she announces at last. Then she pauses, her face a shade lighter despite the clouds wrestling the celestial body above. 'You're pessimistic. No matter when or where. There is always someone, something. It's dark, it's cold, it's late. Someone will turn up at the right time.'

At the right time.

'That's a possibility,' I say.

'You're not convinced.'

'I'm not convinced.'

'You're not convincing,' she replies.

I can't help but stifle a low laugh. Her ways are having that effect. She even lets herself laugh too.

'Listen,' I explain, 'we saw a light in the distance, remember? That red-orange glow or whatever. It was right here, and now nothing.'

'Maybe they went to sleep.'

'There's always someone awake.'

'Where you come from. Not here.'

Where is here? And then I remember the train ticket in my pocket, one way to—where was it again? I left Swansea station at 9.28am this—no, yesterday morning. Arrived at Newport by noon after a delay. Crewe a couple of hours later…I try to feel for the ticket in my pocket, brush against its familiar edges, but I can't find anything. Shit. I might have lost it on the dunes when we sat down or something.

I keep my mouth shut.

We carry on through the streets, guided only by a smattering of stray stars and the moonlight. Everywhere is the same. Same buildings, same path, same square. If anything is different, then the night hides it. And not a sound, as if the world has lost its voice.

'We need to keep moving.' I look up, my blank reply only encouraging her. 'We need shelter. A place to rest for the night.'

'Sure, but where?'

She takes a sweeping glance at our surroundings, now lit by her torch spitting light here and there.

'Well,' she starts, 'if no one is here, then I guess we can just simply walk into any old house, right?'

'Sure,' I say, stretching the word out. Except I'm not so sure. 'What if they're locked?'

She doesn't reply. And yet, somehow, I doubt that would stop her. The way she holds herself here, the fire gripped in her hand; something has definitely changed in her since the crash.

'Let's follow this path leading down. I can hear running water.'

She's right. Down the curving path, sinking a few metres or so, the familiar sound of running water taps against my ears. We cross a bridge, set above a narrow but active stream that is all but consumed by the belly of the night. The water meanders, hitting the bankside, my throat...I hadn't even noticed my own thirst until now.

I hesitate, then watch as she squats, scoops a handful of water and takes a deep gulp. A pause. She takes a few more swigs while I move away and continue to look around.

'Well, at least we have some water to drink in the morning. It should be safe. It's a running stream, so...'

Her voice trails behind, dwarfed by the sight lying just ahead. Though dim at first, the burning torch in my hands brings the brickwork flickering into view. A large building, nestled just beyond the bridge, it stretches beyond the hiss and spit of my light, growing before us as I draw closer—

She's gone. I glance back and she's gone. In a panic I twist around and she jumps back into view.

'Where'd you...?'

But she turns to face the building before us. Her eyes widen, and I notice her feet fidgeting. This time I can see her in the light of my torch. No shadow, only her bright eyes reflecting in the flames, along with that hint of purple that she tries to hide.

'Let's go.'

We approach what seems to be a small courtyard. The remains of a garden soon splinter and fragment into view: statues, ornaments, withering stone both a mottling grey and seeping black, hunched herons, squatting sparrows, even a lone swan standing guard over the empty nest exposed at its feet and I wonder what happened. Up close, light flickering, the faceless faces reveal nothing. At least, nothing I can see.

'Their wings are clipped.'

Her whisper is catching, and takes on a haunting quality in the darkness that eats away at the poor birds' wings. But she soon brushes past these statues and I pace after her, pressing on towards the front door.

'Ready?' Sure… 'Go knock on the door then,' she tells me. I recoil, but she offers no reaction, no sympathy.

I step closer, my own breath running away from the door that seems to tower above me. I sigh before grasping the hook's disfigured face, twisting it, and then tapping on the door. Several taps. I wait. No response. Several more knocks, louder, but still no response. Nothing but the hollow bang of splintered wood. I step back.

'What do you reckon?'

'Try opening it,' she suggests.

'I can't.'

'It doesn't open?'

'No. I mean, what if…'

She lets out a loud sigh that I feel sink into the ground. My own hand remains fixed at my side though.

'We'll freeze to death if you don't.'

Her blunt response hits me. But still I don't move. I'm not scared. I just can't. She sighs once more, then decides not to waste any more time. She pushes past me, grasps the head of the hook and twists. Stubborn at first, a sudden click and the door jerks open. I leap back, the jolt unnerving me.

She leans in closer, but doesn't dare cross the threshold.

'Hello? Hello? Is anyone there?' We hang by the door, with no response. She calls one last time. 'It must be empty.'

'Sure hope so.'

'You think it's strange. That no one else would be here.' She turns back to me. 'Would you rather that, to be by yourself?' I can't tell if she's serious, or if she's mocking me. Either way, she's gone before I can reply. 'Come on.'

I step out of one darkness and into another. I wonder now if outside is preferable to inside. In here there's no warmth, but at least none of the cold either. I fill my lungs and step inside. She's already taken centre stage, her torch crackling, waving snakes of light that slip and slither, quick bursts of sight here and there. The hall, a modest space with several adjoining doors, all closed, ends with a staircase waiting at the back. All these directions...

The light flickers, flings back and forth, only hints at the unknown surrounding us. I retreat a few steps, as if the weight of the room is suffocating me. Then my back hits something. A jolt.

'Hello?' her voice belts across all four walls. She threatens to blow the torch out with those lungs. 'Anyone here?'

Her light slithers in and out of my direction, the spots

of sight no doubt revealing the freckles of anger and fear etched into my skin. But she makes no effort to apologise, instead flicks the torch again, throwing light on the staircase.

'There's no one here,' she says at last. No kidding. 'Or at least so I can tell.' So she can tell. 'Come on, we've found somewhere so let's just take it easy. We can stay here tonight.'

'I guess.' I give in. 'Not like we have a choice anyway.'

I look up at her and, while the flame crackles and whistles, she makes her way upstairs.

I make to follow her, two steps at a time, my eyes shifting left to right, up and down. Everywhere, anywhere. Nowhere. This strange place.

I clamber onto the landing, but she's already disappearing inside the nearest room. A glance up and down the corridor suggests there really is no one, and I hurry to follow her inside. She gravitates towards the window where some curtains are drawn back, and a white light creeps along the dust-coated floorboards that creak with each step. The sound echoes across the bare, lifeless room, climbs up the walls and out of the room. I step closer, and she turns to look outside through the window.

'It's so beautiful...'

I walk up beside her. Her hand brushes my arm, a touch that wakens me.

'It's...incredible,' I reply.

She nods. Outside, a perfect darkness, a blank canvas. No one. No one at all. Apart from us, from me, from her. Her. More mysterious than the night perhaps, than this strange town...

Is this what I chose?

I remember waking up yesterday morning, around 7, ignoring the snooze alarm and disappearing among the bed sheets. I remember the black coffee from Costa that wasn't a coffee, and the still blacker tomcat perched on the wall as I entered the station, the curious thing looking my way as if watching my movements. But all cats are like that, I suppose. And I remember my one-way ticket. I remember she didn't jump. I survived the *train to nowhere*. I check my phone one last time. Nothing. Miles from anywhere, all alone. And this place. Her.

I try to sleep. I imagine the moon as a nightlight, the folds of my hoodie as the soft felt of a teddy bear, and the waves in the distance rocking me gently. But I still can't sleep. I think I hear a muffled cry, like the town is trying to say something.

Should we go back? Should I take her hand now and pull her back? We never had to come here.

Welcome to the town of cats.

*

It's Larkin, and he's caught me. He catches everyone, eventually.

I'm walking up the lane. Early evening, and the sky is already a bruising black. This is home; always dark. The few working street lamps hiss, the light limps from them, and the whole world is a blur. But I see him. Next to the bin, burnt black from the number of fires it's suffered. Larkin likes fires. He likes making them. He's that kid. I know nothing about fires but to stay away. I'm that kid. The wind whips me in the face, and on the fence a black cat purrs then stops to look. I wish I were that cat, a world away.

'Where the fuck you going?'

I dig deep into my pockets, but I know already I don't have any money. I don't even have fags on me, which he might've accepted. I try to ignore him instead.

'Where you going?' Where am I going? 'Dead man walking...'

He blocks my path. I try to reason, but he's not the reasoning

41

type.

I panic and break into a run, but he catches me by the scruff of my shirt with one hand and my arm with the other. He's got a year on me, and his dad's done time; I feel both as his nails dig into me, which I try to resist only for them to dig deeper into my skin. He then says something about him and my mum, and how my dad never wanted me and my mum only pitied me. I spit in his face. I push him and he stumbles backwards. Then I want to point a remote at his face that's now split in several shades of red too dark, rewind, and say and do nothing.

I look for a way out, except others step out of the shadows and the only escape is through bruises and blood. Royston grabs me by the throat and decks me in the face. He shakes me so much my insides dislodge like the contents in my bag; I forget everything I've learnt at school today and yesterday. I hit the ground, and he starts kicking like a mad horse.

'I'm gonna kick you so fucking hard you'll never have kids!'

The others laugh and Larkin lets me have it; so hard that I believe every word he says. They all come for me and I vanish under their blows; I'm nothing more than a wet slab of meat butchered to the bone.

Through one swollen eye, looking up to the little light there is, all I make out is them; several black cats perched along the wall. I want to call for help. But they don't move, they're silent, still. I'm still, silent, and I don't move. I can't. And everything, still like this, makes me scared for my life…

I don't know why I tell her this, Claire, and after a year together and on this beach of all places. Swansea is full of beaches, especially for students living around the university, and this late at night this late in the year, only a romantic, or a fool, or someone lost, would be pulled into its tide. But it's Claire, and as I'm drowning in my own body of water, she pulls the voice back out of me and for the first time in a long time I speak up.

stay as long as you like
(12 days to go…)

Dead. I could be. Except I doubt a corpse feels this much pain. Even feels at all. Then a cough, a *cre-craw cre-craw* that shakes me back to life. A fierce white burns my retina, and I squirm like a helpless child before the brilliance of the light. The train, the wreckage…? I make to move, but a jolt rushes down the length of my back. Even my feet are bent awkwardly, spread across some wall like they're trying to escape. This isn't the train…I drag myself upright, head falling back, drawn to the early beams of light filtering through the layers of dust and dirt clinging to the window. The beach, the town…I look again. How long since this window was last cleaned? I stay still, the beams of light breaking through and warming last night's chill still clinging to my skin, a gentle—

Rasp alerts me. Then the final few hours of last night hit me like a train.

Skye.

There she is, lying beside me. Undisturbed, resting peacefully. She lies perfectly on her side, her body folded over tucked knees like a baby in the womb, her head cusped in the palm of her hands like a pillow. But her face is most striking, now lit up in the morning light, the pale complexion of her skin soaking in the rays washing over her. She doesn't frown but instead her lips curve upwards to resemble a smile. She seems cold still, the exposed flesh of her cheeks glowing red but it doesn't disturb her, doesn't distract from this new image I have of her. I remember last night, the train, her…

I slip off my jacket and rest it on top of her, covering her hands and the bottom of her cheeks. It's then I

43

remember the writing inked on my arm, all smudged and scribbles now, in the past. Shit. Still, I feel I need to be careful, thinking the way Skye talks. I adjust the sleeve of my hoodie so it covers down to my wrist once more. It's then she shuffles and I'm afraid I've woken her until, like a child all snug and wrapped in cuddles, she calms and even pulls on my jacket.

Who, What, Where, When and Why? Reels of yesterday creep forth, each question a little monster stepping up to my ear in turn, each voice in their distinct form and whispering. When did this all happen? I'd like to think that was an easy one, but I'm not so sure. The train crashed around midnight, but I haven't the faintest clue what time it is now. Where are we? Somewhere north. Near some beach. In some town. That just raises more questions. What about why? I'm kidding myself if I know what I'm doing and why I'm doing it.

Who? Maybe the biggest question of all—who is she? She looks peaceful in her sleep and I guess that's enough for now.

I look through the window. Not much save for the backs of some hills hunched over like old men already one foot in the ground, and in the foreground what looks like part of the spire we saw last night. Our divine light— or curtain call—who knows? Beyond that there's only this small bridge, the walls and faces of other houses and the like, now lingering in view. There's detail in them now, grey and red alternating bricks creating patterns, like giant Lego blocks trying to break free. That's what I used to think growing up, looking up at these funny adult Lego pieces sprawling across the houses and flats on the council estates in Swansea...But then the questions come back, and I feel just how stupid that thought really is, as if this kind of place could be full of Lego and laughter. I pull away from the window.

I tread past her, careful not to press too hard on the wooden floorboards that moan under my steps. I glance back once more before disappearing onto the landing.

I drift between the rooms, peer inside like I'm stumbling upon some secret. As if this house could be some kind of mind's eye and I'm wandering the corridors of its memory. But there's nothing but blankness. Everything feels different in the light though, it brings an ease, as if there were a familiar sense to each room. Like there's a piece of me in parts. The staircase, with its large rectangular window, sheds light onto the landing. A strange warmth wraps itself on the walls, has the damp scent of yesterday, the day before. The staircase is also lined with a row of oil paintings covering the discoloured wall behind; a collection of period portraits, yet of a cat, a black tomcat that stares directly at me, drawing me in. How many times have I seen a cat like this? Too many cats, too many times. After a few more portraits the last is of a red telephone, rotary dial complete with cord and everything…with another cat. Looking past him at the telephone it's the one I imagine my nan would have used in the 50s and 60s. I can't help but laugh a little, knowing that even the shitty decade-old Nokia I'm stuck with isn't as ancient as this. I wonder how people communicated back then—but then they probably communicated more. Stepping closer I notice that in the paintings the lines blur, smudge even, the original lost in the folds of grey and charcoal clambering over the walls like shadows. But not this telephone; the red rings across the landing. I take a step back.

The whole place wraps itself around me and I have to shake it off.

The last room, tucked away at the end, is the only one with the door firmly shut. I press my hand against the door frame. A dark oak, or at least what I think is oak, this deep dark colour with rings of light and grains smooth to the—I prick my finger, curse, then pull away. My hand twitches, my legs seize up, and the blood pumping through my veins beats that bit faster. Beats I can hear climb the inside of my ear.

I clasp the handle. Why am I scared? I turn. After everything that's happened since yesterday? A 'click' and the door teases open. More portraits of cats?

I push the door—too fast—and the room sweeps into view. Nothing. A sigh. Bare save for some metallic tub pressed against the wall.

I let the door swing open in full before wandering the full breadth of magnificent nothing, stopping just before the window's ledge and lean over. I grab the long handle, pull at the squeaky, rigid metal. Stubborn, it soon gives, and a smack of winter, of December, stings my skin. Despite the morning, the sun—

'There you are.' She leaps into view and I stutter. 'I was starting to think you'd abandoned me.' That's a strong word. She stops, now staring, taking me in. 'Are you okay?'

I can feel my pulse pushing under the surface of my skin. I nod to reassure her.

'Yeah, fine. You just, uh…had me going there.' I hesitate. 'And you?'

She nods. 'Well, let's go then.' She's eager. 'We should find something to eat. At least there's fresh water nearby. Afterwards we can work out a plan.'

Maybe it's my head; this feeling of being pulled in all directions, the train last night, but there's no denying her energy, her movement, her tone of voice.

She stops again to look at me, a long, drawn-out pause, and I wonder if I should say or do something. Then I remember.

'I have some food.' I start rummaging through the

pockets of my hoodie and jeans. 'Not much like. Just a snack.' Pathetic scraps I'd scavenged at the Costa before boarding the train, a mere couple of sticks of KitKat. Hard to believe that was only yesterday. I frown, digging deep but can't find anything. 'In my jacket...'

'Oh,' she says, and it's not clear if she's thinking about the bar of chocolate or the jacket that I'd left with her. 'Good. I'll fetch some water then.'

'By yourself?' Instinct. Perhaps I am, I'll admit, concerned about this place.

'You can come with me if you like.'

I nod. 'Nothing here anyway.'

'Yep. Just an empty, soulless house. And cats. You don't like cats.' Maybe she caught the frown—however subtle—etched in my forehead at that moment, because she says that as a statement, a matter-of-fact.

'I'm not keen, let's say.' But her stare demands an explanation. 'I had a pet rabbit when I was six.' A poor rabbit who was at the mercy of the neighbours' cats.

Skye though merely shrugs, as if what I said didn't matter. Or was somehow obvious.

'Maybe you were right,' she continues, changing track, 'maybe there's no one.'

No one. In this manor, in this town, in this nowhere. Is that what I want?

She makes her way out. I follow her, and—

Something appears, a darting white flash only to disappear shortly after.

'Hey, you coming?' her shout pounces from downstairs. A flicker of the light—that's what I tell myself.

I glimpse the clouds outside now invading the glass panel of the window. It could rain soon.

'Yeah,' my soft, uncertain sigh follows her outside and I wonder if, like these rooms, the rest of the town is just as dead.

*

Calves white to the bone, that's how cold they are. Somewhere between girls and women, between wearing skirts and shorts, the queue outside Oceania is full of them. Then there are the fully clothed peacocks in Welsh rugby jerseys flapping around them. A zoo, Claire laughs, an odd assortment of animals outside every nightclub in Swansea, shivering in the long arms of the British October weather. After an hour or so we're at the front of the queue, and I can hear the noise inside, so thick and heavy I could chew it. I'm hesitating.

The doors open again, the mass of muscle throbs and the skinny legs dance and we're pushed inside with the stampede. Like all good and bad nights, I hardly remember a thing. I remember I probably drank those extra gin and tonics because Greg offered, and maybe I helped him into the toilets afterwards. I remember Martyn probably danced like a monkey and Becky maybe watched him nearby, close enough to smell the mix of sweat and fear lining the creases in his smile.

But I remember one thing that definitely happened. I escaped the squash and squeeze of bodies and drinks for a fag outside. Where I found Claire.

Before I ask her what she's doing all by herself, before her knees have another chance to clack and dance, I take off my jacket and wrap her inside. I offer her the last scrawny strips of a KitKat. I never liked the stuff much anyway. It never gave me a break from anything. And yet here we are.

She pretends she doesn't want it. I start to unfold the wrapper, the crinkling—

She leans in, and I hold out the two sticks that she swipes, soon ripping the foil packaging open. I watch as her jaw snaps away at the crumbling KitKat like a hungry lion. Not a crumb would survive, yet she pauses.

'I've had some,' I lie.

48

I gave her the last. She watches me, observes me before stretching her arm out and presenting the half-eaten stick. Before I say anything, she takes the remaining stick in her mouth and lifts it up to mine.

*

At the water's edge I hesitate, watch the ripples pulsate like tiny hearts before I do as I'm told. Skye watches, watches as I plunge my hands deep and throw the water up at my face. I gasp as the tiny icicles nab my skin and tap at the back of my throat. At this point, what could be any worse? She throws her head and, without thinking, I do the same only to snap myself back out.

'Damn that's freezing!' Makes me miss the simple luxury of taps and warmer water.

'If you were tired before then you're fully awake now.' Water cascades down all angles of her.

'I guess…'

And I do feel better. So much so that I lean closer and, shaking my head, splash her with water still clinging to me. I sit back, running a hand through my hair, squeezing the last droplets out.

'You're mean,' but her face lit up all nicely in the pale light betrays her tone. I can't help but grin. 'So you can smile after all.'

I hadn't realised actually, but yeah, guess I can. Then her eyes narrow, no longer looking at me.

'What is it?' But my voice trails as she looks right past me.

Behind, I turn and look to the path upwards leading to the bridge and beyond where—

I definitely see it, that white flash.

'Did you see that?' But she doesn't respond. 'The sun's glare…'

'The sun's glare,' she repeats, snapping awake and

smiling once more but not with her whole face. I don't know what to believe. She could just be tired; she could still be under shock. I don't even know how I feel right now. Then, the sails back in her voice, 'Come on then, let's go.'

'I guess,' I say, though I doubt we'll find that much around here. 'The sooner we find someone, the sooner we can get out of this place and be on our way.'

She nods. 'We need to sort out our priorities,' she says, her eyes focused once more. 'We have a place to sleep. The manor should be fine. It's safe, well located. We have water. We have wood for a fire. And now...' She's looking around, then back to me. 'Maybe not all the doors are locked, you know. Maybe we can find some supplies: food, drink, internet if we're lucky. Or even some pillows!' She exaggerates, her hands clasped together, but her face lights up once more.

It's nice to see her this way, even if I can't help but feel sceptical.

'Yeah right, now you're dreaming.'

'Maybe. But you never know.'

Maybe.

'We'll do a quick tour of the town,' she continues. 'We should stick together and not wander too far apart.'

'Agreed,' I say.

'Agreed,' she echoes.

She stands there, staring at me while the silence works its way around my throat and presses hard. Then a release.

'Let's get this over with then.'

We follow the winding path of cobbled stones, up towards the first row of terraced houses lining the path, coming up towards a sort of square I remember from last night. It's unusual at first. Under the sun's eye everything looks different. Colours come to life slowly: a muddy brown slapped on the signs with black, bulging letters and the rustic, tainted reddish-grey brickworks with the odd flecked green climbing the walls. Like an uninspired council estate, more a place you're stuck with than choose, more house than home.

'It's rather dull, huh?' I say.

'Hmm?'

'I mean it's all so grim, right? The grey, the black, the clusters of burnt red and brown smudged over like some sad brownie.'

She stops, confused, maybe even annoyed.

'I guess it is,' she says. 'Now that you mention it.'

It is, I know it. It could be the place I grew up, the same grey brush that they took and plastered over everything. Just missing some railings, make us feel locked into this life. And up above I can see the same sun, struggling to break through the gang of clouds that thinks it owns the skies. Great, dull blotches of grey oozing across the speckled sky. It could be that place…

She's gone again. Damn it. I have to run after her.

'Hey!' I call. 'Don't do that again,' catching up to her shadow.

'Do what?'

Great. I wonder how many times she'll wander off like that. She's like a child. And this damn chill—my right hand is twitching and I have to grab it and press with the other instead of a fix. No, after everything, after last night, I can't let these little things get to me.

'Never mind.'

Maybe all these colours are getting her excited because I can't say anything else to her. I just let her wander, trailing behind, trying to mimic her newfound energy. This isn't the same woman. No doubt she's broken free from last night. And what about me? Who am I after all of this? All I can think of is going back;

back to the carriages, finding someone, some way to get out of here and just go back. Maybe I should make my way now and she will have to follow me. Maybe...

We carry on through this long, winding street where we try a few doors, knocking, later trying to break in but all of them are bolted up, not even budging when I—heck—when Skye tries to force them open. We abandon the idea and just explore the surrounding streets. Orienteering, from scouts to GCSE Geography, the little of it I remember seems useless now but here we go. From the main square after the bridge there are three paths branching out. The first, we know, leads us back to the manor at what seems the very bottom of the town, past the bridge and sitting near the banks of the stream it faces south. The second, so she says, leads us to the devil's left, back to the signpost that we stumbled across last night. The final street ventures to the right and takes us down a long path stacked with houses either side, and seems to branch off into other streets, other paths. Little distinguishes one from the other though. Dull, empty buildings with asbestos covered roofs that stand out in the tight confines and smaller houses nestled in-between. But even in these other buildings the doors remain locked, the windows blackened, shielding the inside from view. And, of course, not a single soul. The houses so far, whatever and wherever we are, everything is empty, void, devoid of anyone and anything. The path remains impossibly tidy: no chewing gum, no wrappers, but that only confirms what we already know. A few sad beech trees occasionally sprout in the middle, mere branches, merely a half-formed thing, a blemished black lost against the mud brick walls behind.

The whole scene wraps itself around me and I shudder as I try to throw it off.

Time is tricky here, too. No watch, phone dead. Not

even the sun is reliable with the clouds wrestling it from the sky. And, of course, she has no phone either. So how long has it been? Quarter of an hour, half an hour, an hour, can't say. Perhaps I'm liberated, free from time itself; except I feel I need it, need something to place me in all of this.

Peering through yet another damn shaded window I hear her call. I leave the world that's closed to me and instead go to join her.

'It's almost like no one wants to see us.'

'Do you want to see them?'

I shrug. If only to leave.

'Anything?'

'Have a look yourself,' she says, but she can't hide her glee; once again this emotion that contrasts sharply with the woman I first met.

I cross the last few metres separating us.

'Looks like we have our first invite.'

'Yes!' Her cheeks inflate like balloons.

We set off down the next fork in the path. We pass several more houses either side—packed and stacked like too many teeth in a mouth—until at last we reach it. A door ajar, a tooth peering out of the cat's deceptive grin. The outline is different too, not a house, not a manor; some large pub—not quite unlike the local Wetherspoons—spreading across the space of some three or four houses and boasting at least two floors. There's a terrace up front, crammed with tables and chairs still set up, set under the watchful sign: *The Moon Under Water*.

It is, after exploring what seems like half of this town already, the only door open to us. Skye approaches, grasps the bulky brass handle hanging off the frame, only to let go.

'What's wrong?'

'Huh?' Like she's woken from a trance. 'Oh...'

'You okay?'

She looks away from me, away from the door just next to her.

'Sure, I'm fine. It's just...'

'You look like you've seen a ghost.'

She doesn't look too impressed, but at least she's with me again.

'I'm fine, it's just that...'

Her voice trails off. It's then that I make out that white flash once more, clear as anything, cutting across my path and inside.

This is no glare of the sun.

Something is drawing me closer. There could be people inside, voices, laughter, warmth. The *Three Golden Cups*, the *Westbourne*, my grandad sporting his trademark Panama hat and lifting me up to the flashing lights and buttons of the fruit machine, and the roar behind me as the Baggies score their goal, and I win a shiny golden quid that I turn over and over again on the pier as both Mum and Nan lick their 99' strawberry vanilla cones. But I'm not five anymore. All I want now is to see that white flash again and answer at least one question this morning.

I step inside.

A pub, like any other. A bar with enough drinks behind to send me to a long sleep, a few tables out front in open quarters, and here and there paintings of ships and—cats? Then again, I've seen pubs featuring horses, dogs...What's a cat to that? I pass them by, try to get to know this place, growing all too aware of that musky odour that usually sits comfortably in these parts; of alcohol, of smoke whispering from the walls from a bygone era. But before I can notice any more details, I notice them.

All these people. Except when I blink they disappear, like they were never there. I take a step back. I look again, but nothing. I step outside.

'Are you okay?' It's Skye.

'Yeah.' Still nothing. 'I thought I saw people in there—'

'Is there someone?'

I hesitate. Even from here I can see that there's no one. I think of how early it is, how the train crashed only last night, how exhausted I am...

'No.' Maybe I just wanted there to be people? 'No, just reminded me of something, that's all.' When family was family, and friends were friends.

I feel a hand on my shoulder. I'm surprised, but also comforted by her gesture.

'Let's keep looking.'

'Right.'

There are plenty of other places to explore, and what's a pub compared to a whole town? I glance upwards, the sunlight struggling as the clouds beat the sun black. I don't even know how long the day is this far north, let alone in late December. Questions still hover around me, but either I'm too concerned for her or too much of a baby myself to tempt the unknown alone.

'We'll come back later,' I add as an afterthought, hobbling off the last step. If just to sample the beer, to dim the senses...

We veer towards the right, pulling away from *The Moon Under Water* to follow a path that leads us back down. She's quiet now, and that unnerves me. She's even walking beside me instead of running on ahead. I think of last night, of what almost happened. Open and energetic one moment, sad and withdrawn the next. This is how she is.

We continue to whittle away what little is left of the morning, mostly stop and stare, or for her to press her hands against some bricks or doors. No great discovery, nothing that'll help us.

Everywhere is sleeping; this town was born sleeping, I feel.

Aches and cramps clamber over my body. My lower back is killing me and, despite her protests, I collapse onto the empty wooden frame beside me. A few branches droop over my head, splitting the few rays of sunlight into fragments that trickle down the side of my face. I could do with a fag right about now.

'There really isn't much around is there?' I say, talking to myself. 'Nothing, no one.' I have the urge to cry. Instead I clench my fist. I shout. 'No one at all!'

She doesn't answer. I turn to her, watch as she throws her head back, her thoughts running white streaks through the grey, gloomy skies.

Eventually those lips part ways.

'The sun is so bright,' she whispers, dreamlike.

She seems lost in her words, the world around her. It's just as well. I'm lost in mine.

'Darkness,' I correct her. 'It's winter, and there's not a single bird in the sky.'

'Huh?'

'Not a single bird in the sky,' I repeat. 'Look.' I give her a moment to scan the empty skies. 'There hasn't been a sign of any down here either. No birds—not even pesky pigeons, and no stray cats and definitely, definitely no other people...' Heck, I can't even pretend to have seen so much as a fly. 'All alone.'

'All alone,' she echoes. Then shivers. 'It's cold,' she says.

I nod, but I can't help thinking; all alone.

And no stray cats.

*

They say there's a pub for every 448 lucky people in Powys. That's almost three times more pubs per person than Swansea. But who needs a pub when there's a Tesco Extra opposite the flat and all your mates live within a mile? I never liked pubs much anyway, the beers or the 'birds'. Just the mates, the chat, the food. So we used to meet up every Friday for pizza, on my sofa in front of the 40-inch Toshiba and Xbox, before it became every other Friday, then one Friday here and there. But today is one of those Fridays.

There's the clap of hands on shoulders, the inevitable jumping and lurch to the right as the left side of the sofa contracts from the impact of the crash landing. Yoshi has won. Mario has lost.

Martyn turns to face us all. 'That's how it's done.'

Looking back, we all remember Martyn's face, the red flush in his cheeks, swollen with heat or pride or too much pizza. We didn't remember Greg, didn't notice him disappear into the folds of the sofa or the bottom of another can.

At some point, long after midnight but before the rising sun, everyone has gone. I crash in my bed and wake up in a foetal position like I'm born again. I get up, eventually, shower and eat and the weekend goes without much notice. It's only on Monday morning, with the week stretching and yawning ahead of me, do I find out.

Greg, early hours of Saturday morning. He took his coat, his hat, no notice of his friends, his leave, a taxi, some water, some pills, another pint and, once it had all mixed in, eventually his life.

And he was gone. Gone on to become another number, a statistic, the 1 out of 12 every single day. They say men don't talk.

On the weekend Claire asks how I am. I'm fine, I talk, I'm fine.

*

Smoking can save a man's life. At least that's how it feels

57

right now. The questions keep piling up, and without any answers a solid smoke can fill the void. Like carbon dioxide to oxygen; you won't live as long, but you'll remember the feeling, remember the warmth in your body. Smoke can start conversations with strangers, it can start fights as well. It can spark a common interest, or provoke a heated debate. Either way, I need a smoke, but got nothing on me. I'm checking just in case, jeans and jacket, fidgeting all over. I just need something to keep my head in place, in this strange place...And she's still staring up at the sky, entranced, fixated by the large empty promise filling the void in her eyes. She's weird. She doesn't smoke.

'So, what now?'

'What now...' she repeats. 'We have shelter, water, wood for a fire, but we still need food, And...'

A fag, she doesn't say.

'And a pillow,' she adds.

'A pillow?'

'Yes.' I frown, willing her to explain. 'I can sleep on the floorboards, but I need something under my head.'

'Anything else, your majesty?'

But she takes my joke head on, her face full in the little light that is left. 'Careful not to give me too much authority,' she teases. But she later gives me this look and I say nothing in return, just glance around instead.

'It seems everywhere is the same—'

She stands abruptly and makes her way to the nearest house. I don't follow, only watch as she rummages, bends down to collect something in her hands, hidden from my view. She resumes her march up towards the house—

I grip the bench with both hands. A piercing crack whips across the air. If there were pigeons, they'd scatter at the broken shards splintering across the ground.

Another crack of the glass, then another as she removes every remaining fragment from the window. I run up beside her.

'What are you doing?'

'Looking for food.'

Her laconic reply. She continues to beat the window panel, the stabbing of her arm almost too brutal, too barbaric, the black tinted fragments falling to the ground like the tears of an animal.

'Christ...'

She twists around.

'Look,' she continues, now breaking off the last of the glass still clinging to the panel for dear life, 'if anyone still lived here then they would have made a sign hours ago. You were right. The fact is we're out here in the middle of nowhere, starving and cold, and if we don't do something soon, we'll never leave this place.' I fall silent. She clears the last of the glass. 'Understood?'

I don't know how to feel, how I'm supposed to feel. Maybe even—sad? That no one is here? If only I had a smoke...

'Yeah...'

She checks the panel and, once satisfied, grips either side of the frame and hauls herself up. The next moment she's gone. I steal a glance around the street—as if someone were there—then clamber inside after her.

My feet land with a soft thud and the room leaps into view. It's cramped, the four walls pressing against me while the ceiling sinks towards me. A couple of old, shoddy cupboards line the walls, but there's nothing else. Dull and dreary, it's a mirror to the rest of town. Another door beyond the entrance lingers in view, branching off to the right and heading into a kitchen, with the staircase opposite. She's already darted off to the right.

I hang back, if just to give her space. I check the

cupboards, some drawers, but if there was any life before then, it's been erased, forgotten. I lean against the wall—

An echo. I think I make out something; a regular, pumping action. A sort of beat. No more than a whisper—

A sharp 'clang' crashes into the room followed by a curse. Makes me smile. She's not paying any attention, occupied with whatever is in the kitchen. I think about joining her, to see what happened, but this ringing echoes nearby. This—

Beat. Fast, irregular like a baby's. No—the sound tightens, grows clearer, a ringing sound. I step closer. Another ring.

I press my hand against the solid wooden frame. Another ring. I slip my hand across the wall, my skin pushed against the tiny cracks and bumps spread up and down its length. Somewhere, somehow, there's this ring...

I listen, the ringing scattered with the occasional clang and bang from Skye, a strange orchestra in the middle of this dead town. How can she be so loud? I try instead to follow the faint rhythm as it draws me towards the staircase. I take each step one at a time until the ring fades, becomes static, then unclear and irregular once again. I try to find it, to chase its last dying breaths across the landing and inside—

Gone. An empty room. No sound. I check the landing, both rooms. Nothing. A—

Clash splinters the air. I hear her voice. I pause, then hear her call again and I step back. I wait for the ringing. But it's just me, some cupboards, and these walls that don't talk.

Another question. No answer. Where's that damn smoke when I need it?

I stand in the kitchen doorway to find her bent over,

head buried in a cupboard, causing a racket of noise that rips into the natural silence. My head aches. My heart thuds.

'It's damn loud in here. You'd swear the whole town was here.'

Of course there's no one. No one but us. She emerges from the cupboard once more, her face twisted.

'Funny.' Sarcasm, but she's grinning.

I say nothing. She dives back into the cupboard again and, before I have much of a chance to take in the otherwise same bare surroundings and mess in the sink, she manages to stand again with both hands thrust in the air. Both full. Both with food.

The ringing echoes once more behind me.

'Great...' A kind of yawn as I let the word slip. My eyes skirt the same dank walls around, the cupboards all open like monstrous mouths spilling out their unwanted contents.

'There's tons of it,' she hurries, tripping on her words. 'Tins of potatoes, tins of vegetables, tins of fruit. All the cupboards have something.'

Some tin, she could have said. She isn't lying. Tins after tins after bloody tins. She seems rather pleased with herself at least, throwing her hand back and pointing out the other cupboards, all with their doors swung open. Shelf after shelf of tins, so many tins, tins that line my eyes from one corner to the next. I feel sick.

'Yummy. I think we should be okay for a good few weeks on this stuff alone.'

'That's great...'

I shuffle forward, grabbing the nearest tin sitting on the worktop. I guess it's sliced pears judging from the image, a cartoonish, snotty green pair of pears with goofy smiles, but the obscure letters scribbled on the side could be anything. Hopefully it's actual pears soaking in their own juices.

'We should take a provision to the manor, build up a nice reserve to keep us going.'

'Why not just leave the stash where it is?'

'No. There's no water here, and if the manor is a good half an hour walk then we should probably just stay over there to sleep, since we need water more than food.'

'Yeah...'

Very methodological. I suppose I should be grateful for her survival skills.

She stops what she's doing, mid-way through stacking the rucksack, another treasure. She's looking at me, eyes focused.

'What's it like upstairs, did you find any pillows?'

Damn pillows...I notice the beat once more. I hadn't even thought about those damn pillows. This strange beat, this ringing in my ears, was someone...?

'Not even a bed. It's like everything has vanished,' I say.

'Strange, very strange. *Someone* must have lived here, with all of this food here, but at the same time...' The ringing continues. 'It doesn't really feel like a home though, does it?'

I look up. It feels like it's the first time in a long time that I've seen her. She tilts her head in the direction of the window and I wonder.

Like home, her voice echoes.

She leans against the wall, running a hand over the veins of paint swelling in parts. Damp spots of mould creep outwards from the corners—another reminder of home and Wales. It does have that...rundown, 'basic' vibe to it. Even the mess in the sink isn't hers. Just some abandoned, manky dishes and the like adding to the lovely, sickly smell of 'home' that hangs in the air. How long has this place been like this? I think she has answered for both of us. What is home? I think of yesterday, of the bed covers, of the sound of a door closing and someone leaving. I can't remember home.

She glances back in my direction before brushing some thought away with a hint of a smile, ignoring it all and scooping up a few tins nearby. She's practically hugging them.

'We can heat up the vegetables and beans on a fire,' she continues, her rational mind racing. Baked beans—that's all I can think of now—baked bloody beans. 'There's the wood stack beside the manor.'

'A wood stack?'

'Yep. We have our tinder, our kindling...And now our food. Come on,' she says, lifting the rucksack with apparent ease. 'Help me carry some of this and let's go. I've had enough exploring for now anyway.'

The ringing fades back into the walls. I couldn't agree with her more.

'Oh, and check this out.' She thrusts a random tin in my hands, her fingers splayed across the bottom. 'These are about to expire.'

I glance at the numbers scribbled on the bottom, clearly set out as dates. Only days away. Twelve to be exact.

'All this food...'

'Slowly turning to mush.'

We go to leave. She heads for the opening where the window once was while I head to the door. At first glance there doesn't seem to be any lock, or anything else holding it in place bar hinges. I take a chance, grip the handle and pull, the door easing open to Skye.

'You found the keys?'

'There are no keys. There is no lock.'

'What?'

I push the door all the way. It creaks as it eases open,

a door handle with nothing else but two rusted hinges strapped to the wooden frame.

'Let's go,' she says simply. Simply put, I could do with a smoke.

Behind me I hear a ringing, the pitch scratching and the tempo twisted, as if the house were crying out in pain; difficult to know if it's here in the now, or then in a past long forgotten, now blurred in a puff of smoke.

Stay here as long as you like.

*

The sink is sad. It lies there, stretched out lazily like a cat, an emptiness in the granite worktop. It's hollow, nothing inside it, never used.

Claire calls me lazy.

I tell her I'm efficient.

We're in Tesco's, and she's dangling a tin in front of me like some bait to a fish, but I won't bite. She says that's odd, given how many of them I consume. I'm the tin man; a tin man. I may as well be. And that poor sink, she says, it has never fulfilled its purpose in life.

She takes me through the aisles like a kid in a toy store, her arms wide open in a grand gesture to showcase every apple every pear, every bean every pulse, every cumin every cinnamon. She'll make a chef out of me yet, she says, or at least a willing dishwasher boy.

She leans in, pleads with eyes filled with the idea of quiches and roasts. Made with hands, made with love.

It seems like so long ago now, but I can hardly bear to see another tin. Everything is made from scratch, sometimes her, mostly me. They say there are several ways to a girl's heart, and good cooking is one of them. As we leave with the shopping on another Monday night, I look up from the car door, lose myself in the grey mass looming overhead; when was the last time I really looked at the clouds, observed their shapes, admired their slow waltz across the sky?

When we get home, I spread this rainbow of food across the worktop, busy myself with the chopping. The sink, soon full of trimmings and cutlery and dishes, swells, blushes with colour, achieves its life purpose.

*

We keep moving, and the last of the afternoon dwindles away. We have a short excursion following the stream that leads us to the edge of a slope and a sharp drop, making us turn back. At least after all this exploring we have some bearings: to the southwest we have the signpost we first stumbled upon at the entrance, and leading through the square we slope down towards the manor house in the south, and then beyond this stream to nowhere only a fall to death; towards the centre and further east are row upon row of houses, all locked and empty; to the north then we have *The Moon Under Water* and the area beyond yet to be explored, but I'm not counting on much. There's a small hill further north— what looks like the highest point of the town, but I can't imagine we'd find anything there except a panoramic view of nothing. After exploring half the town, it feels like we're the only ones here after all.

Evening falls fast, and as the cold gnaws on my fingers, I find myself fidgeting. I never did get my cig.

'We should grab some of the wood from the stack and make a fire, warm ourselves up and heat some potatoes too. We can even bring it inside the manor, light a few embers there in the fireplace. I'm sure I saw something in one of the rooms...'

Half the rooms look like their walls have been singed with a torch, blotches of charcoal black creeping along the walls like shadows breaking free from the night. All the houses too, I've noticed, have a cute chimney hat on their roofs. In any case she's right, and the dark, swelling underbelly of the sky is enough to make me follow.

We head upstairs, to the same dull room that limps into view. I stack some of the wood that she brought to make a small pyre where an old fire place lies opposite us, while she brings up the tins and the kindling. She takes the lead, snapping up the tinder and kindling, her hands trying to call a quick flame. She could be a witch, summoning a spell, how little I know of these things having spent most of my life in the city, however small and insignificant as Swansea is. Waiting for the fire I head back downstairs to collect more wood like the useless half a man that I feel. After another two trips she says it's enough and I shut the door behind me.

The fire lit, light bounces across the room.

'Good.'

'I know I am.'

I let her have her moment, although she's had enough already.

I sit down opposite, ignoring the spasm in my back as I focus on the fire snapping at the air. She hands me a knife which I use to pierce a potato wedge and dangle it over the fire. I watch as, slowly but surely, the dull beige tint of the wedge turns over crispy gold, rough and charred at the edges. A soft scent taps at the air and, mouth teased open, I tear the wedge in two and bite my lips as the heat from the fire scalds my tongue. She hands me a cup—another treasure from among the tins—now filled with icy water which I sip. I'm still holding onto the knife, hesitating before taking another bite.

'No iron lungs, huh?' I say nothing—hate that expression—but keep drinking to cool my tongue, relishing the moment's relief in any case. 'Haven't quite done this before,' she adds. 'I mean, eating potatoes like

66

this.'

'That's alright. I haven't exactly spent the night in abandoned manors either.'

'Guess not.' She grabs the tin and edges it closer. 'Another?'

I nod. The novelty of the fire seems to have given me enough reason to eat. It's…charming, I'll admit. If unusual. Makes a difference from the usual glow of a screen, I guess.

I end up wolfing down the rest of the tin. I didn't realise how hungry I am.

'Careful. I don't want to go back there just yet,' she laughs.

That laughter. In a way it's strange; right now, I still have this image of this same woman on the train, this same woman who almost…Now here she is, with fiery potatoes and a sweet laugh, and I wonder if she's the same woman at all. Then I think—when I first saw her on the train, she was laughing.

'So, what's our plan for tomorrow?' she asks. I shrug. I don't know. 'Explore some more?'

I nod. 'But then what else is there left to explore, apart from breaking into a few more houses, pillaging all the rooms, surviving day by day…'

'Contact. We need a phone, internet, something to *contact* someone else.' But then a shadow crawls across her face. 'Do you think we'll find something?' And she looks at me with those eyes and I lose what little confidence I may have had. 'We should have some long-term plan though.'

'Like getting out of here?'

'Yeah…' She whispers. Getting out of this—

'C'mon, there must be *someone* here.' I'm not sure if it's optimism or statistical chance that I'm holding out for. 'Or if not, maybe there are other towns or villages nearby? There must be *someone, somewhere*, surely. What are the chances of coming across an entire town abandoned, in the middle of nowhere? With all these tins...' I add. And then, I think, probably the same chances as being the sole survivors of a train crash.

'With all these tins,' she echoes.

'Where is everyone?' I may as well have never left my box room, all the words and screens and blankets I ever needed. Then again, here with Skye...

'You're right.' She leans forward, the flames now dancing in the centre of her eyes. 'There must be something...some way of communication. The town can't be in complete isolation!' She pauses, deep in thought, in delight. 'No man is an island.'

No man is an island, she says, I hear. There must be something, some communication, some link beyond this place. Beyond our nowhere.

'You have a phone, right?'

'It's dead.'

'Right. Are you sure?'

Nah, I forgot all about it. Of course I'm sure. I even checked again this morning. Still, to satisfy her curiosity I pull it out and hand it over.

'See for yourself.'

She takes it, fiddles some, only to give up a minute later. But still holding on to it, like a child unwilling to let go of a difficult puzzle.

'Can I keep it?'

I hesitate, but then what good is it to me now?

'It's dead, there's no point.'

'Well, carrying a brick like that I'm not surprised it's dead.'

I stifle a laugh, but neither of us says anything. Funny how she mocks me when she has nothing herself. Guess it gives her some satisfaction.

'Maybe they just wanted some peace and quiet?'

'You can't be serious,' she blurts out, but she soon dismisses what I said. She can't possibly imagine why anyone would want to be alone.

'So what are you thinking? That there's a desktop or something in one of these empty, hollowed out piles of brick? Wireless, Windows 10, quad core processor, and whatever other damn shit they make up that I don't know?'

She ignores my remark.

'More classic than that,' she offers. 'Have you seen any clues pointing to an internet connection or anything? I wouldn't be surprised if their sole thread that linked them with the outside world was a phone line or telegram.'

'How quaint.' So much for my dinosaur brick. 'I remember growing up we still had a landline. And I'm not that old.'

She nods. She looks younger. Or maybe it's my age, or this aching spine of mine that's bringing me down. Maybe the crash did do some damage after all...

'Maybe we'll find something in one of these houses. Maybe we'll trip over some cable running halfway across the town.'

'Maybe,' my voice drifting. But she's watching me. I'm not trying hard enough. 'We'll have to start the search again. First thing in the morning.'

'If we get to morning that is.' I look back at her and can't tell what she means. 'There are shadows in the night,' she says, unflinching. She's playing games with me again. Maybe it helps her cope. 'And it's frickin' freezing in here...' she adds. I think it's the first time I've heard her complain.

I toss another log onto the fire, still crackling over the quiet hush of our voices. It all seems so brilliant, the light, the vivid crimson and burnt orange that skip across the room and our shadows that fidget next to us. I can barely distinguish who from whom.

She says nothing, only plays with the fabric of her sleeve. I turn back to the fire, soon dozing. Then a flash jolts me awake.

'The train.' A sharp ring. 'That train…' I see a crash of scarlet bruise black as the fire falls and the dark rises in front.

I feel something, a hand on my own.

'It doesn't matter,' she says. 'The train crashed. Now we're here. Surviving.' I look up, confused. 'We're just trying to get back home, right?'

'Right…'

'Let's get some rest.'

'Yeah,' I manage, feeling the tug of sleep. 'The fire—'

'I'll take care of it. You lie down. I'll see you in the morning, okay?'

I can't even nod. Her voice hovers around, but I can't register it. I simply give in to whatever ache or pain or tiredness, simply slump to the floorboards, head sinking into the folds of my hood. I catch the last glow of the fire, burning like the final drag of a cig. Then past the flame I think I catch sight of something; some silhouette, some shadows maybe.

Something moving.

*

I could be dead. Except the pain in my back means I'm very much alive. Damn sleep, or lack of. I wake with my dreams snatched from me, the sand slipping through my fingertips lost to memory once more, nothing left but the feeling of guilt in my gut heavy like seawater.

I roll over, hit by the moon's glow smashing through the open window like an intruder. A cold snap of wind rushes in afterwards, crawls over my skin. My heart plunges. Even in the dead of night I can make out she's not here.

Lurches to the right...

I call her name. Nothing. I stand. One leg staggers, the other limps. When did I become so weak? A kind of twitch taps at my nerves, twisting and pulling on the muscles in my legs. I stumble across the floorboards. My head sways with a ringing inside.

I clamber out of the room and steal a glance up and down the landing. No trace of her. I shuffle down the stairs, one large step at a time. I trip on the last, fall onto one knee at the bottom of the stairs. Bloody bang my shin again—going to bruise this time, I bet. I pull myself back up and head towards the entrance door. It's already swung open. I fall forwards, both hands clutching onto the door frame to hold me still. Weak, I feel so...Throbbing, head still...I shake it off, step outside.

Lurches to the left...

The moon. Clouds choke it, mask it, the light suffocated enough so only this silver scythe hangs above. I curse. Darkness wraps itself around me like fear. I call again; maybe she'll answer? Nothing, only the sound of my own voice plunging into the raging currents up ahead. When did the stream turn violent? I call again, shout after her as I pace up and down, past the bridge and into the beating heart of the town.

No answer. Nothing. Just darkness—and in the light—just shadows.

'...'

I snap around. Nothing. Something. I call Skye. Call her.

My skin feels clingy and itchy, like a sweater, like it's not my own. I can barely stand, but this voice calls me forward.

'...'

My legs roll forwards, into a hobbled run up the slope then—

'...'

I wander the square. Pulled—from left, to right—like my body is beyond my control, like I'm on a train about crash...

Skye. Where are you?

I meander through the streets, swaying from one side to the next. The faint glow above guides me, drawing a gang of silhouettes that creep into view from all sides.

'...'

'Who's there?'

I brace myself, shuffling forwards with my fists hanging at my side. This is stupid, but...

Then I see it—no, *them*.

A gang of cats. Beneath the full moon, mere shadows at first, their eyes and teeth and claws all catch the light and reflect in the street behind. Black—no, onyx, obsidian, blacker than black, these are no ordinary cats. They're bigger, their heads extraordinarily so, like they've been snatched from *Alice in Wonderland*. They bob up and down like dolls as they move, and even from here I catch the soft purr that fills the air.

For a whisker of a moment I watch them, watch as they make their way up the street. Watch as they make their way towards me.

I run. Across the cobblestones, down the streets, everything now shaking in waves of light and dark. Did they see me? Can they smell my presence? Do I need to run? Yes, I don't know why, but I know the answer to that final question. They mustn't find me. I need to escape, or at least hide somewhere. The tavern. Just up ahead, I run towards the tavern, all the while hunting for Skye. I can still recall her laughter, still remember her purple jumper.

I crash onto the terrace. A mere murmur reaches my ears, a fragment of a voice. I approach the entrance, the door ajar. I—

Glance back. For a moment there's no one. The next there they are, marching, many of them.

A whole town of cats.

I seize the door frame in front as the ground beneath me disappears, the door now a mouth opening up to the black of the night, the whirling of the wind rushing past inside the train door—

Skye!

'Jump. Just do it.'

And then I see it, my reflection in the hollow of the darkness.

'It's all your fault. You'll never leave this place.'

A blare pulling me back, back to the screaming lights of a train crashing into view. This train to nowhere, the shouts and screams, the shadows on board, and this flash of an image falling out of the carriage...

I'm alive, I tell myself, I'm still *alive*.

A hand brushes against my shoulder—

*

If you can't do it, teach. Which is a nice way of saying you're not good enough but you are good enough to bring up the next generation.

I'm reminded of this on my first school trip, where I'm the teacher—or one of them (re: one of two)—and I'm with a bus load of kids (re: thirty of them). They're some of the youngest in the school, younger than the years it takes for a smoker's lungs to clear after quitting. I know I can't smoke here. But the thought comforts me as I look around the bus full of fresh faces, each one— eventually—turning to me at some point with some question or something.

I'm doing one last check, walking the length of the bus when I spot her—a young girl called Amy who sits by herself, counting on the cold comfort of the two lines of snot running down her nose.

The bus driver shouts and the kids finish buckling their belts. I sit next to Amy, who's five and can't speak.

I learn this on the way to the zoo and for a while I turn to silence—a snotty silence punctured with her attempts to breathe. A silence that I imagine is crushing her.

I can't enjoy myself at the zoo. Maybe it's the 30 kids, maybe it's the fact that I can't smoke for another seven hours. Or maybe it's that shadow in the impression of a five-year-old girl trailing the other 29 kids. The other teacher, older and wiser I hope, points out some black cats on the wall beside us as we wait in line for the toilets. The kids point and bounce but Amy retreats into her shadow, as if the cats could be after her too.

On the bus home I sit at the back again. This time Amy sits next to me. In her silence.

For a while we sit like this, saying nothing and everything. It's then that I notice the book in her hands, Twinkle Twinkle Unicorn. A little young for her, perhaps, or maybe it's for her younger brother. Then I wonder...

'Why aren't unicorns real?' I say aloud, to myself, noticing in the corner of my eye her interest turned towards me. 'Giraffes are real. What's more believable, a horse with one horn or a leopard-moose-camel with a forty-foot neck?'

She smiles. Then silence again. It's only a few minutes later, as the bus leaves the carpark and the zoo trails behind us, like a shadow; for a moment I think she's trying to look past me, at the window, then I hear her voice breaking free.

'Unicorns are real.'

A perfect answer, I tell Claire on the shore later that evening. 'Everything is perfect,' she replies, the last of the sun still caught in her skin, and we disappear under the next wave and laugh into the deep blue.

there's only one way out of a labyrinth (11 days to go...)

Skye!

I snap awake.

'I said good morning!' I tilt my head, the rush of light soon calming like tamed waves and I see her. 'Gosh, are you alright? You look like you've seen a ghost!' A stroke of laughter whips the air—my own—and I stare in disbelief. She crosses her arms. 'Okay, so what's wrong then?'

What's wrong, what's wrong with her? I haul my body upwards, like this other thing still detached from me, the calloused skin of my hands scraping the floorboards. When did my hands become so messed up? I feel a sharp pinch, a splinter from yesterday's firewood maybe, another reminder of reality. Never mind. I look at her again but can't hold back her image. The image from last night.

'Is...Is that you?'

The lines of her delicate skin crease into a frown.

'I see you slept well.' A pause. 'Did you, I don't know, sleep on the wrong side of the floorboard or something?'

I ignore her remark. The palms of my hands glide over the floor, my eyes wander the familiar dank walls of the room with dark stains crawling all over them.

'Here...' I look at her once more, half-asleep, half-confused; the former feeling pulling me away from her, the latter pushing me towards her. 'But I was...' I look to the window. 'There were cats...And someone...'

'Cats? You mean more portraits? And someone, someone who?' she asks, and I turn back to see her frowning once more.

'You really have no idea of what I'm talking about?'

She shakes her head. I sigh. Maybe…maybe it had been nothing all along. 'Then nothing,' I say. 'Just bad dreams, that's all.'

She pauses, as if to absorb the absurdity that had just escaped my mouth.

'Well,' she takes a moment before moving, grabbing the rucksack we'd scavenged yesterday. She's quick to leave again. 'I guess this kind of place can do that to you.' She slings the sack over her shoulder. She sounds upset even, like a disappointed child. 'Anyway,' she continues, 'you should grab something to eat. Tin of fruit or a tin of beans or something.'

Tins.

'Yeah…' I feel so inspired. Still half-awake I try to continue the conversation, to keep her here. 'So, what's the plan today?' Maybe her answer will give me something.

'We have shelter, we have water, we have food…' She states matter-of-factly. 'Now we need to find our way home.' I don't reply, hanging on to that word: home. When I look at her again, she's turned towards the door, the sun slipping into the room and following her. 'I'm heading outside. Don't forget to eat something!'

She disappears, but not without me noticing her shoelaces; undone, dancing around her as she leaves. I don't say anything, too tired and too confused and I let her go. All I can think about now is those tins and the idea sends me back to sleep. At least that's what I want to do, but a flash steals my attention, that same burst of white I've seen several times before. But this time close enough for me to see.

A rabbit.

I look around the room but there's nothing, just me, myself, and I. I wait a moment before curiosity gets the better of me and I drag myself up to head outside. After

Skye.

*

'Finally,' Claire says, walking—no, skipping along the pavement.

I'm not that late. I peek at my phone still nesting in my palm, remove the ear plugs and the call of another world. She stops in front of me, folding her arms. She tells me she messaged me, that I never replied.

I check my phone, an iPhone, the casing alone worth more than the pair of Nike trainers I'm sporting. There's nothing there, at least nothing from Claire. Plenty of other messages, notifications, apps. But she's not there.

She tells me she messaged me, but I tease her for her old Nokia, this relic from another era. After three years together she still has the same one. It's a brave new world, I tell her; one with connections that spiral in all directions, messages and thoughts carried beyond oceans and currents. Even the mermaids are in on it, swimming in waves that travel beyond their waters. They're everywhere, these networks, this web of global neurons linking us in. We're all connected.

Claire laughs.

She takes my iPhone, plays with it like it's some strange artefact, handles it like it's radioactive. Not sure what I was thinking giving it to her; should have just thrown it back in my pocket, but I didn't want to.

She's still playing with it.

'Want me to fix it for you?'

Now I laugh. What's to fix? But she pockets the phone and, before I can protest, she grabs both of my hands and pulls me in. Like a siren. A ringing all around me.

'Show me how we're connected.'

And she reminds me.

*

'So, who's doing what?'

She was expecting me to follow. I'm learning to expect nothing less from Skye. Still...

'Huh?'

'We'll divide the tasks. You're in charge of maintaining our provisions inside. Take whatever you can carry. If you find anything else then bring that too.' All I can think of is tins, tins, and her damn pillow. Saying that, from the pain in my neck she could be onto something. Guess some things in life are still worth living for after all. 'I'll get some more firewood. We burnt through everything last night.'

Images of potato wedges come to mind.

'I can manage by myself you know.'

'Sure you can,' she says. 'Get the firewood then.' She rips the rucksack back open, jams in something that I don't see. 'I'll be exploring. You never know—might find the next best tin!'

I've been too harsh with her but it's too late now. So I end up saying nothing, and maybe that's what troubles her.

'What's wrong?'

I stare at her for a few more seconds, memorising her face, the tint of her eyes that slant upwards. It's like I have doubts it's her, like the events of last night's dream somehow blurred with reality; I try to hold her in place, stop her disappearing again from my view.

'I don't think we should split up.'

She seems confused, caught off guard maybe.

'Now you care.' Half statement, half question.

I hesitate. 'Just that...I don't think it's safe out there, all alone, that's all.'

A moment, then she nods.

'Let's head off together then.'

We set off. I don't show my relief; it's both of us I'm worried about. We make our way down to the square and through the streets, passing the same houses, same tavern, until we hit new territory. We decide to go as far as we can. Eventually I feel like we're pushing up against the edge of town, the clouds so low as if the sky threatens to collapse on us. I can't be sure of what I see, save for a spire that leads us to an empty mound—a cemetery as it turns out—nestled beside a church.

'Well, I guess we should take a look.'

Besides an ominous sign outside, *Good Hope*, there's nothing else. Even God seems to have abandoned this place.

We push further until the very limit of the town makes itself known.

'It's incredible,' she says, stopping just before a vast wall, her small frame swallowed by its immensity. She presses her hand against the bricks, her palm sinking into it. 'The end of the world.'

This world, this place maybe. Another of her strange interpretations. I'd be tempted to give her a smoke if I had a spare.

'That's one big shadow hanging over us,' I say, observing the black stains in the brickwork. 'Rough as anything too. Any idea what it's doing here?' No reply. 'It's pretty big.'

She says nothing so I place my own hand on the brick next to hers. When I remove it there's a shadow, an impression of my hand left behind; like some bizarre kind of messy play, my seemingly small hands painting what little of my story there is onto this giant canvas. Skye draws her hand back as well and I notice her hand leaves no such mark.

'A labyrinth,' she breathes.

'What?'

Eyes still fixated on the wall she continues, 'Do you know the difference between a maze and a labyrinth?'

I shake my head.

'A maze is a puzzle that has multiple pathways, maybe multiple entrances and exits too. But a labyrinth...' She brushes her hand against the wall. 'There's one path. Only one way in, only one way out.' She turns to me. 'Some people don't make a distinction, others do. The first known labyrinth—in ancient Greece—was used to trap the Minotaur monster, but was actually a complex maze with many branches. Historically labyrinths were used to trap evil spirits, or for others to make a spiritual journey. Either way...'

Her voice trails off and I throw my head back, taking in its height, its reach as it threatens to pierce the skies above.

Is this supposed to be our labyrinth? I touch a hand on the wall again only to revoke it shortly after. I don't look for any impression this time.

'Who knows what this is. As long as we get back does it really matter?' I can't be messing with any more questions.

She sighs. 'Yeah...'

We follow the wall, continue along the curving path that never seems to end. It turns out that it loops back around and we find ourselves passing the church and returning to the streets before. Satisfied we've covered the whole town we begin our return, passing by a small park and stopping at a few unexplored parts. The first, a building spread across the space of three or four houses, slips into view. She hangs back I notice, as if waiting for me, and I wonder if she's undecided or testing me.

This time I don't hesitate and step inside.

'It's a library,' I say aloud, somewhat disappointed. 'Except...' She follows me in and we approach the desk, and of course there's no one around. Less than that, there's nothing at all. No computer, no phone, not even stationery or papers. Only yet another portrait of a nondescript cat, the only sign of still life.

I take a good look this time. It's a far cry from the cats I imagined last night though, hardly any connection at all. I peer even closer, but there's really nothing else to it. No mystery. No question. Just a cat. Like any other.

'Come over here.' I break away and turn to Skye, finding her among the books—except there are no books, only row after row of empty shelves. 'A library without books…'

What's a library without books? Scrap that, what's a library without a librarian, a desk, computers and a cat manning the post? I walk up and down each row—not a single book.

'A library without books…' I repeat. 'I guess that's not too surprising with no one here.'

But she doesn't reply. Instead I find her sitting down in the next row, cross-legged and holding onto…

'You found something?' I glimpse down at her lap, her hands covering the one book here it seems.

'Did your parents ever read to you as a kid?' She asks without so much as looking my way.

My parents? Shit, that was so long ago, I have to think. My dad no, my mum? This image appears, of when I was five or six…

'Yeah, my mum used to. But that was a long time ago.' I'd forgotten that. But I remember it clearly now. Sitting in her lap, or on the cushions beside her, the soft scent of her lavender shampoo tapping the air. I'm certain she smelt of lavender, saying it was the only soap worth buying. She read a lot books to me. And I'd forgotten; when was the last time I called on these memories? 'Every night before bed,' I explain. 'She used to read me stories.'

'What kind of stories?'

81

'I don't know.' I really don't. I think really hard; the soft touch of her oversized cardigan, her soothing voice, but I can't remember a single story, a single title. 'It was so long ago. Something about magical creatures—fairies and dragons and all that normal stuff.' Normal. 'I think there was even a talking bunny at some stage. And you?'

'My mother read me stories, and my father too. I remember his voice, but I never got to see him.' Never got to see him. 'Why don't you go on and explore some more? I'll catch up with you.'

I want to ask a question—bring her to the surface from the depths of her past—but I notice the colour lost in her cheeks and I know she needs her peace. I remember the train, remember... I don't want to leave her alone but she should have some time to herself.

Outside the street opens up. More houses with the same empty expressions. It's amazing, despite the five hundred miles distance or so, just how familiar everything feels. I walk up a street which could be any one of the hundreds I've walked before. I step inside another open door into what looks to be an abandoned corner shop, a *Premier* at the end of my own street.

There's no one. No prize there. I look around, nothing much. Again, no surprise. Just a few tins on the shelves that I look straight past—then I find the counter topped with a packet of fags and some scratch cards. My hands fidget and I grab the pack. I tear it open. Lambert & Butler of all things. Only to find just one left. I sigh. Better than a kick in the teeth, as Mum used to say. I take the fag out and pocket it, then move onto the scratch cards sprawled across the counter. Maybe this is my lucky break. I check every one of them but they're all losers. Not worth the card they're printed on.

'Waste of money.' I turn around to find Skye looking down at the scratch cards on the counter and the one in my hand.

I rub the card against my fingers, pressing down hard.

'Yeah, well, when you've got nothing else going on in your life, what's one quid for one chance to change everything?'

'I suppose…' she replies, then turns to me directly, 'but then money won't solve your problems.'

'My problems?'

'Everyone has problems,' she replies and then, as if to remind me, 'everyone who travels this far north.'

The way she looks at me; I didn't even realise the card now crumpled in my fist.

'It'll change enough,' I say, finally.

A flicker of a smile, maybe, and then without another word we both head back outside.

'Let's split up,' she says, after another minute slips between us. 'Have another look around these streets and we'll meet up back at the manor for lunch.'

I nod. She seems upset. Given everything that's happened I don't blame her. But then I regret it when I see her walk away. She moves fast, like she's carried along a wave. Or is the wave. Alone, I resign myself to the nothing and no one of the street, still holding onto the same worthless crumpled card in my hand, still waiting for my spiritual journey to begin in this long, decaying labyrinth.

*

At least I'm still in Britain. That much is certain. Only in Britain could the weather be the same dull, grey lull that lingers overhead, raining or threatening to rain. Miserable, poxy weather. Typical weather is typical. In fact, it's almost a guarantee that, in the event of stumbling across another lost soul here in the town, one of our first questions or comments—in spite of our very lives—will revert to the weather, to the rain. This is what people do when they meet—they say nothing, or talk about nothing. This simple hypothetical exchange reassures me of where I am, at least somewhere in Britain.

Morning passes. I reach yesterday's treasure house and ransack the cupboards; once, twice, and again as I make one trip after another, hoarding a cupboard size of tins, tins of this and tins of that, tins that could last us weeks, even a month without ever having to leave the manor. Live like hermits, like some modern geeks or otaku, or some survivors in some post-world war nuclear fallout. Why anyone would keep so many, and in this house of all of them, is beyond me. Still, I shouldn't question it. It's free food after all, beggars can't be choosers. Like shopping at Tesco or Asda or just about any supermarket at midnight and grabbing whatever's left, reduced to pennies.

I explore the manor again, thoroughly, like I'm unravelling its DNA. Its old, decaying DNA. I count some thirteen rooms in total, seven on the ground floor and six above. God knows why so many. Our room—the room we've hijacked—counts among the largest, while two others are no more than storage cupboards and the rest somewhere in-between. But all of them are the same; all trace of life gone. If people lived here, if a family settled and children once ran up and down its steps, then they're no more now than someone's memory or none at all. Like they never existed. I trace my finger along one of the many empty shelves in one of the many empty rooms, yet nothing. Even dust doesn't settle. Like a tide had swept in and now nothing left remains.

I step outside, embrace the vast emptiness of everything.

A soft crunch alerts me. The few clumps of grass,

beaten brown, easily fold under my feet and the rasp offers a kind of soothing music, an antidote to the silence. I gravitate towards the stream and, bent over with my reflection staring back at me, I plummet under, the chill shocking my senses awake. I hold myself under for a few more seconds before throwing my head back, the fresh sting bringing me to.

As the water settles, her reflection appears where mine once was.

'Feel better?' She asks as I run my hands through my hair, shaking the water out while still gasping for breath. All the while she watches me. 'I'll take that as a yes then.'

She drops down beside me while I rub my skin, snatches of water scattering across the ground around me and running down the slope back to the stream. Sitting cross-legged, her legs fluttering up and down like the wings of a butterfly.

'How was your adventure?' I ask.

'Oh, rather interesting actually.'

'Yeah?'

'Yeah,' she repeats, but the excitement in her voice fades into a solemn tone, the butterfly wings slowing to a stop. 'Here.' She hands me something, some kind of journal—a young girl's, maybe, judging from the rainbow unicorn. 'I found it in one of the houses…'

Her voice becomes lost in the blank space of the page I'm on but I soon find the words she's thinking of. The ink is thick, blotted, and seems to glimmer as the light catches each stroke. I don't miss a word.

You are here for a reason.

I read the sentence several times. Several times but it doesn't change anything, the words don't just disappear. Then I feel the weight of her stare on me, her eyes watching me, searching me. I read the sentence one last time.

'You are here for a reason...'

But my voice drowns out.

'It means someone is here.'

Her words are full of certainty, and she seems to hold onto that thought like some grave omen hanging over her. I turn to the manor, to the row of stone birds that inhabit the isolated space between us. What are these birds, these broken herons and sparrows and swans, unmasked by the sunlight? Wings clipped, heads bowed over empty nests, they look lost in grief. Are they hiding something? I then glance at the entrance door, then the windows of the first then second floor, the reflection of the moment's sun bouncing from the glass panels and now sprawling across my vision.

Then her voice pulls me towards her.

'Whoever it is we should be careful.'

I look up at her as if for the first time.

'Why's that?'

'They may not be very friendly.'

'I see...' I understand what she means, but still. 'More than likely they'll be more scared of us than we are of them,' I say, trying to be confident. She frowns. 'You know, like how the small spider is more scared of us?' I try to explain in ways she'll understand. 'Maybe they're all on their own. It may be another survivor, someone looking for help.'

For a moment I think of Larry, of Bubbles...

'Be careful.'

In these rare moments I feel we've swapped perspectives; she's walking in my shoes and I in hers. Her blunt words—heavy and direct—cut our conversation short. She holds my stare a fraction longer before heading towards the stream. She's upset again, but I say nothing. I just have the sense of our surroundings closing in, swelling in my eyes and pushing against me.

Could it be possible? Did some other poor bastard survive and make it all the way out here? Do we take the risk and reach out, or keep to ourselves and hope for the best? But the words themselves; it's like someone is trying to reach out to us.

Nothing seems right.

I turn back to face her, but I don't know what to say. I say nothing. Not even a comment on the rain beginning to fall.

*

'Rain.'

He says this, the word clinging to his mouth like some stubborn fat raindrop. He doesn't even notice, or at least he says nothing. Rain here, everywhere, all about him, obscuring him, me, us...

'Rain.' I shadow, I echo, trying to hold onto him in some way.

Maybe he said something else, maybe I did. Maybe between the metre or so between us we found some connection; something more concrete, more lasting than his text message that brought me here or the droplets of rain that fall between us, crashing to the ground and gone by the morning. Maybe, just maybe, for once we can be more than just rain.

I watch him watching the rain fall on the early evening pond. Somewhere, a duck quacks and the voice breaks against the bank now soaked with promise that runs back down. Then he turns again—my dad—and for a moment I think he's actually looking at me and not through me. Like I am more than just rain.

It's raining again now. I'm looking outside, Claire's own words in my thoughts. You are not your dad, she says, her hand taking mine.

If he had said anything else at the park then I don't remember. Maybe even that one word I thought I had heard was nothing; nothing but mist and breath and not a single word. Because dads and men don't talk, do they? Before long I was home again that night, just me and Mum and everything said in silence. Upstairs, I crashed onto my bed—like some big fat raindrop. Soon my pillow was wet. After all, I'm just rain.

*

Like a wave breaking, night comes crashing down. I stand outside another entrance, closing the door of yet another house. Just one more then I'll head back. It's like an addiction—that feeling of what's inside, the mystery, the suspense. I can feel the impulse pushing me forward, pulling me inside. I shuffle the few steps next door and, with the crowbar I found stashed away in one of the rooms of the manor, I strike the bolt of the door and wedge in the metallic rod through the opening. Deep enough, I push. The door budges. I push harder. Small snaps and cracks tickle my eardrum. I slam a final time. The door jerks free.

'Great,' she says, 'let's meet back here. I'll continue to pack what's left in the house opposite.'

I watch as she disappears inside yet another house across the street then turn back to my own. The last of the sun struggles through the door after me. I scan the surroundings, desperate for another source of light...

In the corner of the room, a dainty, lonely lamp. I stare, transfixed by the sight. What are the chances? About the same as surviving a train wreck. Why question it? I'm learning. I flick the switch and a beam of light blasts outwards, touching every nook and cranny, bringing everything into focus. Electricity. I smile; never before has a damn lamp excited me so much—all 60 watts or lumen or whatever the heck it is, it's light. For now I just don't dare question it. Skye's influence.

I drop the sack and start rummaging.

Like a kid in a damn candy shop. Cabinets to

cupboards, anything and everything I can get my grubby hands on. It all gets the same treatment. Most drawers turn out empty, save for some candles, small creamy balls of fat which I haul into the sack. A box of matches appears near the wooden drawers and I question the layout of the place. The matches rattle in their box...Shit—if only I could find some cigs. I don't dare using the only one remaining stub in my pocket. I head into the kitchen with nicotine on my mind, only another disappointment. Most cupboards are bare, save for a few tins of potatoes. King Edward or Maris Piper potatoes I don't know, but soppy, soggy potatoes nonetheless. And more damn tins. At this point, regardless, everything tastes the same.

I approach the sink. There, in the dim light from the living room, I make out the fine glint of a knife. I pick it up and balance it in my hand, the weight sinking into my palm. The damn thing then slices the top of my finger and I drop it, clanging and splintering the silence. I curse. I inspect the cut—not a mortal wound but still deep enough so that I feel the pain.

I head upstairs. Nothing. A magnificent nothing. Just the largest room of the house where I find a bed stripped, nothing but a skeletal, wooden frame in place. A single wardrobe shows off its naked interior. Nothing but a few frowning hangers droop from the ceiling above, swinging ever so slightly.

A draft crawls inside through a window left ajar. I imagine someone there now, early morning, opening the window to let the fresh air breathe new life into the stale room. Cold, I shut it. It's then I notice Skye. I can see her as she walks off into the distance. The darkness engulfs the streets around her now and I can barely make out her outline as she vanishes beyond the point of no return. I stare at the spot she left behind for a few seconds longer, before turning away and making for—

My foot catches something and I trip. I steady myself in the ever-fading light, kneel down and grasp a long, exposed cable. I press it between my fingertips, a solid, plastic cord. My pulse twitches underneath, but it's not the thought of nicotine.

Another thought—*a connection to the outside world.*

I freeze. I hear a gnawing of teeth nearby: the cats? I glance across the width and breadth of the room but there's nothing. Another moment. Another breath. Steadying myself, I turn to follow the lead, hands shaking, pacing myself. The long cable stretches across the floorboards, cuts under the wooden frame of the bed, tucked neatly against the wall. It carries on up towards the wardrobe where it disappears behind. I sigh, then curse. Then waste no time. Crowbar in tow I chip away the fragments of plaster surrounding the cable, ignoring the fading light and swarm of questions. I scratch away the hard surface, tugging at the cable. The plaster breaks loose. A hole appears—

That gnawing sound. I breathe, take a moment, then twist my head to the right. And there it is. Staring straight at me, its whiskers poking out either side. Unmistakable. Not a cat. But that flash of white that I've met before.

The white rabbit.

It looks up at me, twitches its fine little whiskers, then dashes off out the room.

'Hey, wait!'

But my voice is drowned out by another loud thud. I stop.

Footsteps scuttle about downstairs, the sound rushing up to the first floor. I stay still. I grip the crowbar. I hear the steps enter the kitchen, roaming…Silence. Shit—I remember the knife, the blood, and I curse under my breath again. Then a screech—drawers sliding open—

nicks my eardrums. I edge closer to the door, hide behind it, just when footsteps clip the bottom of the staircase. I hear the chip of the wood catch, feel the biting metal in my palm.

A shout. I drop the crowbar and walk out onto the landing.

'It's you...'

Her voice shouts back.

'Of course it's me, who else?' Damn it, she's still mocking me, but right now I don't even care. 'Come on, it's about to be pitch black outside. I can hardly see anything except this lamp—it's like a star in the room!'

She's right. Screw 60 watts, it's like a floodlight. But that won't do us good anywhere else—the lamp's electricity is rooted to the floorboard through a cable. I switch the lamp off. I struggle to even make out the steps in the staircase now. It's too risky to stay any longer. We'll just have to rely on the moon's crooked smile.

'Come on, let's go.'

'Just what took you so long anyhow? I was getting worried.'

'Really?'

She looks at me, but the seriousness soon fades.

'Well,' she hesitates, 'you know, I wouldn't want to be on my own here.'

I nod without saying anything. I think about what she said. Neither would I.

'Huh? Did you say something?'

'What? No, nothing.' How did she know?

'Anyways, what did you find then?' she asks as we plunge ourselves into the thick of it. At least the rising moon keeps the dark off us.

She looks at me and then back to the impending night sky, back to the little of the path I can see up ahead. It's biting too, and I thrust my free hand into my pocket, my other still holding onto the crowbar. Just in case.

'Nothing.'

'Nothing?' she echoes.

I open up the sack, the glint of the moon enough to show her the numerous tins inside. She nods, somewhat indifferent, but I can see the disappointment on her face.

'Same old. Tins of potatoes, tins of carrots. Tins, tins, tins. I'm getting sick of tins.' Finally, her confession.

'Me too,' and the start of a smile runs across her face but the darkness hides it soon enough.

'But then again...' She sighs. 'We need to eat something.'

'Yeah.'

Then I wonder what she's been doing all this time.

'So what about—'

I'm cut short by a rhythmic 'clicking' as she bends down.

'The rabbit...'

'Ah, I see you've already met?' She says, picking him up and stroking his white fur.

'You could say that.' I watch as the rabbit doesn't move, only his ears twitch as Skye rubs behind them. 'What an earth a rabbit is doing here I haven't the faintest idea.'

'Oh, they have lots of wild rabbits around these parts. Although technically it's a hare.'

'You don't say.'

'He's a mountain hare, quite common here, although I've never seen one so small like a bunny, and so white!'

Indeed, white as snow.

'Alright, so there's a logical explanation to that.' At last, an answer. 'Let's head back in any case, before the night fully takes over.' As we head out though she continues cwtching the little furball who appears to have taken to her. 'You're not taking him with us, are you?'

'Why not?'

Why indeed. But I say nothing. I'm too tired.

Another night, same room. Eating more pasty soup from those damn tins—the very same—I have to swill my mouth out several times with the frozen water from the bucket we now keep on hand near the door. Hiding under our jackets and hoodie we try to arrange ourselves for sleep. Meanwhile I've no idea where the rabbit has gone—it's run off already but Skye doesn't seem to mind. She's tired, burnt out like the fire at our feet; at this point the heat from the small embers is just enough to keep my toes from falling off. There has to be worse than this, that's what I keep telling myself now, to keep my sanity.

'G'night,' I whisper, my eyes flickering.

'Night,' she echoes.

I turn over, facing the window and, outside, the stars. A yawn escapes and I feel myself wrestling sleep. But I can hear her shuffling behind me. I can feel her stare.

I hear her voice, now a whisper; soft, calm, if not masking something more.

'This wasn't what I imagined it to be like.'

'Not afraid of the dark, are you?'

A faint laugh. 'Funny. No, it's not that…' Then she becomes serious. 'Does this place remind you of home?'

I turn back towards her. Her too.

'Home?'

'Home is a strange place to me. It's not really a defined place so much as a time, a person.' She hesitates. 'Sorry, I don't mean to keep you awake. You should sleep.'

'No, go on,' I encourage, now facing her. At last, I feel this mysterious woman will open up to me, say something to me.

'Okay…Can I tell you a secret?'

'Of course.'

Her lips move but under the veil of darkness I can't

tell if she's smiling or sad.

'Okay... I lived in a small place. It seemed big at the time though, probably because it was always empty. I grew up with my mother all around me, and my father too, but I never had the chance to really know them. Not as much I could have, not as much as I needed...'

I wait for her to continue, but she says nothing.

'Did you not see them enough?' But she doesn't answer me.

Instead, she asks me a question.

'Do you miss your parents?' Miss them? I hardly knew them. I'm about to answer when I hear her sigh, but cut short, as if she's trying to hold onto something; onto some memory, some precious trace of her existence. 'I felt like I was drowning in some vast sea. I was scared...' She stops, unable or unwilling to continue. She looks up at me after a while. 'This place is empty...But it's full of memories too.'

I look across the room at her, trying to bridge the gap between her and me. The furthest north, the loneliest place, and this place, all of this place and no one. No one at all. No one, but us. This place is full of memories, she says, and maybe she's right in some way, like there's a piece of me here in these rooms. This nothing. Then again, I still haven't the faintest idea why I'm here—how the heck did I get here?

The train. The town. Those cats...What does it all mean?

'If I could, I would hug my mum and dad right now and tell them I love them,' she breathes once more, and afterwards neither of us say anything.

I close my eyes. I'm back on the beach, back on the peninsula. The waves rush in, over my feet. I stand and look out across the waves but there's nothing, no one, then...I'm back in that room. I grasp the cable around my fingertips once more. I can hear the ringing, but I can hear the waves too…

Should I tell her? And what would I say, what would she—what could she do? What if I told her that the waves keep raging and the ringing repeats over and over and—

*

Marriage is no question; ever since I met Claire it's been the only answer. An answer to the start of my life after leaving home, a life I never liked and a life that never liked me. But I've always liked—always loved—Claire. And that's why, still fresh out of university and to the wider world, and only three and a half years together, I ask her hand in marriage.

It's a summer's day, funny given it's Swansea and it's April and the rain is more reliable than bills through the letterbox. Which is saying something. A blessing, Claire says, and for once I agree that the sun is shining for us.

It's a simple affair. Two witnesses—both of our mums, neither of our dads—a few friends, and no acquaintances or, God forbid, extended family. It's £190, which I think is a rip-off for the sake of 45 minutes renting a room in the giant lump of brick that is the civic centre—a grey smudge that ruins the struggling beauty of the sand and sea of the shore just in front. Claire says it's a bargain— the average wedding is closer to £19,000. I agree, it's a bargain, and I pay the extra tenner for two marriage certificates.

Outside there are children shouting and bouncing along the stone wall of the pier. It's a Thursday, a school day. There are no parents about. There's a miner's cat, black as coal, and the younger kid chases after it while the older one encourages him.

My mum, who smiles and her face creases in places I don't recognise, helps takes photos. Claire's mam is more natural. We ask passers-by to take a photo of all four of us and when the young couple—similar to us in our age, I think—hand the camera back, I can't help but notice the yawning gaps here and there, the space

95

where others could be.

'The numbers will grow soon,' the woman says, and she has a hand on her bump that I now notice.

On the beach the sun catches Claire's face and my mum, with words I didn't know she had, 'You'll be a great dad.'

I notice the sun shines all day.

follow the rabbit
(10 days to go...)

From the baked beans to the bunny rabbit, life here is becoming routine. Like home. I look from one to the other, from the bunny to the fire to the beans and wonder; if only the wind were as warm as the fire, the fire as enduring as tin after tin of beans, and the beans as unpredictable and unusual as Skye, then it would be a nice breakfast after all. Of course, it isn't any of these things. Nothing. Like home.

I shuffle in my place beside the fire, opposite her, heating up another tin of orange mush.

'Beans...' I mumble.

'Beans,' she echoes. We both raise our forks.

She asks if I've had a good sleep and I mutter something in response that neither of us make out. At least it wasn't as bad as the previous night. Not that I remember anything, except her own story, the little of it I know. I guess she has her reasons. But at least there were no cats, which means I'd probably just dreamt the whole thing, a hangover from the portrait paintings that haunt the staircase of our adopted manor and the rest of this forgotten town.

I don't really hear her next words, instead I'm drawn to the stream. The water touches the brown turf of the bank, like some rising tide calling me. I abandon the remaining blobs that mope about in the centre of my plate and instead edge closer, kneeling down besides the stream now splashing the bank, spraying the ground where I sit.

'Hey little fella, come here.'

Ah, our mysterious friend. How this bunny rabbit came into our lives I still don't know, but I watch her, and the rabbit, and return to my breakfast.

'He must have mistaken the orange-ish beans for a carrot,' I mess with her. Beans. Billy beans.

'Don't listen to him, Thumper. He's just being mean.'

'Thumper? Nah, he's Billy.'

'You named him? I didn't think you were one for animals...'

'What makes you say that?' She's making me out to be one soulless person all right. 'If you remember, I had a rabbit when I was six. It's cats I didn't like.' She nods, but doesn't seem to take much notice of what I said. And now she's calling Billy to come to me. I can be nice. She smiles, at least, and I guess that makes it all worth it. 'Still strange though how a rabbit of all things is here, but nothing else.'

'You question things too much,' is all she has to say. 'You would rather him not be here.'

Once more her way with words, her tone neither a question or a statement. I don't respond. But I do know that I'd rather leave this town. Then again looking down at Billy on my lap she may have a point. Maybe I do question things too much. Caressing his ear, I could be six years old again.

'The water level is higher than yesterday.' A statement, a matter-of-fact.

I take a moment to reply. Billy continues to make himself at home on my lap while I savour the sweet, sickly taste of beans bubbling on my lips.

'Doesn't matter. We'll be gone soon enough.' Then I hesitate. 'You reckon that'll be a problem?'

'Another question,' she replies, but this time smiles. Like she knows she's irritating me and wants to make the most of it.

I follow the fast current with my eyes, the water splashing the tips of my shoes as it rushes by. I look up but now she seems distracted. Then, at once, she leaps back into reality.

'Well, not really,' she answers at last, 'unless you don't like swimming.' Another piece of her dry humour on a slippery issue. Yeah, I can play her game too. I don't say anything though, merely poke my sad, sloppy beans while she does the same. She looks at me across her horizon of tomato-ish orange sauce on the brim of her plate. 'It rained again last night.'

I hadn't even noticed. Not that I can remember anything about last night. I was...I was holding onto something...

I say nothing, instead focus on the fire prickling my skin as she spreads yet another dollop of sustenance across a cream-coloured plate. The sauce stains the otherwise unblemished surface, and I wonder if it's ever been used, if it was anyone's to begin with. Whose hands have touched these, if anyone's? Then she hands it to me. I collect the first few beans. I raise the fork to my mouth. I eat. I survive.

'Maybe we should think about just leaving soon. Just give it another day or two to see if we've missed anything.' I float the idea, but she doesn't respond. I guess it doesn't matter for now. 'Alright, so what's the plan today then?'

She doesn't look up. She finishes her meagre meal first, scraping the last few drops into the back of her mouth. She even licks the plate, her fork, and her lips to finish.

'Hmm?' She lifts her head from her plate, engrossed in her baked beans that aren't even baked. 'Oh. We should continue to look for food, anything else that may be useful. And look for our new friend.'

I look up at her, checking I heard right.

'Sure that's a good idea?'

She nods, ignoring my tone. 'Yep. I think it is.'

'Right…' I fall silent. She seems indifferent. I can't seem to understand her; I'm not even sure she wants to be understood. Then again, it could be the aftermath of trauma. I need to remind myself what happened only a couple of nights ago.

'Who knows? They could be anyone. From anywhere. With any purpose.' She pauses for a moment, reflecting. 'Either way, we go to them, or they'll come to us. It's fate.'

Fate. She's used similar language before, I think, and it's making me uncomfortable. Not that I really believe in it, but in this place…In any case I understand her point, but still.

She slips out of the misty grey air and catches the glint of the sun struggling overhead. I scoop up a few more mushy blobs, dangling them from the fork.

'Ok then.' I drag the words out from my mouth. 'We'll look.'

She seems satisfied.

'Good,' and she knocks back the last of her breakfast before straightening up. 'We'll meet back here in a few hours for lunch?'

'I—'

'Can't be alone?'

'It's just that—'

'And I'll be fine,' she insists, slinging the sack over her shoulder, her shadow stretching out towards the banks of the stream in the rising sun. Like she's heading off to the big bad world alone, and leaving me behind. 'It's you I'm worried about.'

But I'm left to wonder what the heck that's supposed to mean; before I can reply she turns tail and I'm left to watch her disappear over the bridge, vanishing around the corner, her shadow with her. To think, just days ago she...

She even forgot about Billy. Poor kid. I let him finish the beans before snapping up the plates and putting the fire out. He later disappears just as easily as she does, and I head back inside the manor to fetch the second rucksack we'd snatched from one of the empty houses yesterday. I find it lying on the floor with last night's water flask sat next to it. It's a good size, and even brings some character to our lives with its Celtic patterns. Could be a good luck charm, or a curse. I don't know. Either way, I cram it inside the sack before slinging the dead weight over my shoulder. As I do a few flickers of light irritate my eyes, bursting through the window beside. Approaching the looking glass, the town emerges in waves.

The morning light catches the church spire piercing the skyline in the distance, and as my eye passes over the first square I catch sight of her, crossing from one side to the next. Strange, I think, how fast she moves. She glides across the ground, passing through the next street like a ghost until she eventually disappears inside one of the houses perched at the far end. Another house, another haul of tins no doubt. Yay.

I look further ahead. I notice the house from last night leap into view. Illuminated by the light it looks different, exposed even, verging on vulnerable. I clutch my hand, pressing on a pocket of air, pressing on...

The cable.

I hadn't noticed before, yet it's so obvious. At the end of the street, the house towers above the others. I wonder just what side of the house is that bedroom, that...I press my hand tighter. I look again at the house at the end of the street. A faint glow seems to emanate from the first-floor window. I blink. It must have been the glare—

101

'Hey!'

I jump, crashing into the wall behind me. My hands shiver as my nerves inside scatter.

'What the hell are you doing here?' I shout, staggering some. I trip over my own feet and curse. 'I just saw you outside.' I glance back at the window but the light has faded, clouds clutter the sky, and the rain pelts down overhead. I don't understand.

'How long was I—?'

'Just a shower, that's all,' she continues, ignoring my shakiness. 'Probably pass over in a few minutes. I just came back to dump some more tins.' She holds up her sack, triumphant. 'And you?'

'Just…observing.' I say, unsure where the time went.

'Well, come on then, let's get to it. Look, the rain has stopped now, see?'

I peer through the window once more. The rain has stopped.

I turn back to her, confused, my face no doubt quite the picture in contrast to her calm, as if an hour or so had ticked by. She wouldn't believe me if…

I give up, simply head out. Routine. I busy myself with some lunch, pack it into the rucksack along with some other empty containers before heading out, over the bridge. Routine. By the time I reach the square the light has already begun to fade, but at least that's expected. Routine. Forget warmth and the unpredictable.

*

I waste no time.

I head back to the house and upstairs. I rush into the bedroom and collapse to the floor as I fumble around for the cable. I can't see it. Impossible. I look under the wooden frame. Nothing. I swing the wardrobe open. Nothing. Inside, yesterday's hole and the flaking plaster

I'd chiselled away with the crowbar is nowhere to be seen. I curse. This isn't happening—did I imagine it? I look towards the window. Is this right? Then I see a flash of white rush behind me and out the room—Billy!

Follow the rabbit.

I head back towards the door and realise. I've stumbled into the wrong room.

Idiot.

I step outside into the corridor once more, now threatened by the impending darkness. I hurry inside the room opposite. There, to my relief, I catch sight of the cable nestling in the wall just ahead with Billy nearby.

'Curious little thing, aren't you?'

I approach, then stop. Looking through the nearby window I notice the manor. It looks so far away from here, despite everything. I even wonder if Skye is there now, if she might be wondering where I am. Should I even tell her where I am? Then I see Billy in the corner of my eye, sitting beneath the wall.

'Will you tell her?' But he just sits there, whiskers twitching. 'Of course you won't.'

I walk up to the wall above the cable, kneel down, and rest my head on it for support. A deep sigh escapes my chest. Skye. I've found nothing but a cable and I don't dare tell her. I should tell her. Then again, what secrets is she keeping from me? But then I think that's stupid; after everything we've gone through, that the only other person we have is each other. And yet—

It's here. This dull, heavy sound, swallowed by the hollow wall. I step away—the wall itself is soft. I tap against the surrounding plaster which crumbles easily enough. Satisfied, I take the sack and pull out the crowbar, wedging it through the hole, pushing it in deep enough to hold tight. I kneel down once more and drive the crowbar through. I push. Again. A crack. Again.

A *ring*.

I stop. I lean closer. Nothing. I grasp the handle of the crowbar once more—

A *ring*. Another. Then a long screech clambers inside my ear, running and screaming, the noise thumping my head inside. I jump up. It's not here, it's in the next room. I follow the noise, this incessant cry, until I come square up against a wardrobe. I pause. The echo twists and squirms to the back of my mind—

Glory, I wrench the doors open and there it is in all its damn, painful glory.

I grasp the smooth plastic of the red telephone—the very same in the portrait back in the manor, complete with a circular dial and robust, chunky design. I pick up the receiver end.

An empty chasm of sound, a—

Quick, sharp bleep. An utterance. Then silence once more. I press the phone close to my ear, clinging to the receiver, waiting for that next sound, that next connection. Nothing. My hand shakes. Still nothing, no connection. I sigh, pulling away and place the phone back down.

It doesn't ring again.

The wardrobe, the walls, the ceiling. Everything retreats to the advancing shadows. But I don't look away from that fading outline. Night falls. I pick up the phone again. I dial a number—any number—and wait. Nothing. I put the phone back down. I dial another number. I don't know who to call, any number will do. I wait. Nothing. I curse. I invoke Jesus and Christ and some other words in between, but still nothing.

I give up.

Outside, a sea of darkness threatens to pull me under

save for the grace of the starry night. If it thinks I should be grateful, though, it should think again. Stupid stars, damn place. Marching back, I keep feeling the tug of the cable, the hollowness in the earpiece. I soon hear the familiar rasping of the stream and cross the bridge. I struggle to see anything at all now, but the water guides me and it doesn't seem to have flooded anything. The rising tide holds back. For now.

I cast that thought to one side. A yawn forces its way out—loud—as I stumble back towards the manor.

Maybe it's not broken? Maybe even Skye would know—I should tell her. But once inside exhaustion hits me, and I barely think to even close the door and I just head upstairs. Stepping into our room it's steeped in darkness, and I fumble my way until I collapse onto the floor. I huddle up with my hoodie and jacket on, turning on my side and wondering where the day has gone.

I close my eyes.

Ring, ring.

*

We all have a shadow; the trick is not letting the shadow become you. My mum knew this all too well. After I was born, she was often her shadow and nothing more. I'm thinking of this as Claire is getting ready upstairs, ready for our night out at the Millennium Centre in Cardiff—her birthday present—but then I notice that my shadow is in front of me.

I'm at the psychic's house. I have to be here because I'm not allowed to stay at home and my mum wanted—needed—to come here, she said. Because she's her shadow and she's desperate and she wants guidance. Even if she can't afford it, she'll pay whatever the price.

I'm not allowed to enter the room during the reading. I sit by myself, in the room adjacent, a mix of bright lights and their shadows. Because life is full of both. There's a clock in the corner, blessed with the zodiac signs instead of numbers, a sprawl of cards on the coffee table in front, their faces all jokers to me, and cats— lots and lots of cats painted into all four walls of the room.

When the reading is finished my mum smiles and excuses herself for a moment, and the psychic turns to me and her face comes alive; that is to say, the wrinkles in her face move and fill the shadows that only moments ago were etched into her skin.

'You're afraid of cats.' I don't answer her. I don't want to admit to her reading my thoughts. 'You're not afraid of cats,' she says after a long pause, 'you're afraid of your shadow, of everything behind you. The cats know this.'

For the next week I read all I can about cats, everything mitten and magical and mythological. Once upon time cats were revered, even worshipped; from the Egyptians through to (some) Christians and, of course, cat lovers today. But then again cats also allegedly suck the breath out of newborns, and so pregnant women should avoid them at all cost.

Claire calls me from the top of the stairs, and I shake off the memory. I am not a pregnant woman or a medieval Christian, I tell myself. But I am, looking at it tonight, somehow afraid of my shadow.

*

I can't sleep. I call her but there's no answer. I call again. It's early, earlier than the sun. And she's not here, not anywhere. I can't find her, in the room or any other. I see a flash of white sprint across the landing—Billy—and head outside. He disappears and I call her again. Nothing.

I cross the bridge, pass the first few houses and stumble into the square, calling her name. Still nothing. I shiver, but it's the anxiety that's worse; she wouldn't survive this cold through the night.

I stop. The fear is getting to me. What if…?

I call her again. In any and every direction, I shout,

I—

Freeze. There, where the street opens up like a gaping mouth. Not her. No. *Them.* The cats—a horde of them. It's difficult to see, but I make out their unmistakable shape and the legion of teeth that cuts across the darkness like a knife.

I fall back a few steps. I—

'You're not alone.'

A hand grasps my shoulder and I feel myself falling. I'm pulled back. I shout. I twist around—

'Hey, hey! It's me. Are you okay? It's me, you're not alone!'

Two hands lock onto my shaking arms and hold me in place.

'It's okay, I'm here.' Her whisper.

I shake my head.

'No, no. You were gone. They are here. The cats—there,' I point, as if stabbing at the darkness will prove anything. As if mere shadows, the cats disappear back into the dark currents. 'I swear, right behind you, there were cats—a whole town of cats...'

But she shakes her head, at once calm.

'Cats? You think I sound like a cat?'

She pouts, then breaks into a smile. She thinks I'm playing a game with her. But she can't ignore the terror in my eyes for too long, and she holds onto me once more. Her hands grip my own, her touch surprisingly warm.

'Come on, let's head back. It's freezing out here. The cold is getting to you.'

She leads me away, back down towards the stream. I glance back but there's nothing. Nothing but that flash of white bouncing across the ground and, further beyond where I can make out that house, I see it clearly. The moonlight bouncing off the window...

I didn't even notice the moon before.

*

I'm on our beach...And this spot, this feeling; this is not an easy place to find...I know. I can hear the song of the sea, the dancing waves all bright and blue...Soon I look back, see the impressions in the sand left behind by my feet...I look around, but there's no one else to be seen...

I look back and I can't find Claire; but there are traces of her everywhere. In the sand, in the sea, in the whisper 'This is our place.' She had said that only moments ago. Only...

Then a cry, a rush of water, and she emerges all at once from the sea.

I thought she had made it to the shore before me. I thought that she had disappeared. I thought that...I felt that...

'Corey, are you okay?'

I nod. Everything is fine. And I'm reminded of what love is, having for a few moments being caught without her.

walls are built to keep you in
(9 days to go…)

'**Where were you** last night?'

'I told you, I went back to one of the houses.'

Since she woke up this morning, I've been questioning her about last night's episode. Damn thing frightened the hell out of me.

'That's it?' The words hit out. I clench my fists. I don't know why I clench my fists.

'Yes,' she continues. 'It was late, maybe I shouldn't have gone out but I did. But I came back and I'm fine. And it wasn't *that* late.'

I'm shaking my head. My hands are fidgeting too.

'No, I can't just believe that. There's more. I thought—'

But she shakes her head, a gesture now irritating me. I have other questions but she's turned away, a shadow across her face. Then she looks me straight in the eye.

'Are *you* okay? Don't forget, you were out last night too.'

'I've already explained.' I press my hands together, try to calm myself. 'I was out looking for you.'

Impasse. Neither of us will budge. I know that.

'I think something has got to you,' she carries on, provoking me. 'I think you need to lie down.'

Lie down? No. I need her to tell me exactly what happened last night. *Exactly.* I remember the army of cats marching towards me. I can still feel someone's—some stranger's—hand brush my shoulder…

I push her again, but she bats me away.

'Maybe we should just leave. There's nothing here. No one here.' I pause, pacing back and forth. 'We should head back to the wreckage. There'll be someone there by now…' I look her straight in the eye. 'They'll be looking for us: the police, the fire brigade, someone—'

'No one is looking for us.' Just like that, she cuts me short. I bite my lip. 'Lie down, it might do you some good.' She places her hand on my shoulder, a soft gesture that steals my next words.

I take a deep breath, my hands still twitching. It's been too long since my last fag. I still have that one that I found, I could now—but then I feel her hands, feel how warm…

'Just don't do that again,' I raise my voice, perhaps too loud. But I'm shaking, and she's leaving. Is she upset? 'I just—'

She's gone.

I skip my beautiful beans and plush pears and head straight out, but there's nothing here for me right now. I think about the house, the cable, the possible connection; I think about *The Moon Under Water*, and all those people; I think about the shop, the library, *Good Hope*, and the wall surrounding the north-westerly point of the town; I think about all these doors and places and all other sorts closed to me—no, lost to me. I think about leaving. About the train, of that night, of when she almost…

I stop in my tracks. I just can't bring myself to do anything.

I return in the early afternoon, hours wasted and no will to do anything. A few clouds—like waves—crash overhead, flood the skies a bruising black, and now all I can think of is the hunger gnawing at my insides but no real desire to eat. I force myself to prise a few tins open and get the fire going again, that much I've learnt. The crackling of the flames brings a satisfaction to my ears. But then I think of the stack of wood, diminishing, burning away, turning to ash. It's difficult to stay positive when everything is turning to ash.

Then I see her emerge like a siren in the hazy distance. 'Hey!' she calls.

I don't answer. I continue swirling the slices of value peach in the tin with the end of my spoon; peaches drowning in their own juices, tiny bubbles of air surfacing, like a promise, before bursting.

'I said hey!' she shouts in my ear as she comes up behind me, her hands on my shoulders. When did she become so close? She seems excited, as if her past mood has been swept away by the stream now rushing past, buoyed from last night's downpour. 'What's the matter? Cat got your tongue?'

My eyes roll up towards her. Sure, I think, sure. But I make nothing of it. I say nothing, but she's staring at me and expecting me to say something I can tell. I sigh.

'Any discoveries?' I ask, my heart not really in it, hoping she'll leave me be. But she either ignores the tone or is too excited to notice. I look up, her eyes alight.

'I've discovered a wall.' I stop swirling my spoon, pause, then let her continue. 'A great, massive wall that surrounds the town in the west. I haven't seen all of it yet, some of the town remains clouded in that mist. But it's pretty big. Really scary looking, like.'

I look at her, my jaw slacking and my head falling forward. She tilts her own in reply. She's decided to mock me, I'm certain of it. That's my punishment for this morning. She must be really upset then.

'You mean that wall we found the morning after, on our second day? The wall that snakes around the north-western outskirts, that giant of a cocoon that pierces the skies? That one?'

Her head rolls to the other side—too far, inhuman, like some ultra-flexible doll with not a bone in its body.

'Yeah...That one.' She frowns. 'How did you know?'

I grasp the spoon tighter in my hand; I want to feel its raw, cold steel bite my skin. I take my time, weighing my words.

'I saw the wall the day after we arrived. *We* saw it...' I try, but she doesn't move. She merely frowns again.

'Don't be silly, we had never seen it,' she says, like a child playing games.

I pause, my heart on the spoon. I hold my stare, tracing the faint lines that brush her forehead, the strands of hair that fall down the side of her face, her eyes that look back at me. Through me, past me...

My heart skips a beat.

'I see. I guess I was wrong.' I stifle a laugh. Facing such absurdity, it's all I can do. 'Must be losing my mind or something.'

She nods. 'Okay then, well, do you want to see it later?'

Just what the heck would I see? That same damn wall that's been the back of this town—the back of us—all of this time? I struggle to contain my frustration. This must be because of this morning. She's taking the piss. But I'm not going to provoke her. I'm too tired for her games.

'Actually, we need more firewood so I'll head downstream and go collect some.'

'Oh, don't worry about that,' she replies. 'I'll take care of it. You go see the wall. Perhaps you'll see something I didn't.' Is she actually taking the piss? Now I'm not so sure. I scan those bright chestnut eyes of hers as if it will offer some clues, but the dense mist hides everything. I'm lost. 'Go on, I'll work on lunch later too. See if you can reach the other side of town. The mist was there when I tried, but it may have fallen back with some of the sunlight this morning.'

She scoops up a tin of peaches and drops the spoon inside.

'I really like these peaches. These tins aren't actually bad, no?' She beams.

I swirl the slices in my own tin, with my own spoon. I bite my lip. I don't say anything.

*

I head for the wall.

I come up to the main square and carry straight on. I throw a glance here and there, wary of the houses surrounding me. I focus on that one particular house; is it taller maybe, maybe the bricks in the wall are a brighter red? I don't know. I do see the room in my mind. I see the wooden frame of the bed, a skeleton, dried up history. No telling whose it was or what it all means. I see the wardrobe door. I step closer. The phone...A ring...

I glimpse the path behind now fading in a blanket of mist that invades the street. I guess she's right about one thing. I drag my feet so the soles of my shoes scrape the path to reassure and give me a sense of direction. I see far enough to know I've passed *The Moon Under Water*. *Good Hope* won't be far, and then the wall.

I have trouble recognising my place. Streets, buildings, let alone the signposts here and there. A mist—this collection of watery whispers of the town suspended in air—is drowning me in this fantasy, this fable conjured up by Skye. December, Britain, I remind myself. But it's everywhere, forcing itself down my throat. I disappear around the next corner—

I stop. There it is, all at once.

Before the end of the town, barely at the back of the church. I shuffle forwards some, pause, then take a step back, readjusting my sight. Defying all logic, she was right.

The wall.

It towers in front of me—taller than I first remember. The mist is low, maybe that's why, but the black stones of the wall now seem to merge with the bruising black skies above. Difficult to know where one ends and the other begins. I press a hand against a brick, feel its coarse skin against my own.

How did I get here? How did this train crash, and how did I end up in this town? How can this wall...? But no, all I can think of is her; her way with words, her purple jumper, and those eyes. Eyes neither here nor there.

She must remember it when we arrived, must remember despite the darkness that first night. I wander, head back to where this began, back to where the cobblestones dissolve into sand and sea. Sure enough the path is just as I remember, and the beat in my chest steadies some. I pass the next few minutes watching my step, pacing across the sprawl of meshed cobblestones and dreary, dead lamps; broken promises of light, false hope of seeing. I brush past them all, ignore the mist now hanging onto my back like a second skin. A few more minutes, more steps that I recognise. I allow myself to smile. How stupid is this? How could she possibly have forgotten?

I carry on until I find what I'm looking for. I turn the corner. I—

Stop. There is no sign. If there is then it's lost on the other side of this wall. Now there's no entrance, no exit—no breach, not even so much as a dent in the brick. It just continues, enclosing everything. No matter which direction I turn each brick is further proof, each blink of light tells me. This is the place. This is where we first stepped inside this world. This...

I take a deep breath.

I rush up and throw my hands onto the bricks beaten black; I want to feel them, I want them to resist me, to push me back, to prove this damn wall's existence. I run my fingers over it—smack it, squeeze my hands together, hit it. Nothing. The thick bricks absorb all of the impact. I strike again, kick again, but nothing gives. The wall absorbs all of the impact. I hit again, my fist clenched red in the cold. Nothing. I strike, my knuckles now fresh with blood as the skin peels off. I strike until I collapse to the ground, my hands outstretched, still clinging onto the wall. I—

Shudder. Light trickles over my face and I try to catch the falling sun before it's too late. I pick myself up. I run. I skirt along the wall, sprint alongside the edges until my breath is beaten out of me and I'm all limp and lost. I collapse against the brickwork. Lean against it. Feel it push against me, resist my weight, my will; resist everything that I am.

There's no leaving this place.

*

I call after her. There isn't any wood lying around, the tins have disappeared, and there's no sign of her in the window of the manor. The cemetery seems a more comforting place than here. I shout again. But my voice vanishes in the folds of mist and dark that have followed me here. I burst inside, rush up the stairs calling her, checking each room, but nothing. She isn't here. I step back outside.

I wait, observing the tiny wisps of fire and smoke that ebb and flow, slowly retreating from the approaching night. I cough.

'Hey.'

I sweep my head round. It's her. Walking towards me, her arms stacked with blocks of wood that she drops to the ground, a clunky sound that smacks my ears. She approaches the fire, but not before I step in front and grab her by the arm.

'The wall…'

At first she frowns and then, as if silently remembering, she gives me a half-smile.

'You found it?'

I don't move. I merely repeat the word.

'Wall…' The word stretches before me, spreading across the horizon, surrounding me.

'It's really…intimidating,' she offers, an afterthought.

'This is wrong.' I want to shout but manage to hold my frustration in clenched fists. She pauses at least, looks to me with this mix of indifference, even confusion, even annoyance staining the otherwise perfect beige of her face. 'Listen. The wall, it wasn't here, not when we had arrived. And then the morning after, I saw it. I remember it. But now the signpost…When we arrived there was no more than a skinny sign before the cobbled stones and winding path, you remember?' Like an old, hunched lollipop lady, I remember it too well. 'Now it's…'

As I ramble on she doesn't move. But that doesn't stop her from judging. She places her hand on my shoulder, a gentle grip to calm me. To control me.

'Like you said,' she hesitates, as if collecting her words, 'vanished into the darkness. I think maybe that was all you saw, the darkness.' I shake my head, but she continues, 'It was a very gloomy night. We could barely make out anything. I remember we struggled over those dunes, fell more than once, and it was only the sound of the stream that guided us to the manor.'

Her words remain suspended in the air, but I can't bring myself to speak. The dunes, slipping through the sand, the stream…Yes, I remember all this, but…

'No,' I say. 'I remember the—'

'—winding path? So do I, look,' and she turns around, guiding my body as she does, turning me so that I look

116

past the stream, down to look over the valley, down the...

'Winding path. That was it. Down that slope. That's where...'

'Exactly,' she declares. 'We came up the valley side. And look, on the front side of the manor house, that window that stretches across the front, that's where the moon reflected that night, that glow that we saw; that was the reflection of the moon on its façade.'

I look up, mesmerised.

'Fantastic.' A fantastic lie. She's so close yet feels so far; I notice then the lack of purple underneath her coat and I wonder where's her jumper. She tilts her head, a gesture that's now irritating me. 'You really believe all this, don't you?'

She tilts her head to the other side, giving me this puzzling look.

'Well yeah, that's what happened, silly.'

I hold my fists at my side.

'Aren't you worried? How the hell do we get out of here? How...'

But something snatches my voice. Her head tilts further, like it'll soon snap—is she listening?

'Oh...there's a way out. You got here, you can leave. Leave whenever you want.'

Her labyrinth. Her minotaur. How dangerous is this place, how dangerous are these words?

'Whenever I want...'

Funny how I can't bring myself to believe that now. She shrugs it off, turns her back on me and slips away. Away from me. I stand there, alone, the ashes from the logs rotting at my feet.

'Come on,' she calls, 'I'll prepare the fire. You bring some tins.' I stir awake once more and she looks at me, all serious all of a sudden. 'If you did leave, where would you go? That's the question. We've got nowhere to go.'

'Nowhere to go,' I repeat.

My stomach growls and that's all I know. Train to nowhere, stuck nowhere, going nowhere…Why am I here? *You are here for a reason.* What possible reason? *You can leave. Leave whenever you want.* But I can't. Because I have nowhere to go.

I want to tell myself the two are linked. I want to tell myself that this is a joke, an accident, a dream. But I know it's not; the cold gnawing at my skin, the damp in my shoes. It's just me and time running out.

I turn to leave, leave for the manor, to cocoon myself within more walls.

*

Claire…

If I could buy you any house, I would. If I could win a million (unlikely), earn a million (as a teacher, less likely), or even (God knows least likely) inherit a million, I would buy you any house. If I could turn these hands into a builder's, thick with calluses and the seasons and love, I would build you any house. I would scavenge the B & Qs and Wickes, the woodlands and the forests, take everything from screws to cement, bricks to boulders, I would craft and carve and construct a house worthy of you. Of us. If I could, I would build the walls so high and so thick that not one breath of us could be snatched away by the storm outside.

But then again, it's like you always say; walls are built to keep you in, and I know you can't trap a rising tide.

Any house will do, as long as it's with you.

*

Cries. The early evening gale cries, this baby's haunting sound born from the gusts of wind trapped and writhing inside the cracks and holes in the walls. It takes a good hour or so before the fire gets going, a good hour or so when I pass around a few tins over the crackling flames, and one by one we suckle on their contents, choke on their nourishment. I take another lump of potatoes, coughing and spluttering back to life. When I finally spit it out I curse, and with me the wind—*this place*—cries.

'Hate these damn things.'

A stifled laughter blows in my ear.

'They aren't that bad,' she says, twirling her spoon in the depths of her tin, like it's a teacup and this is a tea party. No dolls were invited.

'That's not what you said the other day,' I snap back.

'What do you mean?'

'You told me the other day that you were getting sick of beans, of tins.'

'Oh,' she pauses. She blushes orange-red like them blasted beans. 'I don't remember. Funny that, I guess I wasn't feeling good at the time. But it's actually pretty good.'

I stare back at her.

'I see…' I drown myself in the liquid languishing in my tin. But she's not finished. I look up and see it in that childish grin.

'Nothing is better than eternal happiness. Beans are better than nothing. So beans are better than eternal happiness!'

A twisted logic, like the last few days. I let her have her fun. In this place someone's got to.

'Yeah…'

But all I think is beans, beans, damn beans, and wonder why the heck I ever liked beans in the first place.

'So,' her voice glides across the fire, 'I was thinking maybe tomorrow you could show me your discoveries.' I look up. She smiles, then looks down at her tin. 'I thought so. I see you travelling back and forth to that house, the one at the end of the road. There's something there, right? Something more than just tins and cutlery...' She looks back at me. I can't avoid those eyes. 'Do you want to talk about it?'

I feel anger, then shame. For all the annoying things she's done recently, it's still only me and her. And I can't blame her for what happened today, nor can I just ignore her. I can't lie. And at this point what else do I have?

'I...I'm not sure,' I say, my words navigating the waters before me. I try to resist, try to hide. She holds her stare. 'A sort of...connection.'

But somehow I can't quite bring myself to tell her the whole truth either.

'Connection?'

I nod. 'I'm not sure exactly...Some sort of cable, but it runs into the wall and disappears. I can't pierce through.' Yeah, I couldn't pierce through.

She breaks away from me, cups her face in her palms, pondering. 'What do you think it is?'

I shrug. 'It could mean many things. It could be just a cable, or...'

'Or a link to the world beyond.'

'A connection.'

She sits back down and shuffles closer towards me.

'What is a cable but a link? A basic human desire, a cable is a bridge, a connection between one place and another. Our world to another, from us to some other.'

Our world to...

She continues, 'It travels distances that would take us days, maybe weeks, months, even years to travel. But a cable—a *connection*—can travel faster than all that. What if...' She pauses. 'What if we could reach the outside world again? What if we could communicate with someone?'

She pauses for a moment and I wonder; she looks at me, excited, I can tell, and perhaps I feel the same.

I remember, then, when she told me that if she could, she would tell her parents she loved them.

I pause, my hand twitching. Some strange, far-flung feeling grips me and I'm not sure what to think. I just simply *feel* something. Then I turn back to the image of the cord, and imagine the cold over my body when I see it cut. And then I realise; to escape this place, to reconnect with the outside world...

She moves, startling me some.

'Connections, relations—what's life without them?'

'Without who?' I ask, a whisper. I'm not even sure if she heard, if I was even asking her at all. 'Who would we contact?' The words linger at the tip of my mouth, unable to find a response, and I'm not sure she has an answer either.

But she looks away again and I run my hand through my hair. I press her and she turns back to me, but she seems distant, somehow disconnected from it all.

'You know, you never asked me who I am.'

'What?' I ask, unsure I heard right.

'You don't know who I am, or where I'm from.'

'I know who you are. You're Skye. We met on the train. Okay? But what about the cable?'

But she's no longer listening.

'You don't know who I am,' she repeats.

And at that moment, I realise, I can't ask her anything else.

'Alright, I'm sorry. Who are you then?'

But she says nothing. A tear forms in the corner of her eye, shaking, ready to fall down the side of her face. I go to speak again, but she stands up and walks off. I want to call after her, but her footsteps are already fading, her shadow already consumed by the darkness.

Damn it. Why did she have to ask? And now she's gone.

Some time passes until a soft light pierces my eyes and I look up. That house, that room. What's going on? What is it?

A faint cry rustles in my ear.

Ring...

I stand up and head inside after her.

*

Ring, ring. Ring—

I shuffle, squirm under my hoodie. I was on a beach not far from home. *Ring.* I try pulling the hood up to my neck but the rest of me is cold. It was warm on the beach—no, the clouds were closing in, it was starting to rain. *Ring.* I cover my face, my ears. The waves surged upwards, crashing onto the shore at my feet. *Ring.* I could hear a voice. Her voice. And I could see her shadow, in the sea. *Ring.*

Ring. I jump up. A few beads of sweat trickle down the length of my back and my chest heaves as it fights the rush of blood thrashing about inside. I drag myself towards the window. That faint, yet undying voice echoes once more. *Ring.*

A lurch to the right.

Ring. I need to breathe; I need a fag. I know there's at least one left here somewhere...I've got my lighter here too. I grab both and, trying not to disturb her, sneak out and head for the stream. Red Ronson. I take out my lighter, a quick click and the flame licks the head. Just a few drags, need to drag this out as much as I can. A few breaths, some warmth in my lungs then I stop. That's enough. Gotta make it last. I stab the end and slip it back in my pocket before heading back in and upstairs. I lie down and try to go back to sleep. *Ring.* I sigh. *Ring.*

A lurch to the left.

I pull myself up. The darkness mopes around but I

can make out the flask, the rucksack—no. I look closer. No, not again...

I dive outside, the moon now falling from the sky and lighting the surroundings somewhat. I reach the remains of the fire, throwing a glance here and there. I catch a glimpse of the stream and the winding path. This path that I know and don't know all at once.

I take a few steps closer, then I wonder; what if the cats are lying in wait? What if they really exist and they've caught Skye? I can see them now—those teeth and claws lit up with the moon, their giant heads bobbing up and down. I shake my head—no, there's nothing up ahead. At least for now.

Who or what are they? No, I'm asking the wrong question, as she would say. Why are they here—what is the *reason* they are here?

I hear a shout. Behind me. I twist my neck around. There. I see her. Just up ahead.

'There you are!' I shout, fear giving way to anger. 'Where have you been?' I struggle to hold back the following words crouched on the end of my tongue.

'Me?' she fights back. 'I was inside, where were *you*?' She leans in closer, sniffs, then snuffs. 'You stink. I thought you were trying to quit.'

I stop, frozen, shaking my head.

'What? No, I was just...' Her look shoots me down. Thought I was trying to quit? When did I...? I point a finger at her. 'No, no, don't try this. I was upstairs, just now. There was no one. Just the flashlight and sack, there was...'

But she raises her hands to her head, her eyes closed, her head tilted towards the skies. She inhales deeply.

'I woke up. I went to the toilet, *outside*.' As if to remind me. 'Then when I went back up you weren't there! Then I heard this, this screaming like a little girl and I came running.'

I bite my lip. It's just her dig at me, either to lighten the situation or provoke me, I can't tell.

'Impossible.'

Then I wonder. Is it possible? Had it been that simple?

She's shouting at me, then she starts crying. When did she start crying? Why didn't I notice that before? I step closer to her and wrap my arms around her shaking body. I hug her—tight—and I can feel this coldness on her, this otherness. It takes some time before the waves inside her calm.

'Come on, let's go back inside.'

She looks up at me.

'I can't lose you again.'

I stare into those chestnut eyes and I can't hold myself back. Her words stun me, lock me in place; I didn't realise how scared she is. As scared as I am. I simply draw her in close once more, embracing her. Her body now feels warm against mine, and I can feel her tears break on my shoulder. It's all I can do to stop myself.

Lose me…again? Who am I, who is she? But I feel her body shiver and I hold back the questions, just hold her and not let go.

Meanwhile the night—and our shadows—watch over us.

*

I know life is going to change when Claire gives me this look; this special look she gives after she's cooked a Thai curry with lemongrass for two, and between tasting and talking she gives me this smile.

Lately she's been eating more kale and lentils, less kebab and lemon drizzle, drinking less and walking more, working harder and saving a lot. It's even rubbing off on me. Smoke doesn't taste the same, doesn't fill the hole that it used to.

'How do you feel about being a dad?'

For a moment I think she's telling me she's pregnant, but I don't remember any morning sickness, or finding any testing kit leftovers in the bathroom bin.

I've always wanted to be a dad. It feels like the natural thing to do, and I've always enjoyed my job being around kids. Kids have the answer to everything: life, science, and the reasons why we love bouncing on the bed when we're silly enough to do so. Claire knows that.

She has her hand on her belly, just for a moment, then continues to snack on her kale. She hasn't eaten much. Only her greens. The bottle of red remains untouched.

I take her hand in both of mine, say nothing, and everything at once.

it's a dog-eat-dog world
(8 days to go…)

'**Hey!**'

Fun. Today is going to be fun.

'Hey!' Something, someone. 'Wake up, wake up! Please…wake…up.'

A bright light rushes over me and the room leaps into view, this ringing in my head and gnawing in my side, like I've drunk too much last night or I've slept on the floorboards of some creepy manor in an abandoned town. I can move at least. I push myself up, her voice like a nagging nursery rhyme echoing in my mind. On repeat.

'Hey…' I say, but it feels like I'm dragging the word out, like I'm a reluctant dad caving into his child's pleas. My head screams. My hand twitches.

'Are you okay?'

Her image blurs then focuses into view, the light washing over her. Her hands are clasped onto my arms, pulling me, her fingers digging into my skin. She's saying something.

'Alright, alright. I'm awake, I'm awake…' My throat drills. 'Water…' I croak. 'Please,' I add.

She thrusts the flask into my hand and I knock it back, water dribbling out of my mouth and splashing down my front, but I don't care.

'What's the matter with you?' she says, her sympathy now sour. 'You had me going then!' she tugs at my arm, finally letting go when I nudge her.

I steady myself, the numbness in my body waking to the aches. I groan, moan some more, then mumble something she doesn't hear. She takes the empty flask from me.

'Sorry,' I mutter, eventually. 'Just…' I can't possibly

tell her about last night. I dread to think of her reaction, she'll think I'm the crazy one.

'After last night's escapade and now this, what's happening to you?' She remembers? 'I don't know whether to be angry at you...' She remembers. Damn it, of course, it actually happened this time. '...Or to worry about you.'

I look at her. She looks...sad. What made her remember last night but not the other nights I don't know, but I don't think it matters right now.

'I'm sorry,' I repeat. 'I don't know what happened.' I really don't. 'It's just...'

'Just what is it then?' her tone rises only to fall with the next few words.

'Just so tired...so much pain.'

Her eyes now take on the light.

'Oh. Are you hurt?'

'No.' Not exactly. 'At least, I don't think so.'

'I don't understand,' she says. Neither do I.

'Where does it hurt?'

Where? Everywhere. Like I've fallen from a train...

'Just aches that's all. I'll be fine. Don't worry about it.'

She tries to say something, but my dismissal cuts her short. Instead we remain still, lost in silence until I feel her hands on either side of my head. I look up. Her hands feel warm. She looks me in the eyes.

'You should have some breakfast. Let me get it for you.'

But before she has a chance to leave, I blurt out after her.

'Will you eat with me?'

She smiles—a real smile.

'Sure.'

I smile back. It's only the second time I have in a long time.

She leaves the room and I sit back. At least the mystery of her distracts from the pain. It's fine. I focus on the light peeking through the glass, that dirty, manky window…

I clutch my hand. There it is again. I can feel it, this distant call; the waves crashing against the shore, the sea singing, rhymes and lullabies…

Ring, ring. Ring, ring.

Deep inside I shout.

*

'So, what's the plan today?'

We're in bed, the morning cold still curled into the tiny corners of our quilt, our bodies coiled underneath like an Ancient Greek urn, warm bronze, beautiful and yet somehow fragile.

Claire turns, almost breaking away, a crack appearing in the urn. Until she returns, seals any space between us.

'Nothing,' she says at last. 'Let's just rest today.'

It sounds strange to hear her say that. I ask her if she's really sure. But she shakes her head.

'No, it's fine. Let's just stay here for now.'

I'm not convinced, she's not convincing. She's worried about me; truth be told I'm worried about me too. But also her. She isn't telling me everything either. I don't dare speak though, don't dare disturb the fragile edges of this moment; for now, I just want to rest, to enjoy this time with her.

We stay under the quilt, shape into our urn, mould ourselves into antiquity and try to stay there a little longer.

*

No one will see me. It's late, it's dark, but the moon is bright enough. I can make out the worn edges of the cobblestones, the signs, and the houses lining either side. I blend in with the shadows.

Ring, ring.

I can't take it anymore. I have to leave. Even Skye. The train crash, the wall, this place. This labyrinth. I have to find out what this is all about—the meaning, the *reason*. Even if there are cats—real, and out tonight—I have to risk it. I can't sleep, I can't lie or sit or stand with this incessant cry in my mind, this lapse, this faulty connection screeching between my ears.

I turn the next corner.

Ring, ring.

I wonder if she's awake, if she heard me or not; I hope she doesn't try to follow. That's the last thing I want. If she's worried then she'll only come looking for me. And God knows who's out there.

Ring, ring.

I turn the next corner.

I mean, I can't imagine now being here all alone, without...*Ring, ring.* Damn it. I mean, I want to say that, I can't imagine...*Ring, ring.* Without her...*Ring, ring.* Here alone...*Ring, ring. RING.*

I push the door ajar and slip inside, easing it shut behind me. At once the darkness returns, absolute. Doesn't matter. I follow the beat of the house, the rhyme, the ring...

Upstairs. Cross the landing. Feel my way, palms pressed against the beating walls, the *ring ring* pumping through the veins of flaking paint and plaster that lead me into the room, the skeleton bed, the wardrobe door ajar...And the telephone. I crouch down, balancing a hand over the curved plastic, feel the chips and dents in the plastic and grasp it.

Ring, ring.

Ring, ring.

Ring—

My hand shakes. I can't bring myself to do it. I can't. It's Billy. Perched on his hind legs, in front of me, those two cute little orbs staring into my own. His nose twitches, and his whiter-than-white whiskers bounce about. He looks to me, then to the phone, then back to me as if to say—

I pick up. A shallow breathing echoes in the receiver, a low, heavy tone rings in my ears. A coldness starts to numb the side of my face pressed against it.

'Hello?'

My voice echoes in the receiver. The shallow breathing and dim tone hover in the background. But no voice. No one speaks. No one replies.

No one replies.

That voice. Or was it a voice, or just the echo of my thoughts, my fears?

I sit here, cross-legged, legs crushed against the floor as I lean and fall forwards, hanging over this lifeless piece of—

I drop the phone. The ringing in the receiver still lingers, a metallic stir that scratches the inside of my ear. I collapse onto the floorboards, arms and legs spread out, lost in the semi-darkness washing over me. I lie here, with no intention to move, none at all.

A crash.

A cacophony of noise erupts downstairs and brings me to life. I roll onto my side. I hear a door slide open, then shut. I clench my fists. But there's only Billy in the room with me, looking up at the window, and I rush towards it.

The moon is bright tonight, and I make out the paths and houses for several streets on end. But one in particular has my attention. One in particular draws me in.

I can hear my breathing. My heart beating, faster and

faster.

There. Not cats. Someone. A shadow, but someone's shadow nonetheless. Our mysterious neighbour, there pacing up the street just ahead.

Billy sprints off. Shit. Follow the bunny, I know, I know. I've come this far.

I leap out of the room, pelt down the stairs, through the door and sprint up the slope veering to the right. The position of the moon and the houses throw me into alternating lines of light and dark, all the while stepping in and out of the shadows. But his shadow—I can make it out at the end of the street, this unmistakable shadow that swerves then veers to the left.

I don't look away. I don't stop moving. Around the corner a gang of clouds close in on the moon and the whole street plunges into darkness, his shadow lost in a sea of black. I slow down, stop even, staring at the vast expanse of nothing stretched before me. Damn. Then something brushes against my leg and I catch a brief flash of white sprint ahead. Billy. I set off after him but he's already gone, and I'm left in the dark once more.

I tread each step one at a time, hands out, pushing forwards. Damn. I don't know what I've done. I glance back but the darkness has swallowed all memory of my steps. This way or that, I can no longer tell. I continue. I've nothing to lose.

Up ahead a glint of silver slithers in the darkness. A flash, a flare, and light snakes up and down, curls and climbs. Then at once it snaps into view, the moon appearing overhead in the distance, revealing the outline of a tall gate emerging in the forefront. Open, like the gaping mouth of a cat, grey steel bars jutting out like gnawing teeth.

Welcome, I wonder, to the cemetery.

I glance this way and that as pockets of light peel back

the mysteries of the night. I wander the entrails of a cobbled path that winds and sometimes disappears, only to reappear shortly after. Gravestones emerge on either side like unclipped claws, only to fade away, soon forgotten. Stranger still are these guardians, more swans and swallows stretching their clipped wings as much as they can, barely hiding their nest of small graves from the prying stars above. What kind of cemetery this is, I've no idea; what kind of town this is, God only knows. I climb the last few metres to the summit and I'm offered a splintered view of the town behind me that clings to my back. I try to make out the manor in the distance when a sharp silver glint flashes before my eyes…

'Don't move.' I don't move. A low, shallow grunt grips me, hovers over the knife, touching the base of my neck. 'Wouldn't want anyone to get hurt.'

'I thought as much,' I remark. I'm surprised by my own bluntness.

The knife twitches, the body behind me swaying, unsteady. That much I can tell.

'Keep your trap shut, boy, don't move. Wouldn't want anything to happen now, like.' His voice catches, the words falling from the corner of his mouth.

'You don't have to. Let's just…just talk about it, yeah?' My eyes flicker but he can't see that.

The knife still dangles over my throat, swaying, nipping my skin. I struggle to breathe. The knife shudders.

'Nah, don't think so. Just spit it out, who are you? Who are you and just what is this place?'

His tone drops in the end as if whisked away by the snap of wind.

'Wa-wait, you don't know?'

'Who are you?'

'You're not from here?' A sudden thought slips into

mind. 'It's you, the man behind the journal? You wrote in the journal...'

But he's not listening, instead the knife teases my skin once more, shaking.

'Who are you?' his voice rises, is that sweat or blood trickling down my neck? I'm almost choking.

'The train...The train...'

'Train?'

'The train crash. You're from the train crash...' The knife presses. 'Please...The train...I'm also...'

A thump in my side and I'm pushed away, the knife no longer at my throat but my side throbbing. After a moment or two I recover my balance and clasp my neck with both hands, a trickle of blood dribbling onto my fingertips. They're shaking. My whole body's shaking but I manage to stand.

I turn and face him, this shadow still, still concealed by the darkness.

'Train 531, *Arriva Train Wales*, departure from Swansea 9.28am, December 30th?' He gives a slight nod. 'And several trains later, crossing the Scottish border...' Another nod. 'You're from the train too.' I pause. '*The train to nowhere.*'

'The *train to nowhere...*' he echoes.

'I survived the crash. I survived.' I have to repeat the words to reassure myself. 'Then I came here. Then...'

But I can't continue, the words are trapped in my throat while a drop of blood dribbles down the length of my neck. Meanwhile he shuffles to the side, looking down at me as I crouch, sink into the ground. My hands shake. They won't stop shaking.

He shifts his body from one direction to the next as if he were on the train now, pulled from side to side. It's then I get the urge for a smoke and think...

'You smoke?'

He cranes his neck towards me. I pull out the cig, the new, crispy one I nabbed from the shop, light it with the Red Ronson and take a drag. Then I hand it to him. He hesitates. Then accepts. I watch him like I watched my mum all those years ago, when I was six or seven—like she was breathing and whole again. That's what she used to say. Like she was alive again. Then I hear him coughing and spluttering back into existence and I'm once more home away from home.

I take it off him and take another drag.

'Got nothing to say?' I raise my voice, trying to force the confidence as his fist and the knife inside it twitches. 'Who the heck are you? Why did you leg it back in the streets earlier?' I look him straight in the eye, but neither of us can ignore the glint of the knife caught in the moon's glow. 'What's with the knife?' Loud, my words violate the silent reign over this mound of dead. Yet to me the sound is comforting, the echo like someone else is beside me.

I hear him shuffle.

'Sorry about that, kid,' he grunts. 'Had no choice, you understand. Didn't know who you was. Could've been anyone, anything, couldn't take no chances, you understand.' Then, moments later, he steps out of the shadows, the moonlight catching his face; a stark, burnt face with hollowed eyes and a grey glint that stares back at me. 'Had to be sure.'

I pull myself up, stand again, wary of the figure looming over me just inches in front, the knife still balanced in his hand. He soon hides it under his overcoat, this dark cover that buries him completely.

'For my own protection, you understand.'

'From what?' I ask, but he shakes his head.

'Who knows? The world's a mean and nasty place, kid. Dog-eat-dog world, gotta be a lion to survive, otherwise the world's gonna eat you all up.' A smile breaks across his face and my body stiffens.

I simply look at him. He looks back at me. His body sways and he slurs the occasional grunt. I stand still. Unmoving. His face twists in reply.

'Who are you?' I ask.

'Who are you?'

I pause, body tense. 'I asked first.'

Another moment's silence while his body staggers closer towards me, his knife still at his side until he lets out a big sigh and stops.

'Old man Dai, that's what they used to call me, back at the works. Not no more they don't, no work, no name, ain't nothing else to tell,' he stumbles. Then he turns to me, his eyes absorbing the darkness. 'But ain't alone anymore.'

Skye also said that. And I've thought it. I pause and notice that he's looking away from me, down at the ground and it's there I spot Billy.

I don't say anything. Neither does old man Dai. Damn bunny rabbit is courageous as hell, or a fool. Dai turns back to me, his one hand still grasping the hilt of the knife, twitching, the other leaning on the gravestone next to him. Difficult to tell, in the dark, where everything else ends and he begins. And his eyes; like the night is inside them.

'I see.'

I hold his stare. Watch his hands shake, his eyes—in the dim light once more—scuttling left then right. I remember the train. That night. Here, his body sways, slurring the occasional grunt. I stand still. Unmoving. Has something changed?

'You was on the train then,' he grumbles, a grunt that's neither a question or assertion. His eyes stray, seem to wander the gravestones. He seems comforted by them,

135

like old friends, rubbing an affectionate hand on one of the stones. It's then I notice an old brush leaning against the stone. 'But you're too late, too late you are.'

'Too late?'

'Too late,' he repeats, throwing his head forwards. 'All alone, for years…'

Years? But the train…

'Listen, I was on the train,' I begin, 'and you were on the train.' He sort of nods, still facing the stone. 'And we both ended up here…Alone. But now we've found each other…' He's still looking away. 'And now—'

'Nothing changes,' he says, standing upright, now squarely facing me, eyes fixed, fixing me in place. I can't move.

I need to keep trying, another stab in the dark.

'You're Welsh, right? Glamorgan or somewhere close, Swansea Jack?'

He hesitates, but I know I have him.

'So? What's it to you, kid?'

He stays at least, and that's enough for me. His accent isn't too different from mine, even if stronger, more guttural, a generational thing perhaps, just an older version of my own voice.

'Home is home, no matter how poor it is.' A stoic Welsh proverb. 'Used to live up Townhill till things fell apart. You know the place, right?'

He nods. 'Yeah, I knows the place. Was on Crole Street. Bottom of Uplands. Shithole.' He grins, and I follow him. He warms to me at least. 'Bloody unemployed for two years, innit, damn Stevo and Jono, they is gone too like, and then my wife gets proper sick and gives up the ghost and leaves me the kid I didn't ask for.' Didn't ask for. 'They don't give me much sympathy at the job centre neither like, austerity this, austerity that, so what's a man supposed to do, huh?' He gestures for the fag and I hand it over. He takes a long, deep breath and leans back on the stone for support. 'Already lost, what's a few hundred miles north in the middle of nowhere gonna do to me?'

He looks to the side again, scratches his chin and bites his lip. Maybe he's said too much.

A shout echoes in the distance. I recognise Skye's voice. I turn back to the gates away from old man Dai.

Her shadow appears in the distance, caught in a stroke of nightlight, just beyond the gates. Then I hear some shuffling behind me and twist around.

'Hey!'

His back to me, further away, he stops. I hear her steps come up beside me but I can't look away from him.

'Is that it?' I shout. 'You going to just abandon us?'

Without turning I hear him grunt in reply.

'Every man for himself.'

Then he limps away, supported by a stick, wandering among the gravestones resting at his feet until the darkness swallows him whole.

'He's gone…'

Skye leans against my side. I can't even move. After a short while her words fill the darkness surrounding us.

'Dozens of gravestones. There's probably one for every person we've ever known, everyone we've ever cared for.' I shudder at the thought. All these memories, now six feet underground. 'Whoever he is…'

'The train—'

'Doesn't matter.'

I hesitate. 'And the journal…' She looks across at me but the light is dim and hides her features. Could it be? I hesitate further, struggling against the thoughts in my head. 'It was his journal. It must be.' I swallow hard.

She doesn't move, doesn't need to. Not a sound either.

Then she turns and walks away, the moon now at her back and partly lighting the top of the gravestone where she had stood. And then I make it out. Heather, it says simply, 2021-2021.

I look up and the last thing I remember is seeing Skye, the look she gives when we leave through the gates and, at the far back, old man Dai standing alone, seemingly lost among the memories and apologies and tears that have long since dried.

And then Skye's face as we slip away; not even the light of the moon could touch her.

*

I hold her hand. Or maybe Claire holds mine. For a moment I'm nothing but this hand, my heart beating in my palm, struggling against the tension as everything contracts.

'I love you.'

Claire says this, her face looking down at the wave now coming in and washing over our feet, claiming the bluebell that only moments ago we held in our hands. I love you, the words drift in the air, like the smell of sea salt, pleasant and uncertain all at once.

It's important to say something. That's what I've been told. Anything. To let go. I watch as the bluebell—our bluebell— disappears into the great blue nothing and I feel I need to cry, but I don't. I can't. Or I just don't. I don't even know. I feel Claire's hand squeeze my own and I manage—just—to speak.

'I love you.'

I hold Claire's hand and, with the other, hold onto this space where another little hand may once have been.

*

We say nothing else all night. I watch Skye as she slowly disappears into the outstretched arms of the night, and I can't bring myself to disturb the shadows all around the room.

They're discussing the recent ban on smacking children—and they have their opinions.

You find all sorts on the bus—a miniature world—and people of all shades, sizes, and singing voices. Like now. The man, the husband probably, and the woman, the wife presumably. They're singing, a cackle, about how children can be 'bad', how as young as one they 'misbehave', and how a red mark on their behind 'never did us any harm'. Being a bus, in Britain, full of people all British in their ways, no one else says anything and we all enjoy their singing merrily all the way until the terminus.

I remember Mum smacking me. Only once or twice, the last I remember when I was around four for 'being so effing naughty'. I don't remember the why, the who, or the what. I remember where— in the street where all our neighbours could see—and how—that is to say how a swift palm of her hand felt on my 'backside' as she always called it when she was mad.

There's the resistance, my body shaking to break free; there's the anticipation, my begging then silence as I move to acceptance; then there's the impact, a convulsion as my body tries to reconcile with the soul. What have I done? Why did she turn against me? Finally, the aftermath where nothing and everything else is said.

The bus is full of the old couple's singing. Another man has chimed in, singing their tune as well, and I wonder; were you singing to me, Mum, in a language I didn't yet understand? Were you, in your own way, communicating love in a strained voice?

Sometimes I feel she was preparing me for years to come; life smacking hard, and I don't understand.

I've never thought of her as a bad mum. But I would never smack my children, ever. I tell myself this hoping they can hear me and that will make them arrive faster.

they fuck you up, your mum and dad
(7 days to go…)

A scream. A shout. That long, drawn out cry that follows afterwards. *Ring, ring.*

It's fine, she's still here. The night hugs her tight. She's agitated in her sleep, but still here. I wonder if I've disturbed her, or if the shadows are coming.

After all, the cats aren't far tonight. Their soft purr rings in the walls.

I take my jacket off and wrap it around her. She shuffles some, eventually calming, a line of sweat clinging to her forehead. I watch her instead of sleeping, not that I can sleep.

There it is, again. This lullaby that the town sings to me.

Ring, ring.

*

'He's following us.'

I like to think it's Billy, but I haven't seen him all morning. No, it's our new friend. I see him now, hiding in the shadows like some timid prey. Watching us, like some shadow.

'I know.'

'We should leave him be.'

She twists around, heading in the other direction. It's obvious, though, that she's agitated.

'What happened? I thought you wanted to be friends?' I tease, but she ignores me completely. 'You know for what it's worth I think he's more scared of us than we are of him.'

She stares off into the distance.

'I don't trust him,' she says. I try to speak, but she

continues, 'He threatened you with a knife. He could have…'

She looks away; hiding from me, I think. I don't believe he would have. Somehow, I doubt I'll convince her, but still.

'No, he couldn't. He's afraid.' He's just an old man with a walking stick, a scratch card, and friends six feet under. And a wife. And a child who may as well be to him. The last makes me clench my fist. 'We should talk to him. He might have answers.' The only thing that makes him interesting. 'He reminds me of someone. He's from the same city as me.' But she's not listening. 'He might know something we don't, can take us to places we haven't been. Maybe he even knows how the train crashed, or even…' *Ring, ring.* That damn echo. 'Maybe he can get us out of here.'

She weighs my words for a moment, only to dismiss me outright with a flick of her wrist.

'No, he can't. He's the wrong version of you.' The wrong version of me. 'There's only one way out.' Her labyrinth, her strange way with words, with the world. *Ring, ring.* 'If he knew a way out of here,' she finishes, 'he would have left by now.'

'Right,' I say. I don't want to admit so easily that she's probably right. 'Probably right. Or maybe he's just lonely. Maybe he's waiting for someone.'

Or was. His friends, his wife…

She looks my way but she says nothing of interest afterwards. She mumbles a few other things while collecting some water and fetching a few tins. The day has flown by.

Old man Dai, meanwhile, is still watching, still hiding among the shadows. He should be careful, hanging out where the cats do at night. I make out his outline in the distance now, the unmistakable crook of his walking stick rooted into the ground. He's not going anywhere. Neither is Skye. She throws me a couple of logs to get the fire going again, and by the time I return to the manor and look back he's already gone.

I stare at the spot where he used to be. The houses nearby come into focus and there, once more, *that* house. *That* room. I can feel it once more. Feel it before I've even heard it. It's inside me.

I bite my lip.

Ring, ring.

I just about catch her calling. Food is ready. The clouds loom overhead.

*

But the rhymes and lullabies don't stop. The town is singing, the cats and shadows. All of them, singing.

'Ring, ring…' I echo, the sound bouncing back from the walls. 'Ring, ring…'

I climb the stairs, one hand grasping the bannister and the other pressed against the wall. And the shallow beat follows me. I reach the landing, turn the corner, still following it. With the room just ahead, I approach and step inside: the skeleton bed, the window drooping beside it, and the wardrobe opposite shut tight. I take one step towards…*Ring, ring.*

'Ring, ring…' the sound escapes my lips.

I seize the doors with both hands and fling the wardrobe wide open. *Ring, ring.*

'There it is, Billy.'

I look down at the fluffy white ball who looks up at me and twitches his little whiskers in return. Then we both turn to the phone. I crouch down, hands wavering over the fragile machine, that flimsy cable, this faintest of connections with the outside world…

Ring, ring.

A lump in my throat. My head sways inside, all heavy. My fingers twitch. I take hold of the receiver—

The ringing dies, replaced by a faint drone that feeds into my ear. I swallow hard. I lean forward. Waves rush over, past my body; a tsunami of beats, of this constant...

Noise!

The drone drags on, but no voice—there's never a voice.

'Never a voice,' my own breaks free. Billy jumps. I sigh. 'For damn sake say something, anything...Who are you, where are you, why won't you answer?'

I'm asking the wrong questions, so she would say.

I slam a fist into the floorboards and a dull thud cuts through the monotonous ring. My knees start to hurt. I press my hand against the floor. I can feel the fluffy white of Billy brush against my side.

'Tell me. Tell me. Tell...me...'

The drone snaps out of earshot followed by a batting, then rattling that erupts from the floorboards. But the senseless noise still claws at my ear, still echoes in my body, still...

'Who are you?' Another thud on the floor. I ignore the crack of bones telling me to stop. 'Tell me...'

I need a fag, a drink—another train out of here.

A distant noise clambers over the smash and crash and drone, growing louder as I slam my fists against the floorboards, the shock leaping up and down the length of my body. This shout and scream, and all the while this distant noise grows louder and—

Something, *someone* grabs my shoulders, my arms, pulls me back...

'.........'

An echo.

'........'

This sound.

'……..'

'I'm here, I'm here!' This voice. 'It's me!' It's…

'It's you.' I stutter back to life. 'It's you.'

'It's me,' Skye replies, her hands grasping my arms, keeping me still. My body sways but I can see it now. I can see my hands trembling.

'It's…you.'

I have to repeat the words as if to hold her in place.

'Yes, it's me. I'm here now. Everything is fine.'

'Everything is fine,' I repeat. 'I'm here now…'

Is she smiling?

'Yes, I'm here.' She draws me in close, embracing me, her warmth running through me. My hands are no longer trembling.

'I'm so sorry…' I say, breaking through sobs. I struggle to hold her stare. 'I'm so sorry. I couldn't tell you, I just couldn't. I'm sorry. I don't know why. I just couldn't tell you…'

But she doesn't shout, doesn't frown. She's just here, with me. Her arms wrapped around me, her body pressed against me, she whispers in my ear. I feel my body rocking from side to side. This darkness, this town—heck, this very room—the only thing that matters is her.

She breaks away and lifts up my face to hers. I can't look elsewhere; I'm drawn into those eyes, the white of them shining through the darkness. Her lips closed I can still hear her speak.

She turns away and grasps the phone in her hands. I jump at her. She snaps back at me. Her eyes locked onto my own. Her arm already caught in my grip, the skin sinking under my fingers pressing down hard.

But she doesn't look away. She doesn't let go.

'This,' her voice defiant. 'This is where it stops.'

My grip tightens, panic pushing under my skin. She lifts her other hand, towards me. She brushes the side of my face, a soft, warm touch.

'We'll do this together,' she whispers, her eyes brighter than ever, the darkness falling back.

She lifts the phone to her ear and draws me close. She taps in a few numbers that I manage to see. 116 123...numbers that feel strangely familiar. The hollow noise on the other side disappears, replaced by the dialling code. *Ring, ring. Ring, ring.*

Ring, ring.

Ring, ring.

The echo fades. She goes to put the phone down—

'Wait,' I throw my hands up to stop her. The ringing continues. She hesitates, the phone balancing in the air and the ringing dancing in the darkness creeping past the dying light of the lamp. *Ring, ring.*

Ring, ring.

Ring...

The sound breaks up. Some cackling on the other side. Short, shallow bursts of noise clutter the earpiece. A strange something. Breathing. Shallow, deep, discernible breathing. The long, drawn in breath and a great heave, a push, an exhale as the earpiece vibrates—

'...Can...I...help...you?'

Static scratches my ear. I hear a voice regardless and I seize the phone with manic hands. Skye's own holds on too, holding onto mine. She's looking at me, looking back at her I see my own reflection and the swelling in my body eases.

'Hello...there...?' The voice on the phone.

'You can do this.' Her whisper, her hand holding onto mine.

I lean in closer to the mouth piece. It feels so cold.

'He-hello...' My voice catches, the echo in the ear

piece taking me off guard. She squeezes my hand. 'He-hello. Hello?' I take a deep breath. 'Can anyone hear me? We need help. Our train derailed just north of...'

She sits there beside me, staying close while I recount our fantastical story to whoever it is on the other side willing to listen. The occasional rough voice spits back, a barely comprehensible cackle that interrupts the otherwise surreal calm as I go through each sentence, each word and syllable, recounting the essential details and reliving the emotions caught between them...And I'm shaking, like anything I'm shaking.

She never lets go of my hand.

The line cuts. A long, drawn-out screech echoes in the earpiece, and I place the phone back on its handset. Silence falls on us like drizzle. My hands still tremble. Eventually, I look across to her.

I can make out her smile.

'You did it.'

There's no way of knowing what I even did, but right now I can't help but believe her—at least I need to believe her. I just want to believe her. And I smile too.

She squeezes my hand once more.

*

A whistle. The soul singing. That's what, many years ago when her face came alive in the artificial light spraying over us in the kitchen, my mum had said. She was whistling, like Claire is now whistling in the shower. I hear her as I walk past the door on my way downstairs and out; but not before letting myself stop, let myself be drawn into her whistles, her waves. Her soul.

I whistle in the car, and I no longer hear the horns blaring or the traffic grinding against the hot asphalt. I whistle at work, in the staff room beside the kettle, standing over the urinal and again over the toilet seat two hours later. I whistle. I let myself be carried away by the soft waves that rise and roll off the tongue, gently into the distance.

The soul singing. That's what she had said—my mum—in that hazy lime light in our kitchen. Sprawled across the table were papers: notices, demands, reclamations, and enough dirty washing heaped in the sink to distract from it all. But for a moment she allowed herself to be carried away, by the whistle, by the wave. She took my hand and we went outside and left the estate behind us, walked to the park and fed the mute swans. Even they opened their beaks and seemed to be singing with us.

Back home I find Claire in the kitchen surrounded by her soul. It's been too long this silence, I think, and I whistle to join her.

*

I'm waiting in our room. For its spartan design, I've grown attached to its hard-wooden floorboards, the cracks in the walls, and the spiralling chasm full of shadows crawling beneath the window. Then of course there are our own additions: she's left behind the flask, our *Northern Blue*. It's still warm from her touch. This room right here, it's a strange, strangely comforting place. Like home.

She's been gone a while now, and I'm staring out the window after her. But she insisted I wait here and keep the fire going. There's a clang across the corridor and I shout out—a slight pause—then she replies and I know she'll be here shortly. I sit back down, reluctantly, running my hands through each other. They're twitching again. That and they're so cold they're at risk of falling off, and keeping them close to the fire is as much a distraction as a welcome heat. The flames blur her image when she finally reappears in the door frame.

'What the...?'

She smirks then staggers inside, eventually falling onto me as I race to catch her and the massive crate in her hands. A dozen or so bottles bounce across the room

147

after us. I look up at her but again she just grins, shrugs her shoulders, and takes a seat on the floorboards next to the fire. I close the door after her and take my seat opposite.

'Come over here and join me,' she says, pulling the crate closer.

There's something different in the way she speaks, or maybe it's the flames bringing a vibrant colour to her face that catches my attention. That and—

'Is that...' The smell smacks me in the face all at once when she prises the crate open with the crowbar. 'Beer? No, cider? Wait...'

She shrugs again. 'Who knows, doesn't matter anyway.' She twists off the cap and thrusts the bottle up her nose. 'Smells good enough.'

'Where did you—' She misses my words, knocking back a swig. She still finds ways to surprise me.

'Well?'

She splutters, coughing—choking even. I wince at the thought of downing some, but then she gives me the thumbs up and passes the bottle over.

'I didn't have you down as a drinker.' Come to think of it, I don't have her down as many things. She doesn't answer, anyway. I try again. 'Where did you even find this?'

She says nothing, again. I think she's waiting for me to take a swig. When I do, she offers no reaction at all. Then I notice her face, a dark smear like the tainted liquid in my hand. At least that's how it feels.

I'm not sure I want to, but I hand her the bottle back. She takes another gulp.

'You're quiet tonight,' I say.

'You don't know who I am.'

Not this again.

'Then tell me since I don't know.'

But she gives the faintest laugh. Still clasping the bottle in one hand she raises her hands and points at me.

'You tell me. What's a guy like you doing in a place like this? Why'd you take the train?'

Ugh, I can't stand this image of her but I'll play her game.

'Same reason as everyone else. Just heading from A to B.'

A pause. 'Lies. At least not the whole truth. A one-way ticket to the furthest station in the country, some loose change, a shitty old dead phone, and a lighter and two half fags.' How did she know I had two? She smiles at my reaction. 'Just looking for the most isolated place in the Highlands. That's "nowhere" alright.' Another pause, another swig. Somehow, I doubt I've heard the last of it. 'I'm not,' she says at last. 'You and I are the same, except I'm leaving nowhere and,' she pauses, taking a moment as the previous swig hits her in the head, 'heading somewhere.'

'Heading somewhere alright.'

She kinda snorts this time around. Like Peppa Pig. Except I think the drink is getting to her—how many times has she knocked back the bottle already? How many before? Shit. It definitely smacks of something strong. The heat still burns my tongue.

'Anyway, enough about me, tell me about you.'

'There's nothing to tell,' I say.

'That's what you said last time.' She pushes the bottle back to me. I'm pretty sure it's some kind of cider—I *hope* it's some kind of cider. Now it's my turn to laugh. Maybe it's the moment, but I let her have her way and take another swig.

'I guess I'm running away too.'

'I never said running.'

'Shit.' She smiles, encouraging me to continue. She's

149

good at this game. 'You know I've never actually said that before…'

'What, shit?'

'No, I mean…Ugh, never mind.' She doesn't reply though, only waits for me to continue. I look around— nothing but the fire, her, and our shadows all leaning in. I shouldn't be so afraid, just don't see much point. 'I don't know what to do anymore, so I decided to leave.'

'No job, no family or friends?' she asks, but I don't have much to reply. 'No significant other?'

I taste the sea in my mouth. I take another swig. I cough and splutter.

'That's rather vague.'

What else is there to say? I look straight at Skye—the flare in her cheeks, in her eyes—and wonder who she is.

'You're vague,' I say.

She laughs. She takes the bottle back, now that I've almost finished it without realising. It no longer burns, instead it just feels warm inside. She takes her own swig, finishing the bottle in one.

'Why can't you just admit you're lonely?'

'What?'

'You can hardly make friends with a bunny rabbit. I mean how sad and lonely do you have to be to say no to that cute little white furry thing?' She slurs her words.

'Hey, come on.' I pause, unused to this image of her. 'I treat Billy just fine.'

'Fine. Oh, okay then. Fine is good.'

Is this it? Does she know me better than I do? I look back down at the stack of bottles remaining, count more of them than friends or family. She's right. May as well drink the night away then. I grab another.

'Just the rest of the crate to go.'

'You're funny.' She hiccups, and then I really do laugh. 'You're mean.' Bless. She lifts the empty bottle upwards, pointing at me. 'Do you miss home?'

Home. What it was, what it has become, what is left...And this twisting and bruising inside me, like guilt and worthlessness wraps itself in knots and knuckles.

'I don't know...' Those are all the words I have for her.

'I miss my father,' she blurts out. Silence afterwards, and while I watch her, I swear a tear collects under her eye. I hardly knew my dad, hardly know my mum now too. 'He fucked me up, he did, but he didn't mean to.'

I feel it. She needs to speak. I can see from the way her eyes are drowning in the next drink clasped in her hands.

'I'm sorry.'

'Don't be. He loved me deeply.'

I don't know how to respond, but it makes me think of my own. I don't know if or how he loved me. My dad was so late for everything he never turned up: to my Sunday games, my birthday parties, my birth...Mum used to joke that he'd be late for his own funeral. It was just to ease the pain of his absence. He was a sperm donor, that's all he was good for, she said. How much easier, though—how much better—our lives could have been if he'd actually been around, been a real dad.

'I miss my mother, too,' she continues. 'I wish she would tell me stories and sing me lullabies again...' I remember she said her parents read to her, sang to her too. I guess their voice is what she cherishes the most. I'm about to say something, but she continues, 'They do that to us, don't they? They don't mean to, but parents are the worst, aren't they?'

Her voice drifts away and I'm back on Platform 2, Nokia in hand, shouting down the phone and there are drops running down the side of my face but it's not raining yet.

'Why do you smoke?'

'Huh?' She's caught me off guard again.

'You know you're just killing yourself slowly, right?'

I stutter a laugh. 'My old biology teacher at school used to tell us that from the moment we're born we start dying.' She pulls a face. 'What's another minute less with each drag?'

She holds onto my words for a few moments, and as she does, I start to feel their weight and start to regret them. Have I upset her?

'You don't really think that though, do you?' I say nothing, but struggle to hold her stare. 'Why do you smoke?' When I don't reply she moves and takes my jacket.

'What are you doing?' But I see it now. 'Hey, put that back...'

She has both my lighter and the last—the very last—snub of cigarette in her hands. She looks at me, neither of us saying anything. Then she brings the cig to her lips—

'Don't.'

She stops. I can't let her do that for me. She waits, then starts playing with the lighter in her hands.

'It's very nice. It's still warm.'

'It's my mum's. Well, it was until I took it.' Damn. I hesitate. 'You're right, you know.' She's right and I hate that she is. She could draw anything out of me, I know that now. 'I don't like smoking. I didn't used to. I hated it. She always was a heavy smoker, it killed her slowly, her lungs packed it in and she had trouble with everything. It was her addiction.'

'I'm sorry...'

'When I was eight, I thought that maybe if I stole her lighter and smoked her cigarettes then she wouldn't be able to...' I hadn't realised before, until Skye started looking at my hand, that it's now bunched up into a fist. There's a swelling in my fingers, blood pushing up against the surface. 'Shit load of good it did either of us.'

I think of the years I've smoked. What I've done to myself, to others. To Skye.

She looks at me then, in this way of hers, before placing her hand on my shoulder.

'They fuck you up, your mum and dad.' A pause. 'But they don't mean to, really. And we love them, really. Because they're our mum and dad.' She lights the cig and puts it to her lips. 'This is your last one?' I nod. 'Then I'm going to smoke it for you, so you don't have to.'

I want to stop her but I know I can't. She's too drunk to feel anything and she sucks it dry within the minute. She doesn't savour it, only chews on the edges, and later spits out the end. She looks tired now, drained, and I worry she's going to collapse.

'Skye…'

My hands feel oddly calm, and I can't imagine ever smoking another one again.

'Hey, you wanna know why I left…?'

But she can't finish her sentence. Her body sways and I have to hold onto her to stop her falling into the flames.

'I think it's time to sleep.'

She doesn't protest. She only falls onto my shoulder. I slide the bottle out of her fingers and move the crate aside, back into the darkness. She stirs some and I rock her to sleep, like her dad might have done a long time ago. I make sure to lay her head softly on my hoodie now rolled out neatly, her pillow for the night. When she's finally lying down, I sit beside her and watch her for a few minutes. She twists on her side, her eyes flickering, awake once more.

'You okay?'

She nods. 'I'm okay. I just wanted to see you smile.'

153

Then her eyes close completely, leaving me wide awake and alone in the dying of the light, waiting and wondering what's going to happen next.

*

I was nine when my mum confessed that she hated hospitals. It's where people go to die, she said, she knows. I don't like hospitals and I don't like this one either.

'It's a clinic,' says Claire, but I catch the creaks in the paintwork and the mould on the ceiling and nothing else. 'You're always too pessimistic,' she says. If that's true then at least you're too positive to my too negative, I say. She laughs, I smile.

We sit together in a cramped room that's too small for kids, sinking into the sofa, listening to a doctor whose smile promises salvation but her words dim the lighting, all too serious all too adult. We thank her—Claire thanks her and then I do—and then we leave only to return several times over the coming weeks for various tests. This is only because my own results, the first test, were mixed.

I feel Claire's hand on my shoulder, somewhere, while the doctor speaks.

It's very common these days, she says. 'Men today', she says, then corrects herself with 'society today', she continues, and then I hear all my demons past and present: smoking, drinking, unhealthy eating, sedentary lifestyle, depression…and everything else, from air polluting my lungs to antibiotics in my food and the like. I'm not unhealthy, I think, and choose to listen to everything else. Except I leave the room with the taste of ash on my tongue and a sickness in my stomach.

'It's heart-breaking,' the man says next to me. Claire is in a testing room and I'm in the waiting area. There's a man in a black bomber jacket sobbing to himself in the corner nearby after hanging up the phone. Sperm, something he's done, irreparable damage. I try to forget what he says.

I fall further back in my chair hoping Claire will be finished soon and we can leave this place, leave these poor men (and women) and this damn cat that hangs in a portrait in front of me. I just want to leave this place, leave and find some hope. Claire appears then, radiant, despite everything before and after her. She smiles and I smile and I take her hand in mine and, leaving the building, I swear to her that we can do this.

Back on our beach I write the promise in sand and we splash in the sea, try to laugh and forget it all.

Three weeks later Claire is pregnant, again.

ring, ring
(6 days to go…)

I wake to her touch. She's lying on her side like an autumn leaf, full of auburn colour and vivid life. She's looking at me; those eyes, those bright, chestnut eyes hold my image inside them. I hold this picture of her, too, enchanted. She raises her arm and reaches out—hesitating, eyes wide, as if yearning for permission—then I feel her hand smooth through my hair, caress my skin. She strokes the mesh of stubble now covering my face and I wonder just how long we've been here. But then she smiles before pulling her hand away.

Her smile stays with me and I want to hold onto it forever.

She stands up and leaves the room, the door resting ajar. I stay, not wanting to move just yet. I raise a hand to my cheek, the spot of skin where her warm touch remains.

For the first time in a while I slept through the night, and my back is no longer hurting the way it used to. The air feels fresh, like I've learnt to breathe again. It's a miracle. It's become colder and damper in the room without her though, darker even; this shadow on the wall behind me, this strange dark wave continues to climb the wall. Like a Halloween trick, except Halloween only lasts for one night. Maybe these old walls can't stand the harsh weather any more than we can. That's what I tell myself.

Sometime later I haul myself up, standing sheepishly in the centre of the room, like I don't know what to do without her and wondering if she'll come back or not. I make for the stairs, only instead to turn tail and continue along the hallway until I'm close to the window, the one sprawling across the width of the interior.

I glimpse outside.

I see her. She stands near the bridge, or at least where the bridge should be. Now a layer of mist envelops it and threatens to take her too. Strange, how she seems to hover between the light and dark. The mist seems to move in waves, rushing up to her feet, only to fall back before edging forward once more. Next to her the stream continues its ascent, the water trying to claim her and she has to shuffle back to avoid the splash of torrent. She crouches then, her back arched over its bank at the foot of the encroaching mist, and I see her grasp something in her hands only to discard it moments later. From here I can't tell if she's curious, amused, wistful, thoughtful or thoughtless. Not a thought in her head maybe, only the rush of feeling crawling across her feet, her ankles, maybe her entire frame, threatening to whisk her away...

She turns and looks up. She notices me and calls me over, gestures with the slight nod of her head. I smile, but before I disappear I look out once more, past her, into the lowly grey, this wall of mist. Moving, like it's alive somehow. I pull the folds of my hoodie and jacket closer to my skin.

I head downstairs.

'I'm surprised you're not sat by a roaring fire and tucking into some beans already.' She gives a sort of half-smile. 'You joining me?' I ask, and she nods again.

I grab a few log chippings and some tinder, throw it all together and within a few minutes I get the fire going. Not as loud or colourful as hers would be, but enough to tickle the orangey goo to life. Enough to *survive*. I have her to thank for that. All the while, though, she simply stares outwards into the unknown. The fire now stable, she eventually turns towards me and we both sit in the silence.

The crack of a tin as I prise it open whips the air

nearby, only for the sound to be drowned out in a quick, unforgiving snap. I hand it over to her. I take another for myself.

'Strange, usually Billy is here by now,' I muse, cracking the second tin open. 'He loves these damn beans. Must be hibernating instead.' I look up at her but she hasn't so much as touched her plate. 'You okay?' I ask, unsure if maybe she prefers the quiet, or even to be alone right now.

She holds onto the landscape before her; in some way I feel it too, the stream and mist and clouds seem like whispers here and there.

'I had an awful dream last night.'

I remember vaguely how agitated she seemed last night before I dozed off, her body tossing and turning. Was she like that all night? How did I not notice? I slept throughout—knocked out, maybe, from all the cheap cider. My head still feels a bit loose, the pain still numbed by the alcohol maybe. But I feel…good. And maybe it's for this reason that I don't know how to respond, so I let her continue.

In whispers.

'I dreamt that I was lost in the square, surrounded by shadows, the moon above eaten by the night. One by one the shadows and clouds closed in, wave after wave devoured me until I was no more.

'I tried to call out, but no one came.' Her voice stops, her jaw seemingly locked in place, unable to move. 'I felt…so alone.'

I can't speak. Only yesterday I was scared and she was holding onto me, not letting go. And now…Those damn shadows again.

The rustle of the tin settling onto the ground fades away and I wonder where Billy is. He would know how to comfort her. Instead it's just me. I shuffle closer, take her in my arms and just hold onto her; like she had held onto me the day before. I can feel her sink into my grasp, and I imagine the shadows letting go of her—if just for a moment. I shudder upon feeling the warm drop of her tears trickle onto my skin. We stay still, unmoving. Like statues, like two birds, our wings clipped. We aren't going anywhere.

Only the wind later striking my back and the onset of the cold numbing my nose and cheeks stirs me awake. I press her against me a final time before breaking away. She doesn't resist, instead she crumbles like an autumn leaf and I worry she'll fall to the ground when I pull back. I notice the red around her eyes, swollen, like two bulging bruises. She's barely looking at me, distracted, torn away. I run my hand across her cheek, and she slowly comes back to life.

Just what happened?

'It was only a dream,' I say, but my words feel lost as the mist wraps around them.

She nods. 'I know, I know.' She hesitates. 'It's just that...Just it felt so real.'

I don't take my eyes off her. On this obscure day with the mist at her back, she seems vulnerable; with those tears, no longer the same.

'But this is just one dream,' I tell her, remembering every damn night before I had suffered. 'Everyone has bad dreams.'

Bad dreams.

But she shakes her head, and I catch a few tears swelling her eyes once more as I lean forward to take her hand.

'No...No, every night since we've arrived. Every night...The shadows never leave.' Then she throws herself deep into my stare, her eyes pulling me in with the gravity of the moon. 'Like I'm drowning, every night drowning.'

I try to speak, but I can't. I can't break from that terrifying hold she has of me. I try to speak...

'Every night they come. Every night I fear,' her voice croaks. 'I fear it will be the last.'

I feel her hand slip from my own.

'No.' I shake my head. 'No, this place—this damn place does that to you, it messes with your mind like that. But don't let them get to you.' I take hold of her hand, hold it tight. 'You are more than your shadow, you are Skye.'

I link my fingers with her own, and for a while she takes them until her hand slips through my own and my hand is left hovering in the air in its place.

She nods.

'I know...You're right.'

Does she trust me? Do I?

She turns to grasp the tin beside her. Lifting it up, with the orange glow of the food, of *sustenance* reflecting on her cheeks, she declares, 'Let's eat.'

We eat with the stream gushing past, the mist at our backs, and her cheeks red from tears as much as the flames.

At least for the time being the sea of shadows keeps at bay.

*

This morning we stay inside. The clouds toss and turn in the sky, and rain rides the crest of the mist now thicker and darker than ever. Only in the afternoon does the tide subside and I tell her I'm heading out, but she won't come. Too tired, she says, I think I'll just stay in the manor today. I don't argue. Her sudden scare and the red marks that line her eyes tell me everything. When I draw close she shuffles back; scared even as I approach. She hesitates before letting me embrace her, and when I step back, she gives me that half-smile once more. I ask her if she wants me to stay, but she says I should go. I turn to leave, but not before noticing the gloomy skies sweeping across her face.

I walk the short distance to the bridge, make the connection between us and town proper. I notice the stream, high but calm. I turn back to glimpse her one last time at the door but she's already gone. Gone upstairs, I imagine, maybe to lie down, maybe to sleep. I pray—mutter the words under my breath—that the shadows will leave her alone in the daylight. I cross the bridge.

I sigh, a long, guttural sigh that clutches my throat.

'Shit.'

No doubt about what I'm going to do today. I've had enough of all this. Over the next few hours I'll cover the whole town, leaving nothing unexplored, nothing uncovered. And this great wall—her Minotaur's labyrinth, this bizarre, shifting structure that has cut us off from the outside world. But trapped as we may be this town hasn't changed. It remains rather a mystery, but one with an answer, an entrance. And an exit. The north, past the *The Moon Under Water*, past the church and cemetery, is where the mystery deepens.

And yet, when I reach the first square just at the top of the winding path from the stream, I'm aware of just how thick the mist has become, how blind I am in this most unholy of lights. I throw my head back. I lose myself in the skies, greyer and duller, morbid even; like every dark cloud in Britain has come together and formed some giant super cloud, threatening me with eternal rain, a flood to end all floods.

Then I feel a familiar scratch at my ankles and look down at that white, fluffy face.

'Ain't afraid of nothing, are you?'

How many times has he followed me now? In fact, just what the hell is a lone, mountain hare/bunny doing here of all places, with me of all people? There should be a horde of them, the frisky, funny little things. Or none at all. Then I think of the cats. He must hate cats as well. And fear them. Maybe that's our connection. He looks up at me then, up at the mist ahead and I know. We're both looking for a way out.

Screw it, and I cross the square.

I walk blind, barely a metre in front remains visible. I glance down and occasionally see Billy stopping and starting. He's more Shepherd dog than woodland prey in these moments. I'm still nervous as I pace myself, hugging the walls of houses for support so I don't stray. My hands walk along the bricks and the sense of touch breathes new life into their character, the patterns of indents offering a uniqueness to each house I didn't know before. A few loose chippings scratch my skin, history falls in my hands and I push on.

The path invariably twists and turns and I turn with it, unable to venture out much into the open. This could be a slow car crash, my mini adventure. This mist or fog or whatever is so thick it crawls over my eyes, and my vision fades white and black. Reality blurs, everything painted in a single, dull stroke. I edge a few steps more, still clinging to the bricks before I break free. I venture into the unknown and then, like a wave—a fit of nature—the torrent lashes at me and I huddle back to the safety and familiarity of the wall.

I close my eyes, a shocking black; I open them, a shocking white. Still using my hands to guide me, I follow the bricks until at last I stumble across a door. I slip inside, this small world pulling me in. My eyes accustom to the stray light of a nearby lamp and I piece together the entrance room. This room that I recognise at once. I start choking, suffocating in it. I...

...hesitate. Is the room different? Has someone been here? The lamp—now on—is no longer tucked away in its corner and there are coins on the floor. Pennies and two pence pieces scattered here and there, retreating from the staircase like some Dunkirk.

I pick up one of the pennies, turn it over in my hand and rub the smooth face, as if it would magically change into a pound or something. I later drop it beside the others and stand up in the middle of the room. It's then I notice Billy has gone.

'Billy? Where are you buddy?'

No reply, but at least the echo is comforting, like someone is here with me.

I head inside the kitchen. It feels different here, violated even. The light, choking in the window, smears across the walls and hangs in the air. I step further inside, towards the empty cupboards and bare drawers. One is left open, its contents stripped away, ransacked. Was this her doing? I look on, a few knives and forks—even a rolling pin—now scattered across the floor in some struggle. A long knife, outstretched on the floor, reflects in a tiny fragment of misty light. It teases the wood in the floor as I draw closer to it. I...

Grasp it. A glance around and I step back inside the living-room. I...

Head upstairs. Take each step that I've taken many times before. The painting on the wall, this cat in the guise of *Scream*, smudged and dreary; those glaring teeth, a gash smiling down on me. Why did I not notice this painting before? I carry on. I hit the landing. I see it. I...

Step inside. The room is the same—how could it have possibly changed? I glance at the wardrobe but I drift towards the window first. I try to look outside but it feels like the outside looks at me. My image reflects in the

163

window, but it's lost in the mist that breathes on its glass frame. I step back, away from the edge...

There it is. Sitting alone, in the silence. I watch it for a while, this intriguing object that offers so much and yet...

I lean over, hovering just above. I want it to call but I know it won't. It doesn't. I stop. I pick up the phone. Did it ring? Silence, then all at once a faint ring irritates my ear, then a low screech that cackles daggers. I shut my eyes, tight, as if that will help. The screech continues until it dies and then...silence.

'Hello?'

'Hello?' the voice echoes back. It hugs me for a moment. I clutch the phone. A faint buzz on the other end but I can't distinguish any other sound. Just a buzz, a hollowing of the airwaves that jumps at me. No voice, no words I can hold on to...

'Hello?'

I sit there clutching the phone, holding it close. Why is there no one?

I stare a while longer before grasping the cable in a knot behind it, twisting in and out like veins and arteries linking the heart to the rest of the body. I squeeze. Squeeze, twist, and jab each vein and artery that fails to pulsate under my finger. I scratch the tip of a vein with my nail. I threaten it with the knife. I pull on it. Some resistance at first until, eventually, it slips out with ease. There it is, clear as daylight.

The ringing has stopped. It has stopped because the cable has been cut.

A crash downstairs. It whips the air around and I seize the knife next to me. The cats. Other smaller voices clamber upstairs, feet clipping the wooden steps now vibrating along the walls. I imagine the portrait of the cat slipping from its hook. I don't dare move. I follow each step as it sinks into the floorboards, each creak, each moan as each step climbs higher until it reaches the landing. These are no cats. Still, gripping the knife as the steps echo in the hallway, I...

Hold my breath; hand trembles; the knife swaying in the air; the din of footsteps; breathing...

'You.'

He takes another step, his figure swelling in the door frame, blocking the light completely.

'Alright son, sorry, you understand?' A pause. 'It just kept ringing, ringing, it did. Couldn't stop it. No one answered...Just kept ringing, it did.' His voice echoes behind me. 'Had to...' he mumbles, the words dribbling from the corner of his mouth. 'You understand...' He shuffles closer, the shaggy clothes piled onto him weighing him down as he staggers this way and that, his own knife balancing in his hand. 'Had to, you see, you understand. You understand...'

He approaches, making his way towards the telephone as I edge a few steps away, mirroring his pace, circling around, back to the door. He stumbles on his walking stick as he tries to keep his hand close to his pockets, the unmistakable clinging of coins inside hiding away.

'You shouldn't have done that,' I say at last, just as he comes up to the phone, just as I near the door.

His head snaps to the side, jerking back to the other.

'H-had to, you see. The ringing—yes, the ringing. Every day, every night, every hour—every minute—ring, ring. Ring, ring...'

He shuffles, waving the knife spattered with blood. With blood.

'Whose blood is that?' I hadn't noticed before. Shit. Where's Billy? No...

'This,' he explains, 'this saved me. Look—saved me,

165

the ringing.'

I edge closer to the door.

'You…'

'The ringing, yes, stopped the ringing. Stupid fluff ball wouldn't let me, bit my leg—my leg! But I stopped it. Stopped the ringing, you understand.'

My nerves are tapping. It's fear. It's anger.

'That phone,' I hold back the knife, 'that was our only means to get out of here, to contact the outside world, to save us. And that bunny…' I feel the pulse swell under my skin.

But old man Dai shakes his head, throwing it from side to side, his arm and the knife in his hand slicing the air.

'Saved us, son.'

I clench my fist tighter. *Left me with the child I didn't ask for.* You know nothing.

'I'm not your son.'

But he doesn't hear me, or doesn't understand.

'The ringing, yes, the ringing…' I continue edging backwards, now touching the door frame as he hovers over the telephone. He kneels down, a few more pennies slipping from his pocket onto the floorboards, but he doesn't even notice. Instead he continues, leaning on the handle of his stick, eventually picking up the cut cable. 'See, no more ringing—no more ringing! The cats will be pleased.'

I shudder. 'The cats will be pleased,' I repeat.

He grimaces—this shadow of a grin—his face pulled to one side. All colour drained from him; he's become no more than his shadow. And all the while I retreat from the room, take Billy in my arms and continue to take one step back after another. But I can't forget that look on Dai's face, that look of absolute terror.

'You shouldn't have done that…' I repeat, but he's in

166

hysterics, all the while echoing the same words over and over.

As I back out into the hallway, down the stairs and out of the house, I can't stop hearing his madness.

'Ring, ring. Ring—ring!'

The madness that follows me outside, the ringing of pennies hitting the floorboards, followed by that unmistakable sound. *Ring, ring.*

There's no way out, I hear them say. Now there's no way out.

*

'We need to talk.' Claire is back from her week-long stay with her mam. To talk. To heal. She says this while the TV is on. After a slight pause, the TV replies for her. 'I'm serious, after everything that has happened, we need to talk.'

I hold my breath. Then turn the TV off.

I say her name. She sits down beside me and I take her hand—or maybe she takes mine. It's like she's worried more about me than her. I'm fine, I say. I'm not much of a talker, I say.

'At least you admit the latter.' She smiles when she says this—the kind of smile that rises then falls like the end of a wave breaking on the shore. 'But we need to talk to someone. Both of us. And both together.'

She's trying her best not to cry, but she can't pretend for long. The tears, heavy like the sea, come, and I hold her tight and say nothing, just hold her close.

The following morning it's coffee and cereal and off to work as usual. Except for the leaflet on the dashboard of my Toyota. 'It's time to talk', it reads, among other things... Then my alarm screams and I realise I'm late and, without another word, I press down on the clutch, the accelerator, and speed off.

*

Emptiness, my mind drowns in emptiness as I cross over

167

the bridge, pass the running stream that gushes underneath and attacks the bank that's disappearing before my eyes. I don't linger, instead press on towards the house; the knife balancing in one hand—the cut plastic of the cable still smudged against the smooth of the blade—and Billy's soft, featherlight body tucked in the other arm.

I call, but there's no answer inside. I wander towards the stairs—

'Hey!' I hear a voice beam downstairs. She appears through one of the side doors, seemingly less reserved until she notices the knife and Billy either side of me. She steps back, tripping in her speech. 'Wh-what happened?'

I don't know what to tell her. She watches, head tilted forwards but her body twisted away. She hugs the *Northern Blue* flask close to her chest like a doll.

'It's just...' I start, lifting the blade first. 'Don't worry, just something I found in the kitchen. I thought it was better we had it rather than left alone in someone else's hands.'

'Someone else?'

I hesitate. Now she's looking at Billy and I look too, aware of the very real feeling throbbing inside of me. In my hand I can feel the coldness on his body already. I look up a her again. After everything that's happened, I think I should be honest with her.

'I bumped into our friend just now.'

She says nothing, but I can see her waiting for me to speak. I watch as her eyes dart from me to Billy to the knife, watch as she grabs the flask more tightly. I watch as she ever so slowly takes a step closer.

'I'll put the knife away and bury the body,' I say.

'Yeah...' her voice drifts. She doesn't even ask. I don't think she can. I walk straight past her.

I turn around, wanting to speak, to say something that

will comfort her. She sees me and, as if catching the words in my throat, merely nods.

It's a quick affair. A shovel, a small hole, a goodbye. Throwing the shovel aside, I pick up Billy's body one last time. There, in my hands, his big wide eyes staring back at me, I realise how real this all is.

I remember Skye's words. *It's what you feel...*

I grab the handle with both hands wrapped around. It's so cold and I press so hard that the white of the bone shines through my knuckles. That's how I feel. I bury him, both hands on the shovel.

I stand there for some unknown time, leaning on the shovel for support. Then one moment the first images of Billy come back to me, those whiskers, and for some reason I smile.

'Thanks, Billy, you brave fool.'

I grab the few remaining coppers in my pocket and cast them into the stream, the weight of them not worth holding onto.

Back inside I close the door to try to put everything behind me. I need to stop for just a while. Collapse onto a bed. Smoke and drink until I fall unconscious and forget it all.

Just when I head for the stairs, though, she appears and we both say nothing of what happened before. Instead I ask her how her day has gone.

She explains that she took another bath—a proper bath instead of a rinse—hauling water from the stream and heating buckets over the fire, using an old tub in one of the empty rooms upstairs that I remember. She does look better, but won't say as much. She says there's even water left for me. I say I'll head up shortly but that I'm too hungry first. She replies that she'll cook something and that I should get washed. I don't argue with her 'cooking' beans and instead head straight upstairs, but before I reach the landing, I turn back only to see that she has already gone.

There's no way out, they said, there's no way out now. I definitely heard them this time. These cats—these shadows, or demons, I want to call them—are closing in. Of all the questions—how did the train crash, what is this town, what is this telephone, this wall and this mist—perhaps the most urgent question of all now is these cats. They are following us.

I don't know what to do.

Teeny bit by tiny bite, the water in the bath swallows me whole. I don't notice the temperature; I'm only all too aware of my body sinking into the depths of this tamed sea. At least I won't drown in here. At least I can control that much.

I think of the sea back home. How I used to love the beach, the bay, the Gower. I feel the soles of my feet press into the sand, hear the sea sing, look down at the footsteps behind me and alongside me...

I think of Skye. On the train, on the dunes, here. I miss her warmth, her smile, her energy. Now she seems tired, sad, even scared...

The waves crash against the scratched metal of the tub as I stand to get out. I snatch the towel she left for me, hanging from a glum hook, and step out onto the landing. Heading downstairs I call after her. It's not her voice that replies but the crackling of a fire overhead, a sweet song that drifts towards me from the room on the side. I wander towards the siren call, stopping at the door frame.

'Can I join?' I ask, unsure.

She has her back to me. She's facing the fireplace, this well-adorned hearth nurturing a growing flame that snaps and cracks as it whips the air. She turns then and smiles, beckoning me to enter with the tilt of her head. I step inside. I can feel my towel swaying, balancing uncomfortably around my waist. But she motions for me to approach and, after some hesitation, that smile disarms me and I draw closer to its warmth.

I sit beside her, close enough to feel the heat radiate from her skin. She smiles again, her best smile. I mimic her, and a stroke of red brushes her cheeks, but I can't tell if it's the heat or not. It's so warm in here, everywhere.

'Did you enjoy your bath?'

'I hated it.'

A faint laugh. 'Me too.'

I imagine the water already cold for her, but she doesn't bother to say. I look deep into those dark eyes, those eyes that seem to sway, to nod in their own little way.

She twists around, returning with my lump of clothes that she lays down next to me. Leaning over them I can feel how the kiss of the fire burns strongly on the fabric.

'Here,' she says. 'I found some soap which smelt good enough so I tried to give them back some scent. It's not great, but—'

'It's lovely,' I say, the light fragrance tickling my nose. 'Thanks.'

She nods, as if her voice would be too aggressive, disturbing the peace. I step outside to put my clothes on, returning a few minutes later to find her lying in front of the fireplace. I walk up to her but she turns when she hears the soft creak of my footsteps.

She says nothing and I lie down opposite.

'Will you tell me a story?'

I'm taken aback, unsure I heard right. She catches my surprise and gives the faintest of smiles.

'I don't know any stories,' I say.

Her expression changes, this mix of the dark and the

moon, a shadow cast over the side of her face. Like she's slipping away.

'Everyone has a story,' she says.

'Um…okay then. Once upon a time—'

She shakes her head. 'No, no, not that kind of story. Tell me about you.'

'About me?'

She nods, the brightness in her face encouraging me further. 'I still don't know much about you.'

'Well…' I have to think. What can I say? What would she want to know? 'There are better stories, you know.'

'I don't care. I want to know yours.'

'It's not a good one…'

'The story isn't over.'

I like that. Like I have something to look forward to. I like that about her—that despite everything she can still smile the way she does.

But what can I say? Life before this feels all broken, broken into fragments and pieces.

'I don't know what to say.' I'm honest, and she says nothing this time. 'In the end I didn't know what to do anymore. Don't get me wrong, I'm not ill or anything, I'm not pleading poverty per se. It's just that…' What can I say, what is this feeling, this churning and twisting and gnawing of my insides that won't speak? 'Life just felt…empty.'

It feels strange—strange that I'm saying all of this to her, stranger still that I'm admitting to all this. Admitting to my life.

'Empty? In what way?'

'I…' I bite my lip, embarrassed, even…ashamed. Then I notice her hand touching mine.

I lost my job. I lost the dream home. I had no real friends to speak of. Everyone I used to really know and care about now long gone. Greg, Becca, Martyn,

Louise...Either left for the four corners of the pub or the four corners of the world and onto better things. I no longer had any future plans to speak of. I was just...*surviving*. Not really living.

I press the fabric of my hoodie between my fingers. I can feel her watching me, her hand caressing mine.

And even now—after everything—I still can't bring myself to talk to her.

'I lost someone,' she says, echoing these thoughts in my head. 'Or rather, I never really had him in the first place. But you remind me a lot of him.' Her father? Someone else? 'He was a very warm person—optimistic, full of life. Right until the end.'

'I'm sorry.'

'I never thought it would happen, you know? I really thought that eventually everything would be okay.'

Now it's my turn to take her hand.

'It will be, right?' I say, but I don't know if I believe or if I want to believe.

She allows herself to take some comfort, at least, and for a moment I can believe my words too. But then the colour in her face fades and my faith with it.

'Without purpose in what we do, without meaningful relationships in our lives, what are we?' she muses. 'Something less than human.' She pauses, as if to let the words hang in the air for a moment. 'Have you heard the story of the tree falling in the forest?'

I shrug. 'Can't say, which one?'

But she ignores my playing. 'If a tree falls in the forest and there's no one to hear it, does it make a sound?' She pauses, as if waiting for my reply. 'Some say that it doesn't. Well, what if it's the same for us? What if there's no one with us, no one to bear witness to our existence, that we're all alone and no one can hear us—then do we really exist?'

I have to edge closer to the fire to stave off her disturbing thoughts, but the fire is dying fast and losing all spit and crackle. Losing its voice.

'It's only when we experience our feelings, only then are we truly alive,' she continues. 'At least that's what I believe. Like right now, I feel closer to you, I feel...warm inside. And that gives me meaning in life. Knowing that I matter to someone.' She smiles, even blushes. 'That is, of course, if I do mean something to you.'

'Of course you mean something to me.' I wouldn't want her to feel otherwise. For the first time in a while I feel... 'I followed you all the way here, didn't I?'

'You did.'

The light of the flames runs down the side of her face.

'But then again we are very alone.' She surprises me again. 'You don't know who I am, do you?' All at once a shadow runs across her face.

'I know you're lying beside me right now. I know you're Skye, whose hand I'm holding.'

She smiles, my hand in hers, touching the soft of her skin. I feel her fingers kissing my own.

'Do you remember,' she says, lips curled. 'Do you remember when we first met?'

As if I could forget. The damn cold, the...

'Of course. On the train—'

She shakes her head. 'No, no...'

I pause. What does she mean? Then I remember her on the dunes.

'I was on my own, not far from the crash, lost in the night. And then you appeared. There were, this impossible figure emerging in the light and you asked me who I was...'

'No, no. You asked me,' she shakes her head. 'I've never asked you such a question.' She is adamant, but I can't believe her.

174

'But you asked me who I was, and I was lost—I remember, and even in the faint glow of the moonlight I could make out the purple sweater under your coat—'

'I've never worn a purple sweater,' she replies, and I feel the cold from that same night.

'But—I'm sure.' She shakes her head and I feel her slipping away from memory, from reality.

I offer to find her sweater upstairs but she says it isn't worth it. I don't push it any further. I can still make out the faint lines running across her arm, now somewhat concealed by her clothing. I don't say anything, don't feel it will help. She looks at me, but I feel myself sinking into the floorboards. Sinking because I wonder how she could forget so easily this image of her that I have guarded, these words that I have kept safe in my memory. How—

I feel her hand brushing my shoulder. I look up into those large, chestnut eyes. I can't look away. I'm drawn in. Then a reflection bounces back at me—my own—drowning in the whirlpools spinning in my mind.

She leans forward, her hand locked in mine. I feel her hold me, tug me, cling onto me. The warmth of her body washes over me and her face glows in the heat of the fire, that face where streaks of light and dark meet. She's hiding—hiding from them, I can tell.

A tear—all alone—lost in the colour of her eye, falls down her face. Her dark, frightened voice echoes in the room like a haunting lullaby.

'You don't know me.'

And all at once her words, and that tear, are swallowed by the night.

*

A scream stabs me in the chest and I jerk awake. Shit. It's pitch black again but I know where she is when I twist

175

around, aware that the shadows are all over her. I call her name, trying to reassure her. I'm here, I tell her, I'm here. I grab hold of her and notice she's covered in cold sweat, drenched like she's been submerged under water. As the screams ring dry, as her body calms, I search for her hand and don't let go.

In the glint of the moonlight her eyes open. They blink for a few seconds before she turns to face me, those bright, blaring marbles scanning me.

'I saw them. The cats. They came for me,' she blurts out. The cats, her shadows, her demons. 'They leapt out of the darkness and devoured me.'

'It's okay now, it was just a dream.'

I try to calm her, holding onto her, but she insists.

'I was on the beach. The sun was out, and a myriad dancing sparkles glistened in the sea ahead. I even saw fish, reddish-pinkish fish that leapt into the air and dived back into the water again…Then a gush of clouds bled across the sky, the sea began to cramp then thrash, and the waves tossed and turned about me, and then…Then…'

She pauses, her eyes lost in the darkness. Afraid, I imagine, terrified. I squeeze her hand; a reminder that I'm still here.

'The cats…'

Her sobs fill the room with a darkness that disturbs me. Without thinking I start to hum a lullaby, rocking her in my arms until she calms. Eventually, I manage to lie her back down. Her body is cold, and I have to hold her close to share my warmth—heck, I would give her all of it if I could.

I hold onto her, rocking her back and forth still, unwilling to let go.

We are close.

An answer to life; sitting on the toilet, at the back of a Costa, I'm staring down looking for an answer.

I flick through the pages—of yet another site, another forum—but nothing I don't already know, nothing I can graft onto this dry hope I wear as a skin. I wonder how many pages, how many months or years I must spend before I find something. But there's just the facts—the 1 in every 3, the 1 in every 153—and the messages of people who don't really know how it feels—the 'try again and it'll happen eventually', or worse, the 'maybe it's not meant to be'. I have to wash my hands twice, this skin that doesn't feel like my own anymore.

In the mirror I see only questions. What can I do? What have I done?

A man on the wrong side of his thirties pushes through the door. He takes a slash and lets out a ripper, a shot that could kill. I stay still, washing my hands clean a third time, kidding myself I can do something with enough water. The man moves and I watch, in my periphery, as he eyes up the condoms in the machine, like he's got a chance.

He's got every chance, I know, more chance than me.

I watch as he slips in a coin and the machine spits out a packet. He grabs them with knuckles that sprout hair, like lots of little children dancing on the back of his hands.

'You never know,' he gives me his best grin, which is to say he gives me nothing.

I watch him leave in the mirror, the slap of the door as it closes to. I hope he has kids, lots of them – and I hope he treats them well.

the shadows of cats
(5 days to go…)

Words, I try to put words to this place, to her. I have a few words rattling in my pocket, but they aren't worth much; words that seem to hang from the sky and bring a warmth to my skin, but they don't last long; words that I breathe in, only to lose when I breathe out; ones that press against the floorboards when my ribs sink, or ones past me, past her, this dark wave that rushes up, this swelling of shadows now claiming half the wall next to where we sleep. Words that, when I struggle to wake, I'm too poor to express how I feel about any of this at all.

Then I remember the words of a famous Polish writer: *when you describe, you destroy.* And then I let everything be.

Morning. I lie still for fear of waking her. Despite everything: the train, the wall, this place—heck even before all this, losing the job I loved, the house I came to love, the person I've always loved…Our beach…All I know now is Skye, this young woman I met little more than a week ago who's changed everything. I know it. I feel it. And right now, I know she needs to rest and I'll be damned if I'm the one to deny it to her. Damned if I should be her shadow. So I wait, lying next to her, watching over her as she breathes, as she dreams.

Her body stirs. She awakes. Her eyes adjust to what's left of the day and she smiles when she sees me.

'Awake for long?' she asks, a long, drawn-out breath as each word struggles to escape her lips.

'It's fine. I didn't want to disturb you.'

Even in her tired state she can still muster shame.

'I'm sorry,' she says, but I correct her. It's not your fault. In fact, I found you sleeping rather relaxing, I tell her. A faint half-smile, but her face remains a white mask. Her cheeks are pale. More white than pink. I caress the side of her face but she looks exhausted, ready to collapse back into sleep. I grasp her hand, holding her stare as I do for a few moments until I leave her be.

I return a few hours later only to find her half-awake, slipping in and out of consciousness. I ask if she wants something to eat but she only shakes her weary head after my persistence. I ask if she would like to go outside, get some fresh air, but again she doesn't want to. But you haven't been out for two days now, I persist. I'm too weak, she says. Eat something then, I insist. She moans instead, turns over, collapsing into sleep. I watch as her ribcage sinks into the floor with each beat, each beat of her heart that pumps blood, climbs to her cheeks. Those white, misty cheeks.

I leave her be. I spend the rest of the afternoon outside, but only as far as the stream to collect some water, and on the side of the manor to collect some more wood from the stack we had built. That she had built. I have to remind myself. I turn to leave, arms full. I look across at the fireplace, no more than ashes and dust. Beyond that, where the bridge should be, the mist enshrouds it, hides it—*consumes* it, I worry. Worry that her words speak more truth than I dare.

I step back inside and shut out the cold. At least in here there's no mist, no shadows, no cats.

For now.

I wander back upstairs where I find her lying—or rather sprawled—across the floorboards. I ask her how she feels with words I don't have and she replies with nothing all the same, only lets out a terrified muffle and she stops. Without another word I lie down beside her, caress her hair…

This morning she never left the room.

*

The afternoon screams at us. A terrible crying seizes her. She thrashes about like a fish out of water and hits me like a wave, even cutting my lip and drawing blood that stains my hoodie. I try to calm her, to tell her that the shadows who torment her don't exist. She calls me a liar. I ask where she's gone, this strong woman I used to know.

She doesn't reply. She calms and I lie down beside her. I stay close by, my hands linked in hers, my chest pressed against her back. I don't dare leave her, don't dare sleep. I'm afraid to lose her if I lose sight of her.

A few trickles of light shine through the window. She's still here.

I manage to coax her into eating a few beans, beautiful beans that take on the colours of the sun long since gone, but she seems to have lost all appetite, all warmth and day. I convince her at least to take a bath, promising her warm water which I heat from burning much of the wood we have left. I don't care as I watch our reserves turn to ash. Anything to keep her going. When the bath is ready, I step outside to give her privacy. Shortly after I leave she's already calling me.

I step back inside but can't see her. Then her head leaps out of the water, gasping, the slight of a chill running down her cheeks. From the entrance I see her naked shoulders, her chest barely covered in the water. She coughs and splatters, the water in the back of her throat, drowning her completely.

She gives a faint smile when she notices me.

'You're still here,' she croaks.

It's the first she's spoken all day and I jump at the

180

opportunity.

'Sorry,' I pause, calming myself. 'Although it's not like I've got anywhere else to go.'

'You're stuck with me,' she says, and affords to laugh a little. It feels warmer all of a sudden. 'Come closer.'

'I'm fine here,' I reply, not sure what she's asking.

She smiles again, as if my embarrassment gives her pleasure. She can be cruel like that. But it's good to see her this way again.

'Come on, don't be shy.' She shuffles in the tub, the water rising up like waves crashing against the metal, ringing across the room. Ringing…'It's lonely here,' she whispers, but when I look her way she's turned away, lost in the folds of grey and dark etched into the wall behind.

'It's lonely,' I repeat. She twists around towards me, her eyes locked in mine. There's a deep seriousness to her stare, her silence, that I don't dare disturb.

'I see…' The words escape her lips, like a sigh, and she pauses again. 'Can you promise me something?'

I sense the rising tone in her voice, mistaking it for hope.

'Of course, anything.'

'Will you hold me under the water? Hold me and not let go?'

She's lost her mind. I don't speak—can't speak—waiting for her to tell me it's a joke. But she simply watches me. It's no joke. She really has lost her mind.

'I can't—'

'I need to learn to swim,' she interrupts. 'I need to be brave and face my fear.'

'By drowning in a metal tub in a town in the middle of nowhere?'

She sighs. 'You're right, it's stupid.'

I sit down near the tub, staying close, but also giving her some privacy.

'It isn't stupid, I mean, to face your fears that is. I admire that.'

'And what's your fear? What are you afraid of?'

Shit, should have expected that. And what am I afraid of? And then I see her there, naked, vulnerable.

'Well, losing you for one.'

She's turned away from me so I can't make out any smile if she has one. She pauses long enough though.

'You're afraid to be alone,' she repeats. 'At least now you admit it.'

'Admit it?'

'So many of us are lonely these days. Isolated, *lonely*. We all crave some love, someone. This is our silent epidemic, our war with no voice...' She's talking to herself again. Then she turns back to me. 'You lost someone.' She pauses, and I try to speak but can't. 'It's okay. I understand. I know. That's why you were on the train. You couldn't talk to anyone. You were alone, so very alone.'

'I was on the train...' But I can't finish my sentence, I can't think...

'It's okay, I know you won't say it. No one wants to— men most of all. Always feeling guilty, like it's your fault, something to be ashamed of. But it doesn't matter. I already know.' She's playing with me again. 'That's our great tragedy, isn't it?' She surprises me with a question. 'Either we never find home again, or we do.' Because there's no one waiting for us. 'The *train to nowhere*, for no one...'

'I wasn't the only one on the train remember. You had your own reasons. You were ready to jump.' I stop, aware of the shadow now running down the side of her face. I've gone too far. 'Sorry...'

'That's the first time you've mentioned it since...'

But she doesn't finish, the fading light and oncoming

darkness now stealing her from view. I let her finish her bath alone satisfied that, if she screams, I'll be able to hear her.

*

We're on our beach. But we're not on our beach.

We are walking side by side, but our hands aren't touching; we're walking forwards and yet backwards; we're looking out to the sea only to turn away, as if it's no longer ours, no longer something we can bear to see.

Words were said. Words without thinking. This is why I don't speak, I said. She cried. I cried, inside. More words, then the apology, the 'this is all my fault Claire', if only you'd have met someone else instead, then maybe… Words, and the crying hits me harder.

Eventually Claire goes out to the sea. Standing there I don't know what to feel, how she feels. All I notice is my body now swaying, left to right, right to left, like the sea might take me now and cast me aside; leave me like some train wreck on the beach.

I'm falling, Claire, I'm falling. We both are, both in our own worlds, wondering where the sea will throw us next and if we'll still be able to find each other.

*

Before the moon replaces the sun, that's when I get up. Can't wait any longer. Fetch some food, all the tins I can muster: beans, potatoes, pears and peaches, even tinned lemon I carry with me upstairs. I didn't even know such a bloody thing was possible, tinned frickin' lemon. Seen it all now—no, shouldn't say that. No telling what I might see or feel next. She would have none of the tinned sour, of course. I'm not sure I blame her. I say it's for her health. She doesn't respond. I tell her it's for her life. She shuffles and I take that as a sign.

Why are you so resistant, why won't you leave this

room? I ask, but I realise that bombarding her with these questions is only pushing her further, only distancing her from me. Tear down these walls, I tell her, let me in. But, through weakness or trauma—or both—she shakes her head, raising her voice, shouting even, screaming rather. I try to settle her down.

'The shadows, the shadows,' she repeats. I can hardly hear her voice; the words could be an echo in my mind.

Those wide now darkened eyes stare back at me, a white bulge shooting from them, and I give in. I hold her arms, hold that incredible stare.

'I don't understand...'

Her hand slips through my own. I shut my eyes for a moment, pushing back the fear fighting through and then...At last I see a flicker of life in her, something inside that brings an energy to her. I seize the opportunity. I hold up a tin to her and, after contemplating for a short while, she finally takes it in her wilting hands and, after a few seconds more hesitation...

She takes a bite. Then a second, a third. I watch as she slowly, painfully, takes form.

'Come outside with me, just outside the room,' I tell her, encouraged.

She takes my hand and allows me—for now—to help her stand. I feel her hand tremble, her steps falter, but she holds onto me and I'm able to lead her to the window at least. I say nothing and don't let go, and she surprises me when she breaks free, only the tips of her fingers touching my own. They hover in place and I watch as she stands before the window, peering outside, that view of the world in front of her all mist and shadows.

I watch as she holds a hand to her face, shocked at the sight before her. I want to ask her now what she sees at this moment but I fear to scare her, to force reality on her. I simply watch, watch the tear collect in the corner of her eye. She retreats several steps, her hand sliding back into my own. She locks it, and I take her away.

I take her downstairs and across the entrance hall, not without resistance. I feel her hands and arms tense, even her legs seem to twist and scream. She overcomes it, for now. I guide her, watch her as she takes each small, significant step. When her foot touches the floor, she falls and I rush to support her. I feel her weight collapse into my arms, fear the wind outside will whisk her away, but I risk it nevertheless.

I take her to the door. I open it and can't help but shiver.

Life outside rushes up to our feet, followed by this sea of mist. For a moment I wonder if the cats are behind this, behind everything. A veil over our world, I can barely make out five metres ahead. A whistle of wind, then a roar of thunder echoes in the distance and I feel her shaking. She sways so much in the wind it may well steal her away. The shadows will step out of the walls and come for her just as she fears. I can't tell. But I think she knows. I see the way she looks outside, through the mist, all fear, all accepting. Like time is running out. I feel her body lean forwards and fear she'll fall. The wind whips her face, scatters her hair and I pull her back, back inside the warmth, back inside the manor, back into my arms that I wrap around her.

'I'm sorry.' Barely a whisper. 'I'm so sorry.'

I don't know what else to tell her. The world around us is shrinking, disappearing, consumed by shadows. Without a bang, even so much as a whisper. Like we never existed.

I take her back upstairs before it's too late.

*

I drag myself up in the night. Not because of her, no. I

185

hear it. That beat that haunts, that beat that follows, that—

I shudder.

Ring, ring.

Ring, ring.

...

Ring, ring.

I cry. It's in my head. It's all in my head. I know this. Cable cut, there's nothing else to it. I roll over.

I reach out towards her but she isn't there. Squinting in the feeble light I can't make out anything, no outline, not even her coat. Or purple sweater. What happened to her purple sweater?

I scramble to my feet, my clumsy hoodie hanging loosely over me. I clamber around the corner. Damn it. There's nothing here. The rucksack—the knife. I remember her last night, her arms exposed and cut. Damn it.

I jump to my feet and head out the door.

I can't find her anywhere, no trace of her. I call, shout, but my voice simply drowns in the darkness, vanishes through the walls. I throw the main door open, plummet into the cold of the night. I shout again, but nothing, nothing but darkness, but—

There, hunched over, her back to me. She hovers near the stream—on the edge of the world—and I fear she'll fall forward and disappear into the waves. Fall and—

A soft cry. I walk up beside her.

'Skye...' I stop. My stomach lurches to the right. I gag, have to stop myself from hurling. 'What the hell...What happened?'

Her face is hidden, her back still turned to me. And his body. Still twitching. Curled inwards—as if he were returning to the womb—blood flowing freely from the gaping cut in his stomach. What was life, now staining the ground.

She doesn't move. I steal a few more steps until I'm beside her, close enough so that the knife she still clings to now pierces into view. Stood by her I catch a glimpse of her face, her eyes sunken, sinking into the dead body before her. Her body just hangs there, just mist in the air, but her eyes remain focused. It's like she's forgotten all other feeling.

For a moment I hesitate; what if she turned that knife on me?

I shake the thought off and kneel beside her, placing my hand on her shoulder just to let her know that I'm here.

She gives a soft whimper.

'I...I had to,' she croaks, the words tumbling out of her mouth. 'He tried to—to kill me, to kill you! The cats have got to him. They're coming for us...'

Then, all at once, her strength fails her. She lowers the knife clasped in her hand before collapsing to her side, onto me. Now her tears don't hold back. I wrap my arms around her and pull her in close, so close. I don't dare let go. Even when the cold starts gnawing at my flesh—my cheeks now a purple-bluish bulge—I don't dare let go.

The bleeding stops, and her tears dry. I think it's been long enough. She seems too weak to move so I lift her up and carry her back inside the manor, back to our room where I lie her down in the creases of my jacket. I brush the few loose strands of hair that keep falling over her face, and wait for her to fall asleep. I hum a lullaby, and the thrashing of waves inside her seems to calm, and her breathing becomes regular as she slips into merciful sleep.

Above her, scattering across the wall, the shadows of all the cats in town. Watching us. I whisper into her ear that I won't let go, but my words are worthless and I'm losing my voice.

She doesn't even respond, as if I missed her entirely.

*

Japan. Another world. The other side of it, at least. Because that's where we are, where I am; always on the other side of some world or another.

I've lost count of how many times we've tried. I've lost count of all the questions people ask without thinking, about when we'll have children and how many, lost count of how many tests we've had, of how many medicines and alternative medicines. I've lost track of the days and weeks and months we've lost to false hope, how much money we've spent, how much energy we used to have, how many more times I've seen Claire cry and how many fewer times I've seen her smile, I've lost count.

But we're here now and I'll do anything at this point; anything to see her smile again.

We arrive at the Okazaki Shrine just before closing. It's in a calmer district of Kyoto with fewer Japanese and even fewer foreigners. The handful of wandering souls we do see are either pregnant, male, or hoping. There's a middle-aged Japanese man by himself and I wonder what he's lost.

Claire and I roam the grounds, take in all the shades of black and red and white, and we move through clouds of incense and a chorus of claps as people call upon the spirits for their blessing. There are ribbons curled along some ornate pillars. A woman kisses a man, arms thrown around one another. And many, many statues of bunnies of all shades and stripes populate the grounds.

The kissing couple now huddle around a statue of a small black bunny, bow, pour water over its head and rub its belly, all before skipping away with the newfound belief that this is it. This is the one. I feel a tug on my hand and I know it's our turn. We both stand still, staring into this bunny's eyes, my own trying to fight back a rogue tear. I watch as Claire bows her head, closes her eyes, praying for a miracle that only the gods or spirits can grant now.

I don't know what to do. I don't know what we can do. But seeing her there, eyes closed, on the far side of this shrine on the other side of the world, I close my own eyes and try; try to believe. I open my eyes and Claire is gone, and overlooking the bunny I see a black cat yawning. Its open jaw in the background seems to wrap around the helpless bunny's throat in the foreground, and all the guardian statues and all the other souls are too slow to notice.

A call. It's Claire. She approaches; I smile, and she smiles back. I don't know what to believe.

god is love…god is…god…
(4 days to go…)

There are secrets in this town that I need to find out. Before the shadows take her. Take me. I'm here for a reason; that much I've come to accept. I've left this for too long, but it's not too late. I hope. For my sake, for *her* sake, I need answers and I need them today. I grab the rucksack, a flask of water, the crowbar, and a tin full of confidence before heading out. She's still unconscious—could hardly call it asleep—and I leave her be. With my hoodie as well she won't be too cold, at least. Either way, I need to go alone. Where I'm going, she can't come; what I'm doing, she can have no part of.

I step outside. The cats will leave me alone, I tell myself, a mantra, a prayer.

The main square has long succumbed to the winter mist. I have to feel my way, relying on the limited visibility and my own memory of the streets. By the time I reach it I've probably wasted an hour already. Despite it all I have no doubts when I arrive.

The chill and even the mist hold back. The entrance to *The Moon Under Water* remains free from its grip, and the dim light manages to filter through inside somehow. As I approach the door resting ajar, I begin to make out the bar and open space within. I look around back outside, half-hoping Billy would be there, but it's just me. Then, crowbar in hand, I kick the door the rest of the way and step inside.

The light throws me—as if I've become used to the dark. Here though there's a large window at the back that filters in the day, a welcome breath of life in the room. Not that there's much here, enough for two dozen or so, a small open space with some tables and chairs at the back, then at the front stands a bar with its fair share of bottles and booze, two or three shelves stumbling from one far side to the other. I even wonder if this is where she stole that crate the other night. I wouldn't put it past her. For now, and ignoring the portrait of a yet another black cat hanging behind the bar, I take a stool. No one else in sight, I can relax a little, setting the crowbar aside and browsing what's on offer while I'm at it.

'So, wha' we having?'

I twist around and make for the crowbar only to fall head first into confusion on seeing who it is. It's no shadow, no talking cat, but Larry, sitting on one of the stools and casually leaning over the bar while next to him Bubbles is trying to imitate his friend. They both seem oblivious to the absurdity of the situation.

'So, wha' we having?' It's Bubbles' booming echo. It's him alright, right down to the spit spraying me when he speaks.

'What the hell you guys doing here?' Lowering the crowbar some I hold onto it tight just in case. Larry notices.

'Why don't you put that down first, then we'll talk?'

I loosen—then tighten—my grip, throwing a glance around the pub, but there's no one or nothing else save us three. Larry and Bubbles don't seem very threatening by themselves. Bubbles himself just seems like a big baby and would cry at hurting a fly. I take one last look before setting the crowbar aside, still within arm's reach.

'Alright. But I've had enough of questions. I want answers. Tell me. Who are you and what are you doing here?'

'Who are we? Shit, is your head loose or summat? We only met last week.'

Last week, he says. When the train derailed and this damn nightmare began.

'I'm just tired, that's all.'

'I get it. Anyway, come join us. Barkeep, get my friend here another pint of bitter. He could do with another jolt.'

Behind the bar a woman in navy overalls appears, one who bears a striking resemblance to a colleague at the old school I worked at. She makes no sign of recognising me though, and I know it's not her. Just like this isn't really Larry and Bubbles. It can't be. I watch the barkeep as she collects a glass nearby before fixing up a quick pint.

'Uh, thanks,' I say, twisting in my stool to face Larry who's already taking a swig of his own beer. Bubbles, too, is slurping away. The barkeep soon hands me my own and I take a mouthful—the local bitter cracks on my tongue, but soon warms as it passes through my body.

'That good enough for you?' the barkeep asks for my approval. Her accent is straight out of the valleys, bouncing off the hills all over the place. Like I never left Wales, and the rest of it.

'Yeah.'

'A good way to forget.'

Larry this time. His words surprise me, but I say nothing. I'm starting to wonder if this was a bad idea after all. Bubbles, meanwhile, continues to enjoy his frothy beer, the white now staining his upper lip, the sloppy moustache wiggling as his face moves. Yet I can't help but look back at Larry. He's looking away, though there's something sad in the way his lips hover above the glass's rim.

'So,' the barkeep interrupts again.

She's swilling out an old pint glass. Then another customer, face hidden from my view, comes up to the bar and asks for two more pints which the barkeep, who I last saw handling two phones at once, dutifully pours before handing over. No money is ever exchanged. At

192

this point I'm just accepting everything. I have to remember—what's the *reason*, not how, but *why*. So I accept. That and the dozen or so other ghosts who've popped up around the room, followed by the dim clink of glasses, the banter at the tables, and even the fruit machine now lit up in the corner swallowing some poor bastard's coins. Some f'ing this and f'ing that, and the barkeep shouts to control him. The scene unfolds before me, including the layer of smoke that soon fills the air, my lungs. This could be twenty years ago, like I'm six years old again and watching these grown men act out the other half of their lives.

'So…' I echo.

'So,' the barkeep resumes, turning back to me. 'Tell us about yourself.'

I hesitate. After everything, what do I say? No one's answered my questions, but somehow, I doubt they will. I take another gulp, long and satisfying, before settling into my stool.

'Not much to say, really.'

'Come on, kid. You have a life, don't you?'

Her words strike me. She was definitely my senior, but her directness still takes me aback. I'll just give her what she wants.

'Well, honestly, I'm feeling kinda down.'

'Yeah, where you to?'

'Well, let's see. I'm recently unemployed after losing my last job as a substitute teacher. Near Swansea, south Wales.'

'Swansea, eh? No wonder you're depressed.'

I can't help the slight smile in response.

'Yeah, it's all the rain.' She looks like she's listening, and the beer feels warm inside so I continue. 'Well, where to begin? I lost my job, lost my house too.'

'Damn.'

'Don't know my dad. And my mum is a mess. She's spent the last half of her life as half the person she used to be, always waiting for some Prince Charming to save her, and now someone needs to save her from him.' I pause, waiting for her next remark but she says nothing. 'And...'

There's something else, there's always something else, but my mind is foggy and I can't think straight. Instead I notice Larry looking at me—he's definitely not the same Larry as before. Something has changed. I stare back into my glass, half-empty, and wonder if there's anything left to say.

'I've lost a few friends recently. Heck, I've lost them all, it feels.' Just say it—say the *real* reason. 'I lost someone...' I can't continue. All these people here, these memories, she could be here right now—it certainly feels that way, like she's one of those hooded figures on the other side of the pub, so close and yet so far all the same. 'I was just waking up to go back to sleep. I had to go. I was a burden. So I eventually left. Didn't pack anything, left no notice—I just left. Woke up, the same world, bought a one-way ticket to the most remote place I could find...'

'*Train to nowhere*,' Larry speaks for me.

I stop. For a moment I just let the sudden hush of the bar wrap itself around me, comfort me. I knock back the remaining bitter from the glass and wipe my mouth. Now there's nothing else left.

Larry puts his hand on my shoulder. He says nothing. None of us do. He pulls out a pack of cigs, pops one in his mouth and lifts the packet up to me. Good old Lambert and Butler, an old favourite of my mum—and me.

I hesitate, but he holds the packet out under my nose. 'Screw it,' I say, and Larry smiles.

I bring the cig to my lips, light it with his Red Ronson and suckle on its teat. But I can't help but remember that night with Skye, remember this image of her, and now all I can taste is the filthy ash in my mouth and none of the good stuff. Meanwhile, Larry lights up his own.

'It's good to talk, let it all out. Men most of all forget that sometimes.' The barkeep breaks the silence. 'Sorry about all that, kid, don't sound good at all. But you know, you can't let it get you down for too long. Life's too short and all.'

'Easier said than done,' I reply. 'I have no friends, no one I know—'

'Shit.' It's Larry, surprising me again, his face emerging from the bottom of his glass. 'Even after all this time here you can't see what the real problem is, huh?'

'The real problem, the real problem,' Bubbles bounces in his stool.

'You're running out of time, kid.'

'Running out of time!'

I look away, look across the back of the room. But all the ghosts are gone now, just her again, all by herself at the back surrounded by empty bottles. I turn to Larry and Bubbles.

'Hey—'

But they're gone too. Only the barkeep left, scrubbing several empty glasses with the same efficiency she handled three or four conversations back at the call centre. Or so I think.

'I lost my first few, too,' she muses, but I can't tell what it is she lost or even if she's talking to me. Then she looks me in the eye. 'Careful, kid. Take my word for it, as a woman myself. Losing something so precious, we need love, not left alone. Don't feel guilty, don't "give her space". No need to say anything—just be there for her.'

I look around the empty tavern. That's it, right?

Larry's last words hang onto me, while the barkeep's last words have a strange stickiness to them, too.

'She's all I have.'

And with that, the barkeep is gone too.

She says nothing, the young woman at the back. But now she's changed. It's definitely her though.

Skye—it certainly looks like her, but at the same time I know it's not. Skye is back at the manor, suffering her own nightmare. Everyone else here—they're just part of my own 'bad dream', as Larry once put it when we first met. And yet I can't see anyone else but her at the table— drowning in her empty bottles, no one else with her. All alone.

'That's why you didn't want to come here, wasn't it? We're both the same. Why we always stayed away from this place.' I speak aloud so she can hear my voice, whoever she is. She doesn't move or reply. 'You were afraid of me finding out who you were. All this time you wanted to be strong for me, to help me, but you have your own demons, don't you?' I stare down into the bottom of my own glass. 'You're as screwed up and lonely as I am.'

It's not Skye—that much I know now. The woman doesn't move. She may not even be listening. She may be drunk or drugged for all I know. Knowing my imagination, she could be any or all of these. It doesn't matter—I have to say this regardless. To myself, maybe.

'I'm sorry, you know. For not being who you needed me to be.'

I close my eyes.

I'm back on the beach. The salt and pepper sand kisses my feet as I leap and laugh, the crash of the waves against the shore drawing me closer...But I can't remember where it is. I can't find the footsteps once alongside me. I can't go back, to this secret place...

I open my eyes, feel her stare. I sigh.

'I should have been stronger, or at least admitted my feelings and got help. But you've made me realise— realise how much I need you. It's like Larry said, the reason I'm here, it's all to face my bad dreams...And move on, right? It's what Skye had said. *It's only when we experience our feelings, only then are we truly alive.* And that's why we're here, why I'm here. To discover—re-discover that. Find you—me, escape from this isolation before it's too late, right?'

I smile, then push and smash the beer glass onto the floor. The splintering has the desired effect—she shudders, and I find myself staring across the room at her, trying to hold her in place, keep this image of her here. But I can't stop the mist behind from taking her.

I wipe my mouth and stand from the stool. It's getting late now and the mist is making its way in through the window, through the door, through everything. I have to go. Go to her.

To Skye.

*

God is taking a piss. The rain falls on me the entire way to *Good Hope*, this other place she never went, another place this town is keeping answers from me. I keep the crowbar close.

It doesn't take long to find the church, or maybe it's the curiosity pulling me in. I have to keep going, for her sake. For my sake. Outside I find the familiar double doors, and on the right-hand side is a sort of community board. Another thing that only now I notice. Full of posters, of real words, it's the first sign of other people— of *community*—that I've come across. I read everything there is on here, try to imagine the lives of all these people.

Karaoke at *The Moon Under Water*! Every Friday 7-8pm.
Piano lessons with Mrs Bell, call…for inquiry.
Have you seen this cat? Contact…if you have any
information.

I look at the cat. There's nothing peculiar about it, just another black cat. It could be the same one as in the portraits, it could be the one I met on the way to the train station before I boarded last week. And yet, there *is* something peculiar about this cat. I just don't know what.

I head for the door, haul the one side open, the blotchy light rushing inside before me. I step inside, crowbar raised to my shoulder.

'Anyone there?'

'Anyone there?' An echo, a voice deeper, more guttural. Like someone choking.

I walk down the corridor, row hugging row of benches passing me by, boarded up windows meaning the light falls back as I approach the darkened pulpit. What I can see comes to me in blinks and snaps, but there's no doubt about it, no doubt this is a strange place. Paintings of Jesus, yes, and plenty of crosses and crucifixes too, but now I notice there are other symbols I recognise: the Jewish star of David and the Muslim star and crescent among them. It seems everyone is welcome here. I continue down the path, the crowbar raised to my head, only to find more paintings, more portraits.

Of babies.

Another sign. And more words beneath this one portrait, of a woman, presumably Mary, pregnant with an unborn Jesus. But the woman is crying. She doesn't look like any portrait of Mary that I know, and other women—and men—are kneeled and weeping next to her prominent stomach. Beneath there's a quote,

Lamentations 3:33.

'[God] does not enjoy hurting people or causing them sorrow.'

I look back at the picture. Who is this woman and why does she look familiar? I think about who painted it. I know hardly anything about art, less so about painting or religious ones, but even to me the way the strokes rise and fall look and feel different. Was the painter observing, or part of this picture as well?

I continue to the end of the hall where a prominent plaque draws everything else to it.

God is love. God is...God...

Then nothing but a blank space afterwards. Just...God.

I wonder if God exists and what his or her plan is with me and this place. God is love. If that's the case, then can God forget someone? I try to think of the last time I went to church or something similar. School? The choir? Definitely not with family. Or friends.

I think of the last time I prayed. I know when I last prayed.

I never abandoned God—I never found him in the first place. If he knows I'm here, does he know the reason?

I approach the pulpit, climb the steps and call out.

'Anyone?'

'Anyone?'

Another echo. I swing around, a sweeping view of the church revealing the emptiness hanging over me. Not a single soul. All alone. I lower the crowbar.

Nothing.

I climb back down the pulpit and walk a few steps, head down, looking at the old floor, bare save a single stain. No, not a stain. A book—no, a journal. Old man Dai's journal again? I pick it up, but I can't find the same pages or the same scribble. This writing is neater, clearer, the letters looping and curving and dancing on the page like...like...

'It's me.'

I swing around, throwing the crowbar into the pocket of air behind me and tearing through the echo. Nothing. No one. That's all it was. An echo. That's what I tell myself. I turn back to the journal.

Did Skye write in here? It's definitely her, except... There's just a single entry. Dated the morning of the day we met, before all of this happened.

There's this man nearby. Picking cigarettes from the ashtray of the bin, carefully, like his life has been reduced to the hand that picks them. He doesn't even notice me next to him. Passing me, I'm still unnoticeable. When our eyes cross, still I'm no one.

It's here. Sitting on Platform 2. Waiting. The train to nowhere. What if someone found me—anyone, before day's end. Anyone who'll care to speak to me...

Phone's ringing. Straight to voice-mail. Can't talk to anyone now. Everything, everyone behind me. Take out the battery from the phone. Stop the ringing—stop them all trying to reach me. Cut myself off from that world...Because there's nothing left in that world.

A call. The train is about to leave, leave behind this city, this liquid city that moves with the unpredictability of waves. I can no longer see the sea from here—there's no danger of drowning. That much I can take comfort in.

A final blare, then a screech as the train hauls itself from its slumber. I look for the man again but he's already gone.

I tell myself I'm no one.

There are other pages—other entries maybe—but

they're ripped out, just small shards of paper like teeth marks where memories used to lie. And many blank pages. Instead, I read the single entry once more and think about how she is now.

Like the sea will take her.

My hand clenches. My nails dig into my skin. Like they'll rip through. Fear. That's what fear is. Like I'm angry and incapable.

I close the journal and pack it in the rucksack. Another look around. All these symbols, all these religions, and I wonder if it's worth praying, but I don't know what to pray for or even who to pray to. But I don't want to gamble on bad faith. At the very least, I should pray for her.

I don't know which God to believe in. Then I think, they're all praying to the same God, right? All asking for the same thing, all asking after someone?

It's late. Time to leave. I've seen enough. I turn to leave only to see a cat.

A black cat. Nothing distinctive, and yet the cat *is* distinctive. There it is, I understand. It's distinctive in the way it turns its head towards me, distinctive in the way we share a moment where we can both see and be seen.

We know where you are.

They know where I am. The cats—these shadows, these demons. My shadows, my demons. That much I understand now.

The cat turns and disappears. For now, I'm safe. God sees to that. It's time to leave, to see Skye before it's too late.

Outside it's still raining, like God is pissing, my mum used to say. Through the unholy water falling around me, I see it again, the community board. If God is dead, I tell

201

myself, then he still has his followers. They still have faith.

*

I'll talk. Talk to anyone. Talk to the big man himself. But he's not here to talk. No one is. What's more, like faith, everything here is stripped bare. Nothing but the hollow remnants of the church remain.

I take a seat. When was the last time I sat down in a place like this, in a state like this? I'm looking down and then— awareness creeping in—I look up. To the heavens. To a glimmer of light, like a sign or a miracle or just the green glum light of an alarm system. I watch the faded white panel for a while, the hesitant colour, its own flashing heartbeat slow and dying. I stand back up.

Claire is right. I'm too pessimistic. But then life is too pessimistic. I will talk. But there's no one here to listen, is there?

*

We know where you are.

Night. I snap awake and the beach, those small footsteps, and that voice all disappear. Wide awake I worry I'll hear it again. But I hear nothing. For now. Instead, I find a calm in the still and I can fall unconscious. But now it's that very calm that frightens me. I turn to my side—to her side, but she isn't there. My eyes dart across the room in the semi-obscurity, but no outline; no white of her eyes, no faint sound of her breathing. I throw my hoodie on and head outside.

I pray to God.

I hear her calling—is that her calling? I can't be sure. The first few notes glide across the air, of that lullaby I know all too well. Of course, I follow, of course I trip on the stairs, stumble two, even three steps at a time as I hurry, worried where she is, what might have happened.

The lullaby rings in my head and I head outside to find her.

The moon is barely visible tonight. This crescent-shaped scythe with spots of magma red staining its tip. A halo glow drifts around its edges, later swallowed by the night sky. I come up to the bridge where the stream has now become a torrent that rages and drowns out the soft notes. I fall to my knees, lost in the vast nothing of the night.

I follow the current, down the winding path shaded by the rocky outcrops on either side. At once I hear her voice, that soft, melodic chant that glides and soothes and...

Claws at my skin. A loud, sharp scream lunges from the darkness and I stop.

'Run!' She screams.

I can't move, not until she pulls me forwards, clinging onto my arm and hurtling us both down the path leading back to the stream. I try to shout, to call her to come to her senses, but she only tightens her grip. She won't listen. The tension in my wrist from her fingers is too strong, she won't let go...I won't let go—

We cross the bridge, abandon the stream to the cries and chants behind us. I don't want to believe—I can't believe...Are they real—have they really found us—

She breaks free, now running off into the distance and I have to chase after her but I struggle to keep up. I burst into the square and just metres ahead she stops. She turns, panting, her face masked in the dark, her image a blur, a faint outline that I fight to rescue from the shadows in the background. A faint warmth emanates from her body when I approach. A faint whisper that I know is her. I swear I catch her as she opens her mouth to speak.

Silence.

A cry, the night turns thicker and a shadow leaps onto me from the darkness. I shout. I crash against the ground, the weight crushing me, digging into me. I struggle to resist. I feel a sharp dig in my leg—like daggers—and a gentle flow of warmth trickles down my thigh. I thrash out into the darkness. Another scream. Her scream, I think. I try to break free, try to fight the shadow. I—

Shout. Another shout, the sound of crying. I thrash the darkness once more, strike the shadow and throw it off. I jump and hit again, and again, the clash of my knuckles scraping off the tip of the chin to release a spurt of blood that stains the ground. The screaming dies away.

The darkness pulls back and the moon, smeared crimson red, hangs from the sky like a limp body and reveals everything.

I'm on our beach; the sea, I hear that ringing once more, that lullaby that sings to me. And the whisper of *'this is all my fault'* echoes all about me.

*

The bathroom is miserable with laughter. The echo from the laptop, from some re-run of Friends, *is a world away from the tears and sweat and blood in the bathroom. Here the world is a mess of borders and boundaries, a knot of arteries and veins and chewed up umbilical cords. And I stand here, just stand here as the phone mumbles into my ear as the operator speaks but I hear nothing.*

Without a drop of drugs in your system your body tears itself apart and I think there is no God. There is no God when I see your body shake and vomit and throw out a piece of you. Of us. I glimpse the thin thread of red between your thighs that I imagine fell from your heart—that's the sound you're making. There is no God when you fall off the toilet, reduced to squatting and sobs over the seat, drops thicker than water tripping down your legs. There's no God, I think, when the sound of silence is the echo of someone else's laughter.

I close my eyes—does that make me a coward? I open my eyes—is this all my fault? I look down as screams and laughter blink then blur—God, what have I done?

'I saw her...I saw her.'

I don't know what to say. I don't know what time it is when I finally move and you let me help you up. I don't know what the darkness outside means to say when I clean up the stains of life smeared across our beige floor tiles and toilet rim. I don't know how to feel when I finally bring myself to collect the remains in a black box and flush the toilet.

I don't know, Claire, how to look you in the eyes.

Days, weeks—I want to say something, anything. Just bring you back to life, Claire, but I can't. I'm not God, no one is. I want to tell you everything you need to hear, but I can't. I don't know how to fix this. Not when there's this hole inside me as well; it's not the same, I know, but I've got nothing left to give.

I say nothing, and all you know is the cold space where my arms could be.

Sometimes, at night, I still hear that laughter, the cry of 'I saw her, I saw her' as God closes the door behind him.

the cats catch the bunny
(3 days to go…)

Morning. The sun splinters through the window, a light that filters through and stains the darkness clinging to the room. I struggle to open my eyes. I shift between shades of light and dark. Light. I think I hear a light tapping, someone touching my arm. Dark. It's just the cold and blood that covers my skin in scabs. I turn to my side, hide from the morning. That's life. Just wake up to go back to sleep. Hide from the day, wait for the night.

Skye.

Light. I stare at the space where she used to lie, that space that only a short while ago her warm skin had touched. Dark. Now there's just an empty crate, empty bottles knocked over, and not the faintest hint of her where she slept, where she…

Light. I press my hand against the floorboards, wondering if I might feel them press back against me. Dark. Not even the warmth or sweet scent of her remains. It's as if she hadn't even been here…

I lie still. Just lie here, still.

Afternoon. Light. I get up. Hunger drives me. That survival instinct is all I have left. I drift, wander, my body willing but my mind elsewhere. I have to drag my feet down the stairs, falling down the last few steps. I lie still. I listen to the beat of my heart as it thuds inside, pushes against the floorboards; small echoes of life and I stand up again. I stagger across the hallway, through another door, into the kitchen where I…

…take some tins, a fork. Dark. It's when I discard the pans that I notice it, remember that slick slippery slicer. I take it, grasp it, wield it. It dances in the air, taking a life of its own. I lose it for a second and it nicks one of my

206

fingers, drawing blood. I curse, I shout, and throw the damn thing to the floor. Then I stop, my own panting echoing off the walls of the kitchen relaxes me, makes me feel like someone else is here. I watch as several fragile pearls of red slide down the digit, fall from the tip of the nail and crash and splatter across the worktop. I step back, retreat out of the kitchen. Back to...

...the stairs. Light. It's full of steps. It's a journey to the summit. On the side of the staircase the portraits of cats come to life, wander off the walls, and follow me like they're my own shadows. And of course, who could forget the red telephone; it stays put, hanging there, just some painting, nothing to hold onto, no connection to anywhere or anyone else. Dark. I brush past only to turn back, rip it off the wall and smash it into my knees before throwing the remains down the stairs. I watch as the frame hits each step, bouncing about like some ragged doll, each crack of the wood like the cracking of bones. I watch until the remaining splinters break away and float in the air, a sound and a scene that comforts me... Like someone else is here. I turn back, head up the last few steps and trip onto...

...the landing upstairs, I cross the window, a bright, illuminated portrait with a view of outside. Light. I dare to look out, if only briefly. Dark. She's no longer there, a ghost that rides the crest of the waves, a shifting mass of mist. I try to imagine her there, paint her image on the crest but nothing. A magnificent nothing. The rising tide presses against the glass and threatens to break through the window. I step away from...

...the shadows, retreat further inside the room. Away from it all. Dark. I sit in the corner. Dark. I down another half bottle of whatever I find from the other night and add it to the mix. Dark. I'm worse than her.

Her. What was her name again? *You don't know who I*

am. I don't know who you are.

I look to the space next to me and imagine her watching, observing as I scoop up another spoonful of orangey gooey stuff. Not even that fluffy ball of white is here to join.

'I bloody love these tins,' I mutter aloud. Just to hear the sound of my own voice. 'These damn tins.'

She doesn't reply and morning fades to night.

*

I try to burn some candles, to see something in this darkness.

I try taking a bath; wash myself clean, clear of yesterday, every day. Or maybe I'll just drown myself in these waves and find her there. I wash myself with the soap she found for me, a scent I now think to be her own. She had a hint of lavender about her I'm sure, I think, maybe. I let the scent fill the bath, wash over me, stay with me after I've left. Distracted by her I can forget the cold for now.

I take the journal—*her* journal. I don't know. Or maybe it's a different one? I don't know. I just want to write something in the blank spaces, carve out my name next to hers but I have nothing to write with. Just paper that refuses to listen. Then I see the knife lying still on the floor and I grasp it, balance it in my hands and, thinking of her, carve out her name in the paper, tearing into it. But the paper gives way so I carve her name wherever I can. The floorboards, the wall…

A final stroke and I sit back and call her again, but she doesn't answer. She doesn't even notice me.

With nothing to do they come for me, these little monsters dressed up as questions that lean into my ear and ring. How did the train crash? What is this place? Why is there no one here? Who are these cats, and why are they after me? And that biggest question of all—who is she? I have no answers, nothing to bat away these questions. Then I think about God, about the meaning of life, the number 42 and I realise I know nothing. Then I think about what she had said. Why did I board the train? Where did I want to be? Who am I? I don't have answers but she told me to be honest. I sigh again.

'I boarded the train because...' I open my mouth, try to speak, try to unravel the meaning in it all.

I dare to wander outside as if doing so the little monsters will leave me be, except I hardly manage two steps past the front door. The mist is closing in, so close that I can't go to the side of the manor to collect any more firewood. I'm afraid the outside will swallow me whole. I fall back inside, one step at a time, facing the mist as it threatens to follow me even here.

But not before I see them—their grotesque, oversized heads, tilted to the side, mouths agape with row after row of teeth. There's blood on that white shine, and in one gaping trap I find half of the remains of a white fur.

The cats have caught the bunny. They said they would. It was only a matter of time.

Silence. They don't even speak. They know the silence is worse.

I shut the door and bolt it. I check it works, pulling then pushing the door. Then I jerk the bolt again, pull and push once more. It's definitely locked. I think. I push the bolt again, pull and push once more. I take a few steps back. It must be locked, must be, but I haul myself upstairs, unsure it'll keep anything out.

Besides, this room is full of little monsters and these walls surrounding me are full of shadows. Waiting. Leaning in.

I call her once more but she doesn't reply.

There's nothing left to do.

*

I'm fine. I'm not fine. I'm fine.

I'm reading, for the fifth time this morning, 'Sometimes I feel Sunny'. Here it goes:

'Sometimes I feel sunny, like a great big smiling sun. Sometimes I feel sad, as though nothing will be fun... There are days when I'm the King! And there are funny, floaty, empty days, when I don't feel anything...'

Because that's what depression is, right? It's not all sad and slippery days, is it? Except that's all I remember these days; that's all I can think about tomorrow and today, well, today is almost over. Because that's what depression is, right? It's reading every other page in the book and missing out on life. The reason for everything.

I turn to the alarm clock in bed. 9.05am. I'm late for work. Claire has already left. Outside a black cat licks the window; all black and shadow and demon, and I lose myself in the folds of bed sheets.

I'm fine. I'm not fine. I'm...

*

'...'

Night. It's so dark. I don't dare leave the room. I've shut the door. Pushed the crate of empty bottles against it. I'm keeping them out. I check it all over once, twice, and once again. Awake. I don't dare leave the room. I saw them approaching earlier. I swear. I can see them now, here from the window, creeping towards me as the light of the last candle dies away. Awake. They're already inside the room, emerging from all four walls. I'm locked in.

The shadows won't leave me be.

Leave me alone.

All alone.

*

Half-life.

It hangs over us, sprays the room all white all nothing. The lightbulb flickers; sometimes light, sometimes not. Light. There's a small table opposite with blood-red orchids; blooming—and plastic—a promise both alive and dead all at once. Dark. I shuffle in my seat; my wife is on her side and I'm on mine, despite this small sofa squashed in the corner. Light. I look at her, the room, back up at the bulb; take in everything in one breath. It's a curious thing; shaped like a seed, but unable to grow and give off any light. Dark. Faulty, only half-awake, half-alive. Something you take for granted will work, then you're left in the dark without. Light. That's what we thought; that's what I still hope. Dark. Does she still hope? From the sofa everything feels far away, despite the room. Maybe it's the black of the sofa stealing the little light left that creates the illusion. Is this my fault? I could never reach it, no matter how many tries. She doesn't seem to notice though. I'm on the edge of my seat; she's sunk into the depths of hers. The cheap leather rubs against my skin; she hangs back, like she's her shadow and no one, nothing else. Light. A tap at the door and I think I see her stir; it's just a trick of the light, and no one else enters. Dark. Just us, the bulb above, and everything caught between all white all nothing.

Light. The bulb clicks too, like a cricket's cry. Makes me think of last summer; Ile de Re, the two of us on the beach, September sun setting, this halo disk in the sky above and crimson haze bathing us as we rolled through the salt and pepper sand and cried out. That kind of cry. Dark. Here it's different; the ebb and flow of waves has gone, and the light spots and bleeds. Light. I look for the switch—bring new life to the room—but there's nothing. Dark. Just this faulty bulb dangling from the ceiling, out of my reach. Light. On the beach last summer, we'd planned it all. Dark. She's looking away, like she doesn't want to remember the cricket's cry.

Dark. Nothing, I say. Dark. Nothing, she says. We keep to

ourselves, the bulb blistering overhead, and the light wilting unlike the orchids that never were. Click. It's the midwife, the door shutting behind her. She takes a seat opposite; the lightbulb flickers then fades. My wife shifts in her seat, her hand beside mine. Dark. 'Sorry to keep you both waiting…'

Light. I take her hand, hold onto it—and when the light shudders—squeeze it tight. I want to find the switch, just turn this light on, to fix it. Fix everything.

There are documents on the midwife's lap and, seeing us, she gives this sort of smile.

Dark. The bulb goes out. Then I feel—
feel my wife's hand,
squeezing back…

…Claire.

true remembrance
(2 days to go...)

Silence. Nothing but silence. I strain to hear something, and I hear the blood as it rushes through my arteries. I frown, only to hear my scalp move over my skull followed by a strange metallic stir that I can't explain. I tense, only to hear the skin slide over my muscles, my tendons creak, and my bones pop like chicken bones. Then I realise, this isn't silence at all. I'd have to be dead for absolute silence.

That can only mean—

*

Platform 2. It's early—I'm early, at 8.13am. But then there's no one else at home. Home. I figured I may as well just go straight to the station. Just wake up, take a piss, a shower, some breakfast— two rounds of toast, cow suckle, and black smack—then get changed and take my leave without taking time to say goodbye. Not so much as a note, not like I have any words left in me. 8.14am. Platform 2.

It's 8.15am, and my phone starts ringing. I let it go straight to answer phone.

I think about the things and people I'm leaving behind, but it doesn't take long. I don't even need all five digits, let alone both hands. The job centre won't miss me—that grumpy, judgemental cow that interrogates me every week for a measly £73.10 or whatever. It's not my fault there are no jobs. It's not like I haven't tried...And who else? Friends, the only friends these days are digital or downloadable. Family, what little there is left of it, of my mum, whatever there was of it, of my dad. And money—can't miss what you've never had!

And the sea. I hear the waves over the grisly speaker phone announcing the next train, and I'm there once again. Then the voice

213

dies down, the waves retreat.

It's 8.17am, and my phone starts ringing. Straight to answer phone. I won't miss home, I tell myself. I won't miss—

8.18am. Ring, ring. Ring…

8.19am…8.23; 8.26; 8.31; 8.36; 8.43; 8.46; 8.59; 9.01; 9.04; 9.10…

No one's going to notice I'm gone.

'The next train at Platform 2 is the 9.28am train for…' The station announcement drones across the platform. 'Calling at Neath, Port Talbot Parkway, Pyle, Bridgend…' I rub the ticket between my fingers, this one-way ticket, my only way out of this labyrinth. 'The next train at Platform 2…'

*

—*Ring, ring.* Damn rattle in my ears. I stir, but it's hard to make out anything. Night gives way to night. Missed the day, passed out on the floorboards; or maybe there was no day, no light at all. Can't remember. Then there's that damn rattle—

Ring, ring.

I hear something. This itch in my ear—

Ring, ring. Ring, ring.

Faster, slower—silence. I roll over, my body collapsed, sides bruised and swollen and my back cracked worse than the floorboards. I drag the palm of my hand along the splintered wood. My face itches with stubble, and my eyes are sore and red. I scratch at them, real hard like so it hurts and I know I'm awake.

Ring, ring.

I slam my hands against the floorboards and push myself up onto my knees, head still sinking to the floor. I can't shake this throbbing pain that—

Ring, ring. Ring, ring.

I shudder. I look up. It can't be—

Ring, ring. Ring, ring.

214

But it is. Of course it is. With the light piercing through the window, I'm able to snatch a glimpse of the opposite corner of the room. There, in all its damn, painful glory. The red telephone. I wait for the ring, but nothing. It's sitting there, still broken, without the cable, and yet—there it is again.

Ring ring—

*

I check my coppers—£2.63. Too little for some smokes, too little for lunch, too little for life. I head inside WH Smith, grab some KitKat, Tic-Tacs, and a scratch card at the counter before coughing up the money. I leave the shop, head to Platform 2, only 13 pence to my name.

9.15 am. I slip the phone back in my pocket. The train arrives. This is it. No going back now. I get on the train, carriage D, bang in the front of this shitty train. And I'm stuck in seat 4, facing the wrong way. I can't see where the train is taking me, and they've got me looking back onto the same platform, the same city. Guess I have to wait before I can turn my back on everything.

Think positive—I'm turning my back on everything. The sea is already a few miles behind me.

9.29am. The train is late. Does that even surprise me? Static in my ear followed by an announcement, some voice scratches in my ear for a couple of minutes then, with a screech and a pull, it's off. 9.32am.

Ring, ring. I don't need to know the time anymore, so I just switch it off and cram it back inside my pocket, instead checking my one-way ticket out of here. Only 16 hours to go...

Another screech and another pull and the train grinds to a halt. It's another station, the first of many. I look out of the window.

9.40am. I slip the phone back into my pocket, hearing the rattling of coins as I do. I take out one of the pennies, along with the scratch card—Lucky 7s. I wonder, of all the times I've seen this done, when you see the old men in Wetherspoons at 10am knocking back a pint and playing on the fruit machine, when Mum brought a ticket and won 100 quid and lost it all to paying off debt, or when Greg boy bought a lottery ticket at 14 and won a grand but had to split it with his old man because he was underage, I wonder, what if?

The penny is blunt, no shine, and it scratches at the grey tint on the card with no love. Still, despite everything, even I can't hold back that flicker of hope at the £100,000 prize when, one by one, I peel away the numbers. A 7, another 7, a...

Money has never been on our side. That's what Mum used to say, among other things. She said it all the time; we lived in austerity before austerity became fashionable. She was right of course, even up until the last time we spoke, how this is it. No going back now.

*

—Did I bring the telephone here? But when? And the broken cable. How is it ringing? I stare at it, not moving, instead listening with both ears sticking out, waiting—

Ring, ring. Ring, ring. Then *ring, ring. Ring, ring.* Then nothing. I approach, crawling towards the phone like I'm nine months old again, or ninety years, I fear. I collapse. I cry. Tears trickle down and splash on the floorboards. Why won't you ring? Why—

Ring, ring. I can hear it—I can hear it! *Ring, ring.* It isn't this telephone. It's coming from outside. *Ring, ring.* Get up. *Ring, ring.* Get up, damn it. I shout, shout at myself. Shout, curse. I slam my fist against the floorboards and push myself upwards. The broken red telephone disappears. I pause. Wait for it. *Ring, ring.* I hold myself up, drag this broken body and stumble forwards, staggering out of the room with my hands clinging to the wall.

Ring, ring. I push the door, shake it, then unlock and cast the bolt aside, kick the crate of empty bottles and throw the door open. Ring, ring. It's coming from down the hallway. I can hear it. Ring, ring. I drag myself ever further. Ring, ring. The irritation grows louder, swells in my ears, echoes across the landing and I have to focus to make out where it's coming from. I push myself faster, hobbling towards a door I don't know, locked...

I grab the lock and smash it, push and kick the door all I can until it budges. A final charge and I push right through and stumble inside...

I see it. By the window. A cable, poking through the wall and clambering over the floorboards, attached to a dainty red telephone. Just like the other one. Ring, ring. Then silence. I stop, hanging from the door frame, swaying in the calm air, legs shaking and hand, I realise, now outstretched. I can see my fingers balancing, trembling in the air...

Ring, ring. I leap forwards, tripping and falling to the floor. Come on, keep ringing. I drag myself closer. Ring, ring. There's only so many times it'll ring. Ring, ring. I pull myself forwards by my elbows. Ring, ring. My body is shouting. Ring, ring. I'm shouting. Ring—I throw my hand out and knock the receiver off its stand. It clamours onto the floorboards, rattling, scratching my ears as I fumble...

My heartbeat echoes in the receiver. A buzz in the background, a heavy, dull beat. The two sounds clash and propel each other, the beat then quickens, the buzz drops and...

*

Another station, another text. Like someone is concerned, maybe, like she can help; she can't. I hear the cackle in the station of the speaker once more, of announcements, this rising tide that I have no control over. Another text, just a minute apart. I'm drowning in everything. I'm trying to escape, but the waves won't let me go.

217

Cardiff. 10.02am. First change. Ten more minutes until the train to Crewe pulls in, so I take a moment near the yellow line to take a few drags, to save me.

It's then I see the small girl coming.

For a moment I hesitate, focusing everything on my next breath, the next inhalation. Then, when she touches that yellow line, I grab her and hold her back. A scream behind alerts me to the group of onlookers, these ghosts turned people, eyes fixed on me, on no one and the small girl in his arms.

I let go. The woman—her mum, maybe—approaches. She hugs her, then draws back and clutches her arms tight.

'Never do that again, you hear? Never. You scared me! Never...' She embraces her again. 'I love you.'

She looks up at me and for a second her attention is on the fag jutting out of my mouth and the dark circles around my eyes, this statement about who I am in this time and place. Then she looks me in those same eyes, even smiles, and I think...

Another stranger, looking from afar, may mistake us for a family.

Even when I board the train, I tell myself she wouldn't have run off the edge like that. She's just a kid, I tell myself. I never did anything to save her, she didn't need me. But I still feel it, that ache inside. That pain. I see the mum's face, see the colour in her eyes swell—this all too familiar pain of the worst kind.

Of losing everything.

I pick up my phone, ready to call. Only I take out another fag instead and head to the toilets, to drown myself in a sea of smoke until the next station.

*

My mouth opens, but nothing comes out. Then—a whisper at first—my voice breaks free into the mouth piece.

'Hello?' My body sinks. 'I'm sorry.' I shout inside. 'I know you're out there, somewhere,' my voice drops again. 'Please, answer me…' A pause. 'Claire.'

A voice echoes, strangely familiar. Then a pause. The heavy, shallow beat, the rasp of breathing over the line. My own body thumping. My own breathing caught in the receiver.

'Is that you?' I ask, both hands now clutching the phone. Silence, and breaking through that void comes that flash of purple. *Her.* Did she do this? Is all of this her doing? I can't hold back any longer. 'Skye, is that you?' my voice echoes down the line.

Nothing, then—

. . . .

. . . . . .

. . .

'It's me.'

Her voice fills the room, my body. Her. I feel a thump right in my chest. I hear crying on the other end.

I try to speak but I want to hold onto her echo.

'It's me,' she repeats. 'Corey, where are you?' My name. For the first time in a long time, I hear my name. 'I'm here. Corey, I'm here, you hear me? I—'

The phone beeps, then silence. I hold onto the phone for a few seconds longer, even shake it to hear the rattle of the plastic in my hands—nothing.

We have you now.

A shadow in the corner of my eye. I turn to face the window. I see it, the cable cut, and I can just make out an outline leaning over the remains. The darkness hides its face, but I don't need to see. I put the phone down and scramble for the knife beside me.

I want to live.

'I'm done with this place, you hear? I'm going to find her, and we're both leaving this place and never coming

219

back.'

No reply. They know that the silence is haunting, this darkness that breaks away from the walls, these long arms of the past that wrap around me.

I stab the air.

'I don't need you anymore.'

The shadows approach, the cats taking form in their wake. Several of them, a dozen of them, their oversized heads bouncing up and down, their teeth jutting out of their mouths, their swollen eyes consumed with darkness. They back me against the wall. The knife shakes in my hands. I balance it in the air, waving it, pointing it forwards. I shout. I cry. Then nothing. Nothing, then her voice.

Skye.

The cats close in. I shout. Shout for as long as I can until my lungs give out. The cats drift towards me, riding a sea of black that rises up from the floorboards. I stand still, hovering by the window, the knife still poised in my hand.

I shout again, my voice dying in my throat. But I can hear her voice. As loud as I can, staring down the dozens of cats now pouring out of the walls around me, a final shout. Then they all disappear. Gone. In her wake.

Skye.

As real as my heart beating, there she is. I say nothing. She says nothing. But I can hear—hear my heart beating, hear hers. And now, looking at her I believe; all of this, I believe, was her doing.

She shuffles forward a few steps.

'It's you,' I mutter. Then my body stiffens. The cats, the shadows...

She doesn't say anything, instead approaches me and, where I'm unable to fight back the tears, she wipes the first away before it trickles down the side of my face. She smiles, then wraps her arms around me and holds me tight. I can hear her heartbeat against mine, a whisper.

'You can talk now,' she says and then, the touch of her warmth on my skin. 'Do you remember?'

But my eyes are closing, the cats appear behind her, and the whole world vanishes under the next wave.

*

'Shit.'

The fag slips through my fingers and onto the platform, mixing with the dirt and gum. Yum. I scratch my hand but it still itches, so I end up bending over—back complaining—and swiping the fag back off the ground. I light it and bring its putrid, pure taste back to my lips. Anything to warm my body this early in the morning. But this brick in my pocket keeps calling, but I'm not going to risk this fag again. I'm going to kill it for all it's worth, worry about the phone later.

The light at the end dies away and I toss it on the tracks, coughing as the cold air seeps back into my lungs. And in my pocket, the ringing continues.

18.22pm. The train will be here any minute. Enough time for a final fag. Shit, none left in the packet, no time or money to nip back in the shop either. I glance around—several half-chewed fags lie squashed on the bin tray. Without thinking I grab a few, shove them in my pocket and bring the last one to my lips and light up with Mum's stolen Red Ronson. I kill it for all it's worth, hold onto that feeling in my lungs—that warm feeling inside, like nostalgia, like yesterday, before the cold invades and I lose it only seconds later.

Only seconds later the next train arrives. Platform 2. Swansea to Highlands, already four changes, another six hours or so.

And then nothing but me and the ends of the earth.

*

'It's okay,' Skye says. 'You need to remember.'

221

'I can't…' I say, I lie. I don't want to, I *can't*.

'I'm here,' she continues, her hand in mine, and I imagine we're walking on that beach…

*

September, 2022.

It beats down on the salt and pepper sand, scatters across the deep blue, the last of the sun. I catch her then, riding the crest of a wave, crying out—calling me, arms in the air and throwing herself forwards. I leave behind my coke and pack of Lambert & Butler on the towel and run after her, before it's too late.

Too late.

She falls with the waves before I reach her, and I have to dive to find her as the sea carries her under.

July, 2022.

'Let's go to Langland. I want to stroll on the sand, sing in the sea, let the sky fall on me!'

I follow her—to the ends of the land, any land. Summer finally here, she lets it carry her away. I can't even see her now as she races ahead, a dot in the sea.

I reach the coastline, listen to the swash and backwash of the waves along the shore. She's nowhere to be seen.

May, 2022.

Langland Bay blushes before us, sun alive and waves whistling. Even the dunes welcome spring with raring rabbits and lush green grass. We climb the slopes, race down their backs and roll in the sand that tickles our skin. Life like we were before.

Maybe, just maybe, everything will be alright.

March, 2022.

She's waking up, now that she's returned to her beach, her Langland.

'It's still cold,' I say.

'It's fresh,' she says, and her smile warms us both.

She takes a step into the sea, the waves licking her feet, and I have to push forward to reach her. But she stands there, not a word, nothing but the waves all around. The clap of each crash, the rush towards her...

I pull her back, take her hand, her arm, and pull her back from the waves coming for her.

December, 2022.

The anniversary air is heavy with fog, with small, sharp bursts of light. Sun, no sun.

I see her now, on the edge of the sea, the waves thrashing all about. Like the earth is contracting. The sea will take her, I worry, swallow her whole if she lets it. Just one step...

I try to follow, but the winds hold me back. Despite her frame, she resists it all. I remember her then, one year ago, riding those waves and shouting. One year ago, we had it all. One year on, I know she's still waiting, know she's still watching the waves, waiting for her little one who couldn't be here...On her beach, her Langland.

One step forward, the waves rush over her; one step back, the waves fall short of her.

I run. Her cries drown out, the sea bleeds blue, and the wind breaks against my back while the waves charge forward as I run. I reach out for her hand, reach into the deep blue womb before it's too late...

Too late...

...

*

'You need to remember.'

A smack to my face and I'm out cold. When I wake up it's colder still, and the night embraces me. I shift my weight and feel the earth moving under me. Then I realise; it's earth, dirt, and when I look up, I can hardly see the moon, just this silver scythe hanging cleanly above me. I see her too, standing some way up there as well.

'Skye…?'

'I'm sorry, Corey, but it's for your own good.'

'I don't understand, what…?' The words are stuck in my throat, but she doesn't reply. 'Where is this place? What's going on?'

'The reason you are here. You need to die in order to be reborn.'

I look up at her one last time before catching the end of my breath as everything drowns in darkness.

you can do this
(last day…)

A newborn's scream. That kind of scream.

I snap my head around. What time is it? Dark, but I feel…_Alive_. I glance around. I'm in the middle of a room I don't recognise. Before I know where I am or even who I am, I know her: Skye. Leaning over me, her bright, chestnut eyes watching me.

'This is your choice now.'

She makes to leave, but I grab her by the wrist.

'I'm getting out of this place.' A faint smile brings her to life. I can't help but smile too. Then a shout crashes in the distance. I already know. 'The cats.' She nods.

At the window she steals a glance then pulls back, turning to me.

'Can you run?'

I shift my weight. The swelling and aches are still there, but more of an afterthought. The danger—no, the hunger to live—brings everything to life.

'I think so.'

'Come on, no time to waste. It's time for you to get out of this place before it's too late, before the exit closes.' I need to leave the labyrinth. Before it's too late. 'Follow me.'

I say nothing, only haul myself up and stumble out of the room after her. Hurry down the stairs. Bolt across the entrance hall. Throw the door open and there, outside, the world hits me; above, a bruised swelling of clouds splinter and crack across the sky, like some broken double helix, and below the mist spots and the water in the stream gushes like an open wound. The shattering of thunder overhead could be mistaken for some inhuman scream, like the earth seized in some great contraction. I run, on unsteady legs, as I feel the world—this town—closing in.

Up ahead I catch the chanting and crying dancing over the blurred horizon, a procession sweeping into view in the direction of the square. A dozen or so shadows, cats, swarm the path, the mist a tidal wave at their backs. I hesitate, only to feel a grip—Skye's hand—throw me forward.

Body lurches to the right.

She grasps my arm, my drawn out, flailing arm that flounders in the air, detached, disconnected from me. My eyes swell in the faint glow of the magma red that slides freely across my skin. My flesh. My soft, braised, pierced flesh that writhes and snaps out of my control. My eyes pass over it once more, that arm caught in her hand, her hold, never letting go.

Body lurches to the left.

She shouts but I can't hear her in the downpour. It masks her voice, and even her body becomes consumed by the oncoming mist, in the darkening shoreline that separates her from me. I feel a tug and my body jerks forward. She leaps into the unknown and pulls me with her. The shouts and screams and cries soon fade under the pounding of the rain and I feel my body heaving once more.

Body lurches to the right.

My mind snaps awake once more as she thrusts my body forwards, screaming at me to push on. I try. I try as I have tried again and again. Yet I feel my body buckling, my will leaving me. She tries to continue, to push me on. It's only a little further, I hear her shout. Or whisper. I can't tell. The thunder claps again. The light flashes above. The rain continues to run down the side of my face.

Body lurches to the left.

The high wall on either side closes in on us, like rising tides threatening to drown us. I feel the weight on my lungs, but I still shout.

I'm thrown into the open. My lungs gulp the air roaming freely and she calls again. But this time I hear a jubilant cry wash over me. She cries louder and louder. I can't believe it. It's there right in front of us—it's really there. I see it.

She shouts back and we both leap forward. In her euphoria she breaks away from me to make for the exit just ahead. I cry after her but this time she doesn't hear.

Everything derails and we're thrown about like rag dolls. Then I feel it. Her body falling. Onto her knees, then her whole frame crumbles to the ground. I shout. But it's useless. My own body gives in and I collapse beside her. My flailing, weak arm hovers over her, my hand gently grasping the fingers of her outstretched palm.

Several warm drops creep along my skin. Do not go gently into the night. Do not let the shadows take you.

I call, I cry.

A shadow approaches, leans over and reaches out a hand—then nothing, just this shadow leaning over, hand outstretched, and for a moment I think I glimpse its face.

I know you.

And then, however faint, I hear; hear her voice.

'You can do this.'

the 13th hour

I wake at the beach. I don't ask how I got here. I've learnt that thinking why and finding meaning is more important. I can hear the waves on the shore, the swash and backwash as each one rushes up then retreats back down. A spray of water washes over me. A warm breeze picks up, tickling my skin and carrying the droplets further inland behind me. And the moon, it's full tonight.

For a moment I think I'm back in Wales, on Langland Bay and I see Claire, under this halo high in the night's dark canvas. She stands on the edge of the sea; a sharp division between her world and mine. And then I'm back here, with Skye.

'If I go into the water, will you let me?' I shake my head. 'I'm going,' she says.

Just what does she think will happen? The waves rage behind her, and then I remember her story in the bath and how she wanted to face her fears.

'You don't need to do this. I can't let you.'

She smiles then, this strangest of smiles. It hurts to see it. She takes a step back, the waves rushing up to her ankles. She takes another step back, into the sea, away from me.

I step forward, but she's shaking her head.

'I'm not going to stay.' Her smile pains more than her words. 'I'm going. You can't stop me.'

Another step back, the waves devouring her feet, rising to her shin. I stagger a few steps forward to the edge of the sea, but she shakes her head, forbidding me to cross that boundary. That sharp division between my world and hers.

'The cats, the shadows…'

'Just shadows,' she says.

'That's why you took the train. The *train to nowhere*.'

'To *somewhere*,' she corrects me. 'That's why you took the train.'

That's why I came here. She came all this way, to the unknown, a place of her choosing. And I came here, to this unknown...to find her.

'Is this it?' I shout, unable to hold back the upheaval, the waves thrashing about inside me. 'You told me that we came here for a reason—that we would find some meaning or purpose in all of this. Is this...' I need some answer, anything. 'Is this what you wanted?'

The sea all around me, it catches in my eye. I hover over the edge, staring straight ahead, try to fix her in place, hold her image right here.

'Do you remember now?'

'The train?' I ask. She nods. 'I remember.' Of course I remember—how could I forget how we ended up here? 'I remember when we first met, it was on the train. I found you there, hanging on the edge of the door, the train carriage on one side...'

But she's shaking her head.

'No...It was you. You were the one hanging off the edge, you were the one ready to jump.' A pause. I feel her words hitting me. 'But you didn't,' she continues. 'It wasn't what you really wanted. You were your shadow, you were lost, but that was it. You just had to find yourself.'

I stand here, the waves dancing before me, but never reaching me. The sea won't take me. It won't take me because I've decided it won't. And above, the moon high in the sky, and below, the edge of the sea; hanging on the edge, the carriage on one side of me, the unknown on the other.

I remember.

I'm there again. The last days with Claire, a shadow all over her, the light barely touching her. Grief had become a ghost whose grip on us wouldn't let go; on her, on me. On us. Our Langland, our beach, was no longer a place of birth but a place of burial. We lost something—*someone*, an integral part of our existence and without it we became nothing, no one. But we had told friends, we had told family. We were close this time. We had moved to the bigger house near the stream, close to the community library, the school and the church. We had adopted the fluffy bunny rabbit, my idea, and the cooking fat cat, Claire's love. We had prepared the room and the cot, and she had read bedtime stories from a book, while I had sung a lullaby that I remembered my own mum had sung to me as a boy. We had chosen the name. We never did tell anyone about the visits to the clinic, or why we chose Japan over Peru. We never did find the money to pay off the mortgage. The school was knocked down and converted, and the cat killed the bunny. We tried to forget the name. We tried to stop asking questions. How is this happening, what have we done, why us? We tried to stop feeling guilty. I tried to stop feeling guilty. I tried to tell her we could keep trying, that we could still make this work. In the end, I was the one who gave up first.

We had built a home, a whole town, a whole world. And then it was gone. Somewhere became nowhere; we became no one.

I remember. I remember this memory of mine that I'd buried; the grief, the guilt, I buried this memory along with others. What was it? That I couldn't take it anymore?

Here again, on this far-flung beach, with her. And then I think, before the train, before the town, her...Skye. She stands there now in the water, like Claire last year, neither of them wanting to leave the sea. Skye. She knew everything; it was me who needed saving, it was me who was ready to jump, it was me who wanted to forget everything.

I stare across the water at her, this question in one hand...

'Who are you?'

'Who do you want me to be?'

Her vagueness, undefined, no definition or borders just like the open sea. I stare once more at her, and notice how much younger she is than I had first thought, how much older I am than I care to admit. Without thinking, I hum the lullaby that brought us together, the lullaby that now echoes across the beach, the waves...

'I'm glad I had the chance to meet you.'

Does she say these words? Do I? They are so soft, so innocent and perfect that I can't trust what I hear.

Then she fades ever further into the darkness, the waves ready to reclaim her.

'Wait—what if...' I think over the last few days with her, try to snatch some memory of her, her purple jumper...'What if I can't hear your voice?'

'You exist,' she replies. 'No danger of the shadows taking you.' She laughs, this ever so sweet laugh that she made during those first few moments I saw her.

Then something, some movement below and I look down, but there's nothing there. I look back up but realise it's too late. She's gone. The slap and clap of the sea dances where she used to be, the moonlight bouncing off the high backs of each wave. I stay a long, long while at the edge of everything, and with everything here the shadows stay away.

It's cold. I've only just noticed. I thrust my hands in my pockets, but my hand brushes against the dead plastic of my phone. She's right—a stupid old brick not worth shit. I grasp the phone tight, ready to throw it into the sea—

Vibration. My finger catches the buttons, turns it on. A vibration.

I hold onto it, watch as the screen comes to life and displays the time and battery. The red light is flashing, but there's enough left. It must have been her. Or was it me? I think of everything that has happened so far, of the last few days, heck, the last few months in a new light. Did I not want to be contacted, to contact anyone? Is this all my doing? She found me on the train and decided to talk to me. How much words, someone talking to you, can change everything. I...

Dial a number. Bring the phone to my ear. Up ahead the sea crashes and waves rush up to my feet.

Ring, ring.

What if I told them everything?

Ring, ring.

Would anyone believe me?

Ring, ring.

What if...?

One step forward, the waves rush over me; one step back, the waves fall short of me. I see it now. The edge of my world and the waves ready to take me if I let them. My footsteps in the sand wash away and hers next to mine disappear with them as I try to remember what they looked like. If I take one step forward, I think, then maybe I'll hear.

Hear her laugh, hear her voice.

One step.

Ring—

*

There was a train crash. That much I found out from the police afterwards. They have a whole file on it. Skyeline Trains, train number ZS00, reported late at 01.01am. Apparently the train derailed approximately two minutes past midnight, no known cause besides the usual faulty rail lines answer. The train was an old model due for decommission, and the lines long overdue for repairs. Few people head that way so it has mostly been forgotten. The officer had never even heard of it before it made his desk on Monday morning. Besides that, I learnt little else about the train on a beach. I learnt quickly not to ask any further questions. The officer's patience was wearing thin, unlike his waistline.

I asked other questions, had some answers but also more questions. Who knew there are actually some abandoned places still dotted around the UK, even in these parts? But nothing, I found out later, that matched my description. The officer did seem interested in how vivid my imagination was though.

I didn't ask directly about Skye, for obvious reasons. But I found out that there had been no known fatalities, no one reported missing. But that got me thinking—no *known* fatalities. There are after all plenty of unmanned stations left where someone could easily have boarded and been unaccounted for, plenty of unreserved tickets and no-shows. In the middle of nowhere who's going to know? Sometimes I have doubts that she even existed at all; but then other times I'm all too aware that there are traces of her everywhere. I open the journal on my lap, and there she is all those months ago, her words not mine...

In the end they found me in the dunes, some five and a half miles from the crash site. I was unconscious. Of course I was. Difficult to say how long I had been lying there. I was in the town beforehand, or whatever it was, and on the shore after that I guess. Of course the officer interrogated me, put me on trial with a lot of questions about my whereabouts, what I remembered, but I chose to say as little as I could get away with and what his lack of enthusiasm called for.

He was at least a little bit concerned for me though. When he wasn't able to reach a single contact on my phone, he handed me some leaflets and gave me a number to call. One I recognised. Turned out to have been one of the most important phone calls of my life.

I didn't talk. I didn't know how to grieve. I didn't know how to move on. I had lost everything and everyone I knew, isolated myself in my room and woke up every day just to go back to sleep. Now I can, I hope, move past all of this. I understand that now.

In the end, despite all of these unknowns that I've come to accept, there are at least two things that are nothing less than the truth. I had been missing for thirteen days, and lying next to me they found a mountain hare white as snow and small as a bunny.

*

Sunrise, almost. I glance at the phone on the table, seemingly slipping away, out of reach. Should I check? I hesitate, then flick it on and shuffle through the texts. They're all recent. A text from Mum, or rather, many such texts asking for the hundredth time where the heck I am. But that shows she cares and I'm grateful for that. Then another from, surprisingly, my dad, an unexpected, belated 'Happy Birthday', the first time in years. There are more words that follow than I can handle right now, and whether I want to open that door again I'm not sure, but at least I have that choice. Besides these there are a few other texts. From acquaintances, one or two friends even. And finally, two weeks ago, from an old school mate at the weekly support group I now attend, asking if I was going to meeting that night. I did—it turned out to be the one I needed most.

And for the first time in a long time, I feel like I'm

someone.

I finish writing today's entry. I've taken up the habit of writing in a journal. I could type it up on my phone, but the words seem to come to life in the ink. It helps me stay grounded, and reminds me of the small things and moments in life that make it worth living. For a moment afterwards I just lose myself in the vast emptiness of the blank pages that remain, and wonder what wonders await me. Then I turn to the landscape outside, pregnant with possibility, imagine the glimpse of the sun on the horizon and the whole world slowly coming to life. Feels right, feels like home.

Home.

A cough, a splutter, and I turn to face Bubbles and Larry once more.

'Corey, you in?'

It's Larry, with Bubbles grinning beside me. Of course, it's not really them but I like to pretend they are. I hear their voices and that's enough. This is my second chance; God or life or whatever willing. Larry is nice, and Bubbles is a funny character—it's hard to ignore his childlike innocence, the goofy smile that wraps around his face. He smacks of silly, but in a nice kind of way. And Larry next to him reminds me of an 'older brother' kind of friend.

'The next game. I'm heading out for some fresh air first.'

'Come on, you gotta join us this time, gotta join us.' Bubbles whines, trying to catch me with his big paw but Larry stops him.

'Just let Corey go, he'll be back.'

There's a friendly determination in his eyes, and I offer him a smile before squeezing past Bubbles. Again, it's not his real name, but Bubbles just feels so familiar.

I head down the corridor, past all the empty seats. It's

quiet for sure, but we're saved from the silence. There's still the occasional early bird, some robin or blue tit; the young couple nestled asleep in each other's arms in the corner, all twisted and conjoined like two sides of a Greek urn; the old man a few rows down on the opposite side who's drinking some hot beverage in a flask, closing his eyes and sinking into the fabric of his chair afterwards. Sure, it's a quiet train, but everyone in this moment feels connected somehow, like we're all on the same grand journey.

And I wonder what their stories are and smile.

I glance at the time on my phone once more. Just a couple more minutes until we reach the station, and then I'll catch the first bus of the day to make it the rest of the way. I should arrive just before the sun rises. I want to be there once more.

Back from the toilet I cross the vestibule only to hear the whirling of the wind rush around, and on the side I find the nearest door. Closed, but the window is open and for a moment I see it, this dark mouth opening up into the vast unknown, and like a rabbit I'm drawn to the rabbit hole.

It's calmer than I remember. Guess Wales ain't all just black clouds and pissing rain; instead, there's beauty in this early morning darkness, this drizzle. I take another step, trying to peer outside to grasp the scenery. My head leans over the edge…

'You okay?'

I hear her voice. It's not her of course, but I choose to hear her. She may not have even spoken these words, but I choose to hear them.

Instead, it's another woman, maybe my age or older this time, wrapped in a long night coat but with a hint of purple peeking through underneath, some sweater perhaps. And eyes that look right at me, through me. She catches me unawares.

I smile. 'Just getting some fresh air.'

I grasp the handle and pull the window to, a short shriek as the wind catches in the pressurised space and then the window shuts tight. The woman looks at me, all strange, then manages her own smile before passing me by. I head back inside the carriage a few minutes later.

Back in my seat and Larry has already dealt the cards, but Bubbles is nowhere to be seen.

'He'll be back,' he says, reading my thoughts. I glance towards the window, waiting. There's a faint glow on the horizon that struggles against the last of the night. 'You saw her, didn't you?'

I pretend not to know. Of course I know.

'Saw who?'

'The *train to nowhere*,' he says, placing his cards on the table and leaning forward, eyes on me. 'Doesn't matter what train you take, what ship you sail, or plane you fly, if you don't know where you're heading then you're heading nowhere. And the train to nowhere is full of shadows.' He pauses then, as if to check that I understand him. 'But if you ask me, that train takes us to the place where we can face our own shadows for what they are.'

He returns to his original position, taking the cards back in his hand. 'Only bad dreams, that place. But we have to face them in order to move on.' Then, in a whisper, 'Not everyone escapes their town of cats. She saved me once, too.'

Did I hear him right? Am I trying too hard to remember Larry, or did he say something else entirely? Either way his voice carries and there's a strangeness in the way the words hang from his lips, the way his body sinks into the chair, the way his eyes turn towards the window, outside, and for a moment seem to take on the disappearing night itself.

He places a hand on my shoulder.

'Anyway, it's good to have you join in, mate.'

I say nothing, just nod.

'I'm here, Larry, I'm here I am.'

It's Bubbles again, taking his seat opposite Larry, next to me, and scoops up his cards in his giant paws. He looks them once over. The fool, I see everything the way he holds them, but he just turns to me and gives me the biggest grin and I feel at ease once again.

'So, you in?' It's Larry.

'You haven't cheated already, have you?' I joke. There's something about this moment that feels right.

I pick up my cards: a ten, a jack, a queen. And a king…Just one more card. Somehow, I just know I've got this.

Opposite me I find the woman I met a few minutes earlier return to her seat. She catches my stare and acknowledges me. Strange, I think, this woman here. Opposite me. Sitting the way she is. I can't help but think this is all meant to be.

The sound of a card brushing against the table alerts me, along with the train's wheels grinding against the tracks, ready to ease into the station. I stay seated, staring out of the window as the sun begins to rise. I look at my phone—there's still time, and I relax back into the soft cushion of the seat and close my eyes.

I'm back on the beach, on our Langland. I'm holding her hand as we walk up to the water that rushes past our ankles. We say nothing, instead let our souls speak; our feet splash through the water, our clothes catch in the wind, and I feel the familiar beat of her heart in her hand, in my hand, and she feels the same I know. Soon the sea reaches our waists, and we take out a flower—our bluebell—and hold onto it. And I hear it then, that

238

ringing, that lullaby all blue and bell...

At least I know I won't sleep tonight. Eventually, I guess, the nightmares will stop and they'll no longer be playing over and over again in my mind. Grief happens in waves, I've learnt, and one day the sea will calm. I glance down at the table, at my cards, then at my ticket beside them. A return ticket; I'll say my peace and move on from this chapter at long last. Then who knows—I could be anyone, anywhere. From here on forward all the way. From nowhere, this train to somewhere.

*

Sunrise, sunset, ten thousand stars in the sky and a moon that lights the night. Nights, mornings, Mondays at work (yes) and lazy Sundays (obviously). Sunday breakfast, pancake, pancake with banana, pancake with blueberries, with walnuts and almonds and sometimes honey and always coffee. Coffee with milk, without milk, strong Italian espresso in Milan. Milan in the late summer breeze, Milan in the winter snow with the Alps at my back while I'm sitting behind a fire reading a book. Books new and old, the Harry Potter books (because I forgot about them), the Game of Thrones books (because I thought I never had the time), self-help, cooking, and Booker books and all the books that made me think and feel and smile. Smile, a stranger, a conversation that leads to another that leads to another until we call it friendship. Friendships in the unlikeliest of places, at the support group, at a bus stop, at the ends of the earth. Earth, returning to nature, growing my own pear tree, plum and peach and every other tree, digging and cooking and hosting meetups. Meetups where we eat pizzas, meetups where we watch re-runs of *Friends*, meetups where we play Dungeons & Dragons and we can be the heroes we are in the stories we tell, and meetups where we celebrate birthdays, a wedding, and the birth of a rainbow baby. Another chance. A daughter. A family.

Acknowledgements

A novel is a journey, one that involves many incredible individuals to whom I am most grateful.

To Tony, Rod, and Polly at Black Pear Press for believing in my writing and *All the Waves, Calling*. They responded to my questions, queries, and quibbles and it is thanks to them that you're holding this book.

To Mike, who captured the heart of this novel in an amazing piece of cover artwork and who is a great friend, a beautiful human being.

To Lorraine, whose comments on early drafts of the opening gave valuable direction and encouragement. To Jackie, who understood the soul of this novel and, through her guidance, helped me hone this story for publication.

To Nuala and everyone at Splonk who published my flash fiction story, *Half-life,* in 2020: not only because the story explores a critical moment in Corey's grief, but their faith in it came when most needed. To Retreat West, Flash500, Worcestershire LitFest & Fringe and all the other supportive writing communities I've known.

To Szymon, Ciccio, and Stuart, whose friendship has left an indelible mark that has made its way into the ink on these pages, and JJ, whose conversations and pullups at Morriston Park provided a welcome connection at an unusual time. To the Dungeons & Dragons gang, for the fun and exciting times and for reminding me that we can be the heroes we are in the stories we tell.

To everyone at Morriston Library, for the space and community, and to others who provide a space for books, stories, other worlds in which we are invited to lose ourselves in our shared humanity.

And to family, because what greater inspiration is there than love?

About the Author

Jamie D. Stacey lives in Swansea, South Wales, with his family. He has been a metal worker cutting aluminium and an academic in international relations; has chased after children as an *animateur* in Bordeaux, France, and lived in a martial arts academy in Rizhao, China; spends a lot of time baking unusual bread and even more unusual cakes; is a son, a dad, a husband... He says yes when he can and tries to understand and write the world one story at a time. An avid reader of scratches on walls and scribbles in notebooks, he is drawn to stories that empathise, encourage, and empower. Whether he writes very short stories or novels, whatever the form or shape it's the heart and hope inside each that matters. You can find him at www.jamiedstacey.co.uk.

Author Photo by A. Stacey